The Professional Mourner

Neil Randall

This book is dedicated to the memory of my father.

Sleep well, sweetest friend xxx

The Professional Mourner

Part One

On a rainy, overcast Wednesday in the small town of Velika Plana, a baby girl was born to Dragan and Nevena Stanković. Seen very much as a miracle – the proud parents were in their mid-forties and had almost given up hope of ever conceiving a child – it would be no exaggeration to say that little Milica (as she was soon to be called) came kicking and screaming into this world. A perfectly natural state of affairs, many would assume. Only she didn't stop screaming. Not from the moment she was safely delivered into her mother's arms, to the moment Dragan and Nevena left the local hospital the following morning. Nothing seemed to pacify her. No amount of shushing or cradling or rocking. Even when her exhausted mother, in the hours immediately following the birth itself, presented the baby with a teat, she somehow managed to both greedily suck the milky goodness from Nevena's swollen breast and continue to cry, sob, wriggle around, and prostrate herself in a manner the midwife (a veteran of over ten thousand deliveries) or any of the physicians on duty that day had ever seen before.

"It's the most curious thing," observed Dr. Ivanović. "If I didn't know any better, I would say the infant actually enjoys being in a state of utmost distress."

*

On their return to the family home, a modest apartment in the working-class district of town, the concerned parents did everything in their power to try and settle the baby down – more shushing, cradling, rocking, and feeding. They even let her suck on a wine-soaked finger (a now-frowned upon but nonetheless effective technique routinely deployed many years ago). And while their efforts were rewarded with brief periods of respite when Milica had literally screamed herself to sleep –

it never lasted long. A matter of thirty or forty minutes at a time.

After two sleepless nights, they were nearing their wit's end.

"Whatever are we going to do?" asked Nevena, red-eyed and haggard from exhaustion. "I know all babies cry. But this isn't natural. It's as if God has blessed and cursed us in equal measure, as if He has given us the one thing we most wanted in life, only for that great gift to be the most onerous of burdens."

"I don't rightly know," Dragan replied. "But you can cut out all that superstitious nonsense. Milica is a perfectly healthy baby. You heard the doctors say so yourself. This is probably just a tetchy period of adjustment. I'm sure she'll be right as rain soon."

But that didn't prove to be the case, and it caused untold problems in town.

*

By the end of the first week of constant bawling all through the night and early hours of the morning, not to mention the vast majority of the day, the neighbours started to complain. Not just about the noise, you must understand – though many a resident did bang a piece of wood against their radiators time and again when the crying fit reached a feverish late-night or crack-of-dawn pitch – but because these were still a deeply superstitious people, regardless of the incredible technological advances made in recent decades. They saw something strange and worrying, portentous of evil spirits and bad omens, in an infant who simply wouldn't stop crying.

"Mark my words," they said. "This don't bode well for any of us. That there little girl is possessed by dark forces. She be cursed. If we don't watch out, she'll bring bad luck upon every decent man, woman, and child in the region."

They openly displayed their annoyance, if not outright hostility, towards what, up until the birth of their daughter, had been a popular and well-respected couple. If they saw the father, Dragan Stanković, on his way to the steelworks in the morning, or returning home after a hard day's toil, they either crossed the street or, if they hadn't had the good fortune to see him approaching, turned their back on him completely. If they saw the mother, Nevena Stanković, with her pram, they did likewise. Some of the older women went so far as to openly make the sign of the cross in her direction.

"Be away with you," they hissed. "You should've drowned that one at birth. Now all of us will have to suffer."

Irrational, unkind behaviour which only added to the Stanković's plight. Not only did they have an infant who cried from dusk till dawn, they were now treated as pariahs by the local community.

*

One Saturday evening, around a fortnight after Milica's birth, the family received a visit from Mihailo Pančev, the foreman at the local steelworks, in effect, Dragan's line manager.

"I'm sorry to disturb you so late," he said, taking off his cloth cap and wedging it under his arm, a stiff formal gesture which greatly unnerved both husband and wife. "There's no easy way to say this, Dragan, but if you don't make some changes to your domestic life, I'm afraid we will have to rehouse you and your family on the other side of town."

"What? But why?" he asked, affecting surprise, offence even, though the reason was perfectly evident and, even if he didn't like to admit it, perfectly understandable.

"Your child – ," Pančev peered down the dimly lit corridor where the sound of despairing sobs, fit to break the heart of the most hardened of individuals, was punctuated by a far throatier choking noise, like the gasping death throe of someone being violently strangled in a darkened alleyway, " – there have been many complaints. Every resident, in fact, has been petitioning my office for the last ten days. You must understand how difficult this is for me. You're one of our finest workers. A loyal Party man. A comrade. We've worked together side-by-side for many a year. But, as with everything in life, we must consider the greatest good for the greatest number. If things carry on as they are now, we'll have mutiny on our hands, if not a full-blown strike."

"But what are we to do?"

"That I can't say with any certainty – consult with the doctors in town, maybe even send the child away to a relative or a place where she can get proper treatment."

"No!" cried Nevena. "We would never dream of being parted from our Milica. What you're suggesting is impossible!"

"Well – ," Pančev shifted uncomfortably, " – the decision is yours, of course. I was only told to make you aware of the current situation."

*

By this stage, it wasn't just the prolonged, incessant nature of their daughter's outbursts which worried them, the way her face would turn a worryingly dark, purplish hue, nor the sheer unlikely violence of each heaving sob. It was the odd, curious moments when they could've sworn that she momentarily broke off from crying to critically appraise their reaction, to eye them with disconcerting intensity, to see if her sobbing and wailing had produced the desired effect. Moreover – and this was a physiological phenomenon, thus factually indisputable – despite the force of her cries and the length of the episodes themselves, she never became hoarse nor her throat red or swollen. A bizarre, not readily explainable anomaly, from a strictly medical point of view.

"I see no inflammation of the larynx whatsoever," said Dr. Ivanović, following a thorough inspection of the child's throat cavity. "If I hadn't witnessed these screaming fits first-hand, I would've assumed I was examining a different baby. Therefore, I can offer neither a prognosis nor a course of suitable medication."

"But, Doctor," said Nevena, over the infant's re-emerging, full-throated screams, "as you well know, my little girl hasn't stopped crying since the moment she were born, near as damn it. At times, she's in so much distress, I'm sure she's about to do herself some serious mischief."

"I fully appreciate your concerns. If this behaviour persists, we shall have to send for a specialist."

But persist it did.

*

6

The following evening, Dragan returned home from work to find Nevena passed out in an armchair, and baby Milica sprawled out on a rug on the floor, crying and prostrating herself before a few old ikons the family kept tucked away in a corner of the room. Far surpassing her previous histrionics, which had already been enough to alienate, if not everyone in town, then certainly those within a reasonable distance of the apartment, she proceeded to join her trembling hands together in what looked like prayer, and somehow manoeuvred her body into a kneeling position, as if she were appealing to a higher power, to God, the Almighty Himself. All of which astounded her father to such an extent, he could never tell – not in the immediate aftermath of the incident or in later life, when his daughter had attained a huge level of notoriety, if not fame, in the region – if his eyes were deceiving him.

Before he could take a step closer to confirm as much, Nevena suddenly jolted from her slumber.

"Whatever has happened?" She shot to her feet and scooped the baby up off the floor. "Please, Milica, my love, my darling girl, calm yourself," she beseeched in such plaintive, heartfelt tones, Dragan couldn't help but stifle a sob himself. "Stop that crying. Be at peace, child."

Incredibly – and this was such a rare occurrence, for never had the baby responded to her mother's pleas before – Milica stopped crying and drifted off into a peaceful slumber of her own.

"It was the strangest thing," whispered Dragan, when assured that his daughter's sleep was as deep as it initially appeared. "When I walked in through the door, I could've sworn that Milica were staring up at those old ikons in the corner."

"It's funny you should say that," Nevena whispered back. "These last few days, when you've been at work, I've often seen her eyes wander in that direction. And, well, it got me thinking. Maybe we should take her to see a priest. Maybe we should speak to old Father Miroslav, for instance, and ask for some advice or guidance."

Dragan winced. He knew the contempt in which old world ways were now held. He knew how resorting to such a course of action could affect his already compromised standing with his bosses at the steelworks. But when Milica awoke, barely five minutes after she had drifted off into a seemingly peaceful sleep, and screamed and sobbed even louder and harder than before, he knew that they had to do something.

*

The following morning, he visited Dr. Ivanović and made a formal request for a specialist to examine his daughter.

"Why of course, Mr. Stanković. I'll compose a letter to the main regional hospital this very day. But I must warn you. Our resources have been stretched to the limit in recent years. Things move slowly. It may be many weeks, even months, before a specialist is able to visit your daughter."

"Weeks? Months?"

"I'm afraid so. As much as I sympathise with your plight, your child's condition, worrying as it no doubt is, is far from life-threatening. Like I said following my last examination, the baby is in perfectly good health."

"Is there anything we can do in the meantime, though? Any kind of medicine or pills she can take?"

"Not really, no. I know it's difficult, but patience is key in situations like this. You must continue to love and care for the child, to shower her with affection, to do all the things parents do when a new baby enters their lives."

*

While certainly disheartened, Dragan resolved to follow the doctor's advice. In truth, there was little else he and Nevena could've done in the circumstances. Had he not been subject to one of those suspiciously random coincidences in life, immediately upon leaving Dr. Ivanović's office, they would've diligently carried out their parental duties to the best of their abilities, and awaited notification of the specialist's visit.

The coincidence in question transpired as follows:

As he rounded the corner and made his way onto the town's main thoroughfare – the quickest and most expedient route to the steelworks – Dragan bumped straight into Father Miroslav, nearly knocking the ailing old priest off his feet.

"Oh, Father, I do apologise." He grabbed his elbow, steadied and held him firm, to ensure that he did indeed remain upright. "I was miles away. I wasn't looking where I was going."

Rather than respond in words, or express gratitude, or even a hint of uncharacteristic annoyance at his former parishioner's clumsiness and distraction, the priest's heavily lined face broke out in what Dragan later described to his wife as a 'beatific smile, just like one of the saints from the Good Book', and he laid one of his bony, veiny hands on Dragan's shoulder. So strange was Father Miroslav's reaction, Dragan couldn't help but feel slightly unnerved. He had known the man since early childhood, and had witnessed his painful, humiliating downfall, the way a once-revered personage in the community had been reduced to a figure of fun, a religious fool that citizens either despised, pitied, or treated with a mixture of indifference and contempt.

"Are you okay, Father? I hope I didn't startle you?"

"No, no, my son," he said with the same distant smile on his face, and his hand still on Dragan's shoulder. "You didn't startle me in the slightest. For many days now, I've had visions of meeting you in the street, just as we met a moment ago."

"How'd you mean? I don't understand."

"You are looking for spiritual guidance, are you not?"

"Well, I…"

"Come. Take me to your child. I must see her for myself."

*

When they arrived at the apartment, they were greeted by a scene now all-too-familiar to Dragan – his bedraggled, sleep-deprived wife holding their screaming, writhing baby daughter in her arms. On seeing the priest, however, Milica began to, if not stop crying immediately, settle down to a certain degree. If nothing else, she was clearly curious about the arrival of this stranger.

"Your child is special," Father Miroslav proclaimed. "In such a cold, uncaring society, when man has had his back forcibly turned on his religious beliefs, it was only a matter of time before the Almighty showed us a sign of His displeasure."

"A sign?" asked Nevena.

"Yes. Your baby does not cry merely for herself. She does not cry because of a middling physical complaint that ails her, or because she is somehow simple or mentally defective, or possessed by an evil spirit. No. She cries for the great wrongs that have been perpetrated in society in recent years. She cries for how the word of God has been forsaken. Therefore, you should not fear for her welfare. You should rejoice in her spiritual awakening. For make no mistake, that girl has been blessed with immense powers. She is an instrument to voice God's immense dissatisfaction with His flock."

The priest cited a whole host of injustices that he and his religious brethren had suffered in the name of progress. He spoke of churches, places of worship, being looted, pilfered, and desecrated for a 'handful of gold'. He spoke of despicable acts of violence against men of the cloth, of priests being dragged from their homes to be kicked and beaten to death. He spoke of young people spitting at him in the street. He spoke of moral decay, how an entire generation had been returned to the dark ages.

"Without His word to guide them, they have regressed to a barely human, almost animal state. There is no kindness, compassion, or empathy in society today. Ironically, people have no sense of communality anymore. If an old woman fell over in the street, the vast majority wouldn't blink an eye. They would simply step over her without offering a helping hand."

For the most part, Dragan dismissed this impassioned speech as the empty ramblings of a sad lonely man who no longer felt any relevance or purpose in his life. Bitterly, he started to regret his decision to invite the priest into his home in the first place, clearly envisaging the problems it would cause at the steelworks, rather than feel any succour, consolation, or hope for the future. Men of Dragan's ilk are stirred by actions, not words, no matter how lofty, convincing, or well-meaning. It was only when the priest took a strangely silent and positively entranced Milica from her mother's arms, made the sign of the cross over the child, and began to recite a prayer that Dragan realised that the visit might not have been such a huge mistake, after all. Remarkably, for the first time since her birth, Milica was not only quiet and content, but she actually wore – if only for the briefest of moments – a smile upon her face.

"Did you see that, Dragan?" Nevena gushed. "She smiled. She actually smiled. It's a miracle."

"Not a miracle," said the priest. "More confirmation of your daughter's gifts, that she has been sent to us with a very important message."

*

For Father Miroslav to have had such a powerful effect on the child caused Dragan Stanković untold consternation. Granted, Milica still cried with unbridled ferocity for large parts of the day and night. But now, thanks to the priest's intercession, the parents had methods at their disposal – namely, whispered prayers and hymns – to subdue her.

"At least we can get a bit of respite now," said Nevena. "At least we have a little more control over the situation."

"That we do," said Dragan. "And I'll be grateful to Father Miroslav for as long as I live. Only I didn't like all that spiritual mumbo jumbo he spouted about Milica being 'special' and an 'instrument of God'. Talk like that is dangerous, Nevena. You must never repeat it to anyone, you hear. Not even your own kin."

*

The couple struggled on for the next few months, and while Dragan escaped serious censure for his absence from work on the morning of Father Miroslav's visit (he was a highly skilled and productive worker, a man who had never taken a day off sick or failed to fulfil his daily quota) his family problems *had* affected his standing on the main production line. As someone who thrived on the camaraderie with his colleagues, the banter and good-natured if often foul-mouthed joshing in the canteen, this had a depressing effect on him as a person. Not that he ever outwardly expressed his disquiet to his wife. Still, he was subject to restless, resentful, agitated feelings both during the working day, when shunned by his fellow steelworkers, and on his return home, when he had to perform all kinds of lengthy and elaborate rituals, re-enacting the religious scenes from his childhood, just to quieten his baby daughter down.

"Are you okay, Dragan?" Nevena asked him one evening. "You seem a little distant."

"Yes, yes, fine, my darling. Just tired, that's all."

A half-truth. Because he *was* tired; he tossed and turned at night. He couldn't shake off his growing sense of frustration or reconcile his reduced standing at the steelworks against all the good memories from the past. He couldn't understand why things had changed so quickly, even if he could pinpoint the cause. Each evening, when he passed the town's main tavern, his walking pace slowed and he looked longingly at the bright lights from the windows and listened to the enticing sounds of raucous laughter and bawdy conversation, the likes of which he had been denied ever since Milica's birth. And while he didn't enter – he was well-aware of the perils of alcohol – he felt its powerful allure, a need to be amongst his fellow working man, to talk, laugh, joke, to forget about his problems, even if it was for only an hour or two each evening.

"You're a little late tonight," Nevena remarked, when the lure of the tavern had been at its strongest.

"Oh, I had to do a few bits and pieces after my shift. We've got a regional inspection coming up, and the bosses want to make sure everything is in tip-top shape."

This was a lie – an unnecessary lie. For Dragan had neither stayed behind to perform any extra work duties nor done anything wrong. He had merely stood across the street from the tavern and gazed at those lights and listened to those sounds. But perhaps it was indicative of his state of mind, of how much the baby's birth had affected him. How certain adverse situations in life can lead a good man down the wrong path.

*

In contrast, Nevena, after many testing months, felt positively rejuvenated following Father Miroslav's visit. Having suffered not just through excessive tiredness but a torturous sense of inadequacy, as if it were her fault alone that Milica was the way she was, that Nevena had failed, and was failing, on a daily basis as a loving mother, had been difficult to bear. At times, she couldn't look Dragan in the eye, for fear of seeing his disappointment or reproach at her failings, even though he couldn't have been more supportive or understanding.

Every day, after Nevena had pacified the baby through prayer or hymn (or, as was more often, a combination of both), she carefully laid the sleeping child down in her pram and took her for a long walk through the town. These were particularly blissful excursions. Not just because of the peacefulness or late-summer sunshine, but because Nevena felt a supreme sense of vindication when she passed the old women who had been so cruel before, who had made the sign of the cross and said such unkind things about her daughter, when the baby herself was silent and sleeping deeply, making not a single sound.

"Lovely morning," Nevena would say to them in sing-song fashion, as if none of the nastiness had ever taken place, as if it hadn't had such a devastating effect upon her and her husband, as if she was a better person who had risen above their small-mindedness and backward, superstitious ways.

And while the begrudging acknowledgement of a grunt and a slight nod or a false smile was all she ever garnered in return, it still felt like the sweetest of victories.

*

On one of these morning walks something happened which further validated Father Miroslav's lofty predictions about the baby. In far gloomier conditions – an overcast sky threatening imminent rain, a cold, swirling wind, dreary harbingers of the changing season – Nevena inadvertently stumbled upon a funeral procession, a long line of mourners slowly making their way towards the town's main cemetery. But rather than openly express their grief, each person present held themselves stiff and upright, consciously trying to repress their emotions, to remain detached and dignified, as if the passing of a loved one hadn't upset them deeply. If any of the party did display any momentary weakness – invariably an older man or woman – one of the younger mourners would take them aside and whisper what looked like harsh, admonishing words into their ears.

Struck by the cold sterility of the scene, these black-clad automatons robotically going through the motions, Nevena recalled funerals she herself had attended, both as a young girl and during her adult years. And she remembered the rawness of emotion on display, the grief, where bereaved husbands and wives, mothers and fathers, brothers and sisters, cousins, nephews, nieces, were distraught, beside themselves, barely able to walk or stand, or function in any significant way, so crushed had they been by the death of someone close to them. In comparison, this stilted display was almost gratuitous in its dispassion, bordering upon the disrespectful.

As she pondered all this and more, Nevena failed to notice that Milica had not only woken up but had somehow managed to manoeuvre herself into what constituted an upright position, a position which granted her a full view of the funeral procession. It was only when the baby started to bawl and wail and thrash around in her pram as if subject to the most violent of fits or convulsions, shattering the forced, unnatural silence that pervaded the procession itself, that Nevena was jolted from her reverie. Alarmed, she ducked down to see the most curious of sights. Just like Dragan had witnessed all those months ago, the child had both hands clasped together, as if praying to the Lord, beseeching the Almighty. Even more strikingly – if that were at all possible – her blotchy, reddened face was the picture of grief and despair, the kind of grief and despair Nevena had witnessed at the funerals she had just recalled so vividly.

Alerted to the baby's crying fit – and it was impossible to ignore – the mourners came to an abrupt halt. At the head of the party was a plump, round-faced woman of middle age. Breaking away from the others, she walked over to Nevena and the hugely distressed infant.

"I'm terribly sorry," said Nevena. "We mean no disrespect on your sad day. The child is irritable, that's all. We've had untold problems with her."

Without so much as acknowledging Nevena's apologetic words, the woman ducked down and whisked Milica out of her pram. Hugging the child tightly, she broke out in floods of tears herself; she literally started to choke on her upset, as if drawing emotional succour from the baby's tiny frame, as if Milica were absorbing her pain and loss, sponge-like. All the pent-up emotion that came pouring out of her had a powerful effect on the other mourners. To the last man, woman, and child, they too broke down in tears. They hugged and embraced and comforted each other, until the collective outpouring of grief was so palpable and sincere, it, ironically, felt almost celebratory, like the most fitting and respectful way to mourn the loss of someone close to you.

Eventually, the woman (who later introduced herself as Bojana Miljković, a postmistress from a nearby village) handed a serene and almost ethereal-looking Milica back to her mother.

"Thank you. I can't tell you how much comfort your little girl has just brought to me. It's been a tough few days, all told. Even though my dear husband Nemanja had been ill for some time, the end still felt so…sudden. He were a labourer, see. Asbestos is what killed him. Those bastards from the ministry worked him like a horse. Twelve hours a day for nigh on twenty year. Never gave him no proper equipment, no breathers to protect his throat and lungs. And they didn't even have the good grace to send anyone from the department to pay their respects. It makes me so angry, as if his life didn't mean nothing to no one.

"And I know this will sound stupid, but that baby daughter of yours, it were as if she could feel my pain. Ever since my husband's passing, I've felt numb inside. I've not known what to do with myself. Now, after I've had a good cry, I feel so much better, as if I'll be able to get on with things as best I can, rather than mope around, feeling bitter and resentful."

She half-smiled and brushed the back of her hand up against Milica's cheek.

"You look after that little one, you hear? There's something 'bout her that's different, special. I sense she can do a lot of good in this world."

It took quite some time before the funeral party had recovered themselves sufficiently to be able to continue on their way to the cemetery. As they dried their eyes and blew their noses, and hugged and embraced and comforted each other anew, Nevena couldn't help but be struck by the transformation. Now they resembled the mourners she remembered from the past – real people with real emotions. And it was probably the first time she recognised her

18

daughter's true power, the 'something' different and special that the widow had mentioned.

And it wasn't something that went unnoticed or unreported in the town. Whether via the mourners themselves, or passers-by who had witnessed the incredible scene is probably unimportant in the bigger scheme of things. But for the next few days, it was all the townsfolk talked about – how a strange infant child's crying fit had brought an entire funeral procession to a standstill.

"It were that Stanković child, the one who won't stop bawling and screaming."

"I hear they've had old Father Miroslav out to see her."

"Bad business. Don't know how they've got the front to show their faces in town, to brush shoulders with good, honest folk."

*

Inevitably, the gossip and stories (all of which had the utmost legitimacy, it must be said) reached the higher-ups at the steelworks, senior Party men who were not only responsible for maintaining a high level of production, but the ideological purity of all their workers.

During the course of what had started out as a normal morning, Dragan was called to Pančev's office.

"We're making some organisational changes. For the time being, we're taking you off the main production line."

"You're doing what?" Dragan could barely believe his ears. For over two decades, he'd worked his way up to a position of responsibility; he'd led by example, to the extent that most of the men viewed him as a senior figure, someone to be respected. If any problems were encountered, big or small, he was the first person they would seek out for advice and guidance.

"It's only temporary." Pančev backtracked, if only slightly. "In a few weeks, a month perhaps, we can reassess the situation."

"Well, I don't know what to say. I've always applied myself to the fullest, and took pride in my work and the fulfilment of my quota. But if you think a change is required, I can only accept your decision."

And while this didn't affect him in a financial respect – all steelworkers were renumerated in the same way, no matter what role they undertook – it was a huge blow to his self-esteem. Never before had he felt so humiliated. To be forced to undertake auxiliary tasks of little importance, to work beside young men who'd only just left school, exacerbated his resentment about his current family situation. In the canteen during breaktimes, he sat on his own now; the cooks allocated him derisory portions, or the very worst cuts of meat, and all around him, he had to listen to whispered jibes, caustic words from men he once considered good friends, not just co-workers.

"Look how the mighty have fallen."

"Serves him right. If you don't toe-the-line, what do you expect?"

"When a man can't keep order in his own home, when he can't keep his wife and child in check, what chance has he in front of a smelting pot?"

On more than one occasion, Dragan struggled to restrain himself; he almost challenged them to speak to his face rather than whisper behind his back. But he knew it would've been a pointless gesture, which could only cause him further problems. For now, he had to accept the situation for what it was, and hope that things would return to normal soon.

"I've just gotta be patient," he thought to himself. "They won't be able to do without me on the main production line for long."

*

Meanwhile, Nevena couldn't have been more delighted. She relished the idea of the whole town talking about her daughter. In the weeks and months that followed, she became obsessed with finding out more about Milica's 'special gift'. Unbeknown to Dragan, she'd sought the counsel of Sanja Babić, a 'healer' or 'mystic' to some locals, although in the current climate, she would more likely be seen as a complete crackpot. Ever since she could remember, Nevena had been aware of Sanja's reputation. Most days, the old woman set up a stall near the town's main bus station. From cracked earthenware jugs, she sold all kinds of natural remedies. In the main, dried roots from plants she had gathered in the forest. At one time, her wares were in great demand, and people from the town and its environs consulted her regarding a whole host of complaints, ranging from general aches and pains to fertility problems, to treatment for serious illnesses that had been given a fatal prognosis by more conventional medical practitioners.

"Yes, yes," said the old woman. "I'd be happy to look the child over. Come to my place later this afternoon."

In the same way that Milica had been fascinated by Father Miroslav, she instantly quieted when her mother carried her into Sanja Babić's rundown old shack on the outskirts of town. Maybe this was attributable to the heady smells coming from whatever concoction the old woman was preparing over an open fire, or the way Sanja herself carefully examined the child, cooing and poking and prodding her with a firm yet playful thoroughness all infants adore. But, as Nevena was soon to discover, the connection went far deeper than that.

"I've seen this kind of thing before," said Sanja. "Not recently, granted. But on rare occasions, a past spirit gets brought over into the next world."

"The next world?"

"That's right. We're all on an eternal journey. We all occupy different forms at one time or another. Every now and then, something happens to a few chosen ones that is so powerful and extreme, so painful and terrifying, it becomes ingrained in their very souls."

"Powerful? Extreme? Painful? Terrifying? Whatever do you mean?"

"That I can't rightly say, not with any certainty, that's for sure. But I can tell, just by your little girl's reaction to me, that I've found a kindred spirit, someone with the third eye. For that reason alone, I would like to offer my advice and guidance.

"Never, under any circumstances, should you let her be examined by one of those fancy doctors from the big hospital in the city."

"But my husband, he's already made arrangements. Ever since the child was born, she's worked herself up into such a state, it's worried us half to death."

"That matters not. I'd hasten a bet that the regular doctors have found nothing wrong with her, eh? I bet they've said she's a perfectly healthy child."

Nevena nodded.

"And that's why you have to keep her away from those specialists. They don't like it when they can't explain things with science, if it's not written down in one of their textbooks. Hence, they'll try and take the girl away from you, or they'll cut her up in one of them operating theatres, or pump her full of God-knows-what pills.

"If worse comes to worst, you must give her a dose of this stuff here." Sanja handed Nevena a dusty vial of medicine.

"What is it?"

"An ol' remedy of mine that'll quieten the child down, for an hour or two at the least. That way, you might just be able to pull the wool over those big city doctors' eyes.

"Just as importantly, tho', you must try and keep her away from other people, children 'specially. They can be horrible little creatures when they encounter anything or anyone different to 'emselves. Like the doctors, they're a suspicious, unforgiving breed who feel threatened by what they don't understand."

"But what am I to do when the child starts school?"

"That's a good few years off. By that time, she should be able to control herself a bit better. Be wary, tho'. That there potion won't stop her from having her crying fits, for that is what she were born to do. It's her purpose. But it will help her lead a more normal life."

*

Despite Pančev's reassurances, there was no change to Dragan's situation at the steelworks. Not a few weeks or even a few months down the line. Even during periods when failure to meet their work quota was a very real and worrying possibility, the higher-ups refused to reverse their decision and have one of their finest workers help address the shortfall. In that respect, the other men were particularly stubborn, and voiced their opposition to the prospect most vehemently. They didn't like the idea of consulting with Dragan, someone they had been treating with the utmost disrespect. Perhaps they had always felt jealous and resentful of such a productive worker. Or perhaps, they feared that his return to the main production line would only highlight their own inadequacies all the more. Whatever the reason, it was enough to finally send the man, if not quite over the edge, then certainly in the wrong direction.

One evening, after he had made an open appeal to Pančev to let him assist in the more important operational tasks to ensure that they did indeed meet their monthly quota, only to receive the sternest rebuff yet, Dragan finally succumbed to the temptations of the local tavern. In truth, this had been becoming increasingly inevitable as the dark days and weeks passed into winter. Even though baby Milica was much easier to handle now, and certainly didn't scream and bawl in quite the same manner as before, and certainly not with the same kind of brutal regularity, Dragan's sleeping hours were still often disturbed. The families above and below them still banged pieces of wood against their radiators in the early hours of the morning, or slipped notes under the door – usually anonymous and filled with scribbled complaints, expletives and abuse, if not threats of outright violence against Dragan himself. He still felt the sting of their reproaches, and a powerful sense of humiliation at what had befallen him in life.

From the moment he left the steelworks, this, in many ways, broken man knew that he wouldn't be going straight home to his wife and daughter. Ever since he had exchanged heated words with Pančev, he had been dreaming of the tavern, the smoke, the conversation, rubbing shoulders with his fellow working man, and, of course, the strong consolatory properties of alcohol, the likes of which so many of his forebears had sought to salve the painful reality of their existences. In his head, he played out imaginary conversations, told jokes, listened to stories, and relayed his own. He began to visualise the tavern as a haven, a form of escape, a place where he could forget about his troubles. Even though in reality, when he pushed open the main door, it was a gloomy, smelly, dingy place, badly lit and full of ramshackle old furniture, it was truly a sight to behold for Dragan. For here, no one cared who you were, whether you were an honest man or someone who had once spent time in a prison cell, or if, more importantly, you had a daughter that most of the townsfolk considered to be the devil's own. While far from as crowded as the raucous laughter and bawdy chatter had suggested from the street, there were enough men, most in cloth caps and working clothes, for Dragan to feel that sense of camaraderie he had been denied this last year or more.

"What can I get you, friend?" asked the barkeep, a docile specimen of humanity, with only a few wispy strands of hair on his head and barely a tooth in his mouth.

"A tankard of ale."

"Coming right up."

As Dragan watched the barkeep pour the golden nectar into a glass, a slight, sinewy man in paint-flecked overalls sidled up to him at the counter.

"Buy me a drink and I'll tell you a secret," he said, his bright eyes twinkling merry and star-like in a face covered with dry, dirt-caked sweat.

Rather than express any wariness – and one must remember, even in those days, taverns were still dangerous places to frequent, places where brawls often resulted in men being beaten and robbed, or far worse – Dragan threw back his head and laughed.

"I'd be more than happy to freshen your glass, friend. But I fear there are no secrets in this life anymore, only painful realities."

Despite Dragan speaking in good-natured jest, the stranger's facial expression hardened into an almost painful, ponderous grimace.

"Never has a truer word been spoken. Put it there." He thrust out a hand. "Robert Savović at your service."

"Dragan Stanković."

The two men shook hands with respectful earnestness; their rough, cracked workers' hands telling a story all of their own.

"Delighted to make your acquaintance, Dragan. And to celebrate this most fortuitous meeting, it would be a great honour for me to buy you a drink. If, of course, you don't mind a little company and conversation on this fine evening."

And thus, Dragan Stanković struck up a friendship with who would soon become his regular drinking partner, Robert Savović. And, even though he was a good man at heart, the same Dragan Stanković – the husband and father who had displayed such patience and consideration in the months following his daughter's birth, a selfless, hard-working man who always put the interests of the steelworks above his own – became an habitué of the tavern, as synonymous as the gloom, the smells, the dinge, and the ramshackle old furniture. He became, in short, what is commonly known as a 'drinking man'.

*

Not that Nevena ever suspected the true nature of his newly acquired habit. Granted, she often smelt the alcohol on his breath, and his return from the steelworks got progressively later (on odd occasions, two hours or more after he had typically returned prior to Milica's birth). But he was invariably in such a mellow and carefree mood, she ignored the tell-tale signs many other wives in her position would've despaired at.

"Come here, my darling." He would scoop Milica up off her playmat and lift her high in the air, whether the child was in the middle of a screaming fit or in a rare, placid mood. "I swear you get prettier with each passing day."

And crouching down, he took the time to play with her. Nothing more complicated or taxing than rolling a ball with bells along the floor or shaking a rattle, but activities which fascinated and delighted the toddler in equal measure, garnering one of those treasured smiles that had pleased her mother so much in the presence of Father Miroslav.

"Oh, Dragan," she beamed upon witnessing a particularly playful and tender scene between father and daughter. "I really, truly believe that everything is going to be fine, after all."

*

For around eighteen months, right up until the time Milica was due to attend preschool classes, the Stanković family enjoyed an unlikely golden period. Their homelife became even more settled. They experienced all the wonders new parents experience as their child grows – the first teeth, first steps, first words. In a strange, contrary way, they even came to enjoy her now sporadic (if still monumental) crying fits, for they felt it showed that she had not lost the precious gift Father Miroslav and the old healer Sanja Babić had eulogised.

But it was only a matter of time before Dragan's increasingly heavy drinking had an adverse effect on all aspects of their life, most notably his job at the steelworks. No matter how big, strong, and resolute a man (and Dragan undoubtedly was and would remain all those things for many years to come), alcohol has an unerring, if slow, way of corrupting and breaking down that size, strength, and resolution, until little or nothing remains of the man, only a shell of his former self.

*

For the time being, however, mother, father, and daughter interacted in a blissful manner. There were weekends away to visit relatives at the seaside, pleasant strolls through the forest; they flew kites, played board and card games in the evening. But what perhaps brought the family unit closer together than any of these worthy distractions were the stories Dragan would tell on his return from work, or, more correctly, from the tavern. In no small measure – if not the whole of the figurative and ironically apt glass (we are referring to arch inebriates, after all) – this was due to the power of Robert Savović's storytelling gifts. A confirmed drunkard and not wholly unloveable rogue, he was indeed a skilled raconteur, a man who could hold a whole tavern enrapt with his tales. But unlike other barroom philosophers, whether entertaining anecdotists or morose, crushing bores, he drew his often-fantastical yarns from his vast life experience. As a young boy, he had signed up as a deckhand on a commercial cruiser. By the time he was nineteen, he had sailed the seven seas, and visited dozens of exotic destinations. In his mid-twenties, after a brief spell in a North African prison, he found himself playing piano in a notorious brothel in New Orleans.

"I don't like to talk 'bout my time in Tangier, tho'. Dirty, filthy place, but not without it's more dubious charms, if you catch my drift."

"But however did you end up in prison?" asked Dragan, as enrapt as the dozen or so other patrons crowded around the bar.

"Well, strictly between us – ," here, Savović paused, in all likelihood, merely for effect, but it produced a feeling of great kinship in the others, as if this most worldly of men was sharing an important secret with them, " – I'd been up in the mountainous regions of Afghanistan. I'd ridden the whole of the Great Silk Trail on horseback. I'd heard of the vast amount of money that could be made from the poppy, see. Masquerading as a holy eunuch, I attempted to transport a vast harvest across a dozen or more borders. But, like many a man, I were betrayed by a harlot on me way through the dark continent, and thrown in a prison cell for the best part of a year."

There were other tales, dozens and dozens of them. It would be no exaggeration to say that many a book could have been written about Savović's adventures.

"Did I ever tell you 'bout the time I were chased through a Canadian forest by a brown bear that were all of twenty feet in height, and with a mouth so large, it could've bitten a man's head clean off at his shoulders?"

"Did I ever tell you 'bout the time I tried to rob a bank in Frankfurt? Funny business. Inside job, see. But those Teutons are sharp as a razor. They soon cottoned on to our little scheme. I were lucky to slip away, down into the sewer system. Had to hide out there for two whole weeks 'til the coast were clear. All I lived on were rats, and the odd bit of bread and water I could thieve in the dead of night."

"Did I ever tell you 'bout the time I worked as a kitchen hand in a Parisan bistro?"

"Did I ever tell you 'bout the time I wrestled with a saltwater crocodile in Darwin, Australia?"

On his return home, either after he had played his now regular evening games with Milica, or around the dinner table a few minutes afterwards, Dragan couldn't resist regaling his wife and daughter with some of Savović's more memorable reminiscences (if, in fairness, each and every one of them could have been classified in that category). And while not in his drinking partner's league in terms of telling a story, Dragan had a gift for physical comedy. In his cups, he liked to shoot to his feet and gesticulate and mimic, perform funny, mincing walks, talk in different accents, high-pitched wails or low husky whispers. All of which reduced Milica to fits of giggles just as prolonged and rambunctious as the crying fits which had defined her infant years. The little girl simply adored her father's tomfoolery, the way he would shamble around the dinner table, impersonating the colourful characters from Savović's tales.

"You're pulling our legs," Nevena chuckled heartily one evening. "How could someone climb up the Eiffel Tower? It must be over a thousand foot tall."

"I know, I know. It sounds impossible. But Robert, he don't make these things up. If anybody ever challenges him, he always produces a piece of what he calls 'corroboratory evidence'. In this particular case, he showed me a great big length of puddle iron. He reckoned he pulled it off the tower when he got to the top.

"Now, you know I know everything there is to know about metal and what have you. And I swear to you, it wasn't the sort of thing you'd pinch from any factory or building site 'round these here parts. More to the point, it were an old piece of metal. You could tell by the patina, the wear and tear it had endured over the years. And it were definitely the kind of material you'd use in a large construction project of that kind."

*

31

Unfortunately, as many a philosopher has observed, all good things come to an end. This short yet blissful period in the Stankovićs' life was soon to be shattered forever more.

One morning, they received a letter on official letterhead from the region's main hospital:

Dear Mr. and Mrs. Stanković,

Please be informed that Professor Dejan Damjanović will visit your home on [x date] to perform a full psychological evaluation of your daughter, Milica Stanković. If you could arrange for both yourselves and your child to be at your residential address at 10 a.m., it would be greatly appreciated. At present, our resources are stretched to the limit, and have been for a considerable amount of time now. Requests for non-essential treatment are a severe drain on the medical services. Should you not be able to be present, for whatever reason, you must make us aware of the fact as soon as possible.

Yours sincerely,

The Chief Medical Officer

"Well, would you believe it." Dragan handed the letter to his wife. "It's a letter from the hospital."

"From the hospital? About what?"

In truth, the couple had all but forgotten the request for their daughter to be examined by a specialist. Nearly four years had passed since it was officially communicated to Dr. Ivanović. And now that Milica's crying fits were under better control, the need for her to be examined by an expert in the field didn't seem in any way as pressing as it did back then.

"This is bad, Dragan." Nevena tossed the letter onto the kitchen table. "Those specialists, those scientific people, don't like what they don't understand. If they learn about Milica's gifts, her 'third eye', about her being an 'instrument to voice God's dissatisfaction', they'll take her away from us. They'll lock her away in some institute."

"I think you're overreacting, my darling. This is just routine. In all likelihood, this Dejan Damjanović fella will take one look at our Milica, tell us there's absolutely nothing wrong with her, and then be on his way. We've nothing to worry about. I promise you."

*

In the two weeks before the specialist's visit, nothing out of the ordinary, or certainly worthy of note, occurred in the Stankovićs' life. Promisingly, however, Dragan had (in incremental stages, it must be said) been rehabilitated into his former role at the steelworks. This culminated with Pančev seeking him out one morning and explaining that one of the more senior steelworkers had been taken seriously ill overnight.

"It doesn't look good. His heart has packed up on him. We doubt he'll make it through the next couple of days, let alone ever return to work. Therefore, we really need you back up top, Dragan. Truth be told, we've missed having you at the forefront of operations."

Despite suffering from a stinging hangover, the effects of far too much alcohol the previous evening, Dragan managed to both conceal the fact from his superior and perform his old duties with the same proficiency and vigour. By the time the lunch bell sounded, the sweat was literally pouring out his body. A common enough occurrence when in close proximity to red-hot furnaces, many would rightly assume. But this was a different, and perhaps far more portentous, kind of perspiration. And Dragan knew it well. He was boiling all that alcohol, all those impurities from his system through dignified and honest labour. Coupled with his joy at being back on the main production line, the sensation felt very good indeed, as if he were not only purging his body of the ale and strong spirits he had consumed, but his conscience for having gone down the wrong path. If he could work hard, he contended to himself, in the manner he always had the day after what could now quite accurately be described as 'sprees' or 'binges', then what possible harm could going to the tavern have on anyone?

"That's it, Stanković." Bubalo, one of the workers who had prospered most from Dragan's fall from favour, patted him on the back. "We've worked like horses this morning. Come. Let's go to the canteen and have some beef soup. I'll save you a place next to me."

*

Still worried by the imminent arrival of the specialist, Nevena once again sought the counsel of Sanja Babić. In the old woman's dilapidated shack on the fringes of the forest, Dragan's wife both relayed her concerns, and spoke of the great changes that had come over her daughter in recent months – how she didn't cry nearly as much as before, but seemed possessed of a strange, distant serenity, as if she had been transported to a different time and place.

"It's a delicate situation," said the healer. "From what you've just described, I would say your little girl has ascended to a higher plane of consciousness, that she is, in all probability, projecting herself, in an astral sense. That she is in conference with the spirit world. Hence, she don't seem to take in anything that's going on around her.

"This is both a great gift and, with professor-whatever-his-name-is coming out to see you, a cause for grave concern. Like I said before, those fancy city doctors don't believe in the existence of anything out of the realm of their own comprehension. As a consequence, you need to be on your toes, my precious. You need to be crafty, clever, conniving. At every opportunity, you must distract that croaker, whether it be by offering him cups of tea, or talking ten to the dozen 'bout how well your little girl has been doing since her troubles as a baby, it matters not. For make no mistake – one wrong move and all could be lost."

*

On the day of the proposed and much-delayed visit, Dragan had been given the morning off from his duties at the steelworks. With what was left of his wavering resolve (the temptations of alcohol in any soul who has acquired a taste for it are strong), he had forsaken his nightly foray to the tavern and helped his wife clean and tidy the apartment, and prepare what constituted an elaborate feast – the kind of sweet and savoury foods usually reserved for weddings and family celebrations. In short, food wholly unsuited and unnecessary for what constituted a medical examination.

"We've got to be on our toes," Nevena told her husband. "We've got to be crafty, clever, and conniving. We've got to try and distract that doctor. Keep him occupied."

Such was their state of anxiety when the doorbell rang, they gave off the kind of shocked start people would display if a gun went off in the same room.

"That'll be him," said Nevena. "You go and answer. I'll make the tea. And remember – ," she grabbed his elbow as he turned to leave the room, " – keep him talking. It don't matter about what. Imagine you're telling us one of Robert's unlikely tales. In fact – ," she grabbed his elbow for a second time as he turned to leave the room again, " – you should tell him one of those stories yourself. If nothing else, it will distract his mind."

When Dragan finally opened the door, he was so nervous he could barely form a full or coherent sentence.

"Morning. You must be…Nice to meet…Thank you for coming all this…"

Professor Dejan Damjanović eyed his host with a mixture of vague amusement and tangible impatience. An impressive-looking man of around fifty or so years, impeccably dressed, he wore a checked suit, matching waistcoat, crisply starched white shirt, crimson-red necktie, and had a pince-nez hanging from his neck by a thin strip of tan-coloured leather that matched his deep and wide doctor's bag. With a briskness and authority which took the still-stuttering Dragan Stanković by surprise, he dispensed with any formalities, strode inside the apartment, and made his way into the main living space.

Alerted as much by his purposeful step as by a pesky and creaky floorboard on the very threshold of the room itself, Nevena ducked her head out of the kitchen. Only then did Dejan Damjanović perform even the most perfunctory of introductions.

"Stanković, Mr. and Mrs., I presume."

"That's right," said Nevena, inching out of the kitchen and drying her hands on her apron. "We're obliged by your visit, Doctor. But your journey must've been a long one. Please, before you get started, can I offer you some refreshments? Perhaps a cup of tea and a slice of homemade pie?"

"And this is the child?" He ignored Nevena's words and pointed to Milica, sitting cross-legged on her playmat in the middle of the room.

"That's right."

In contrast to her reaction to both Father Miroslav and Sanja Babić, Milica seemed to positively quake with fear when she saw this tall, intimidating figure peering down at her, and she did the most curious, and very probably the most insulting and ideologically unsound thing a person, whether adult or child, could possibly do in the circumstances, something which horrified her parents – she made the sign of the cross in the Professor's direction, as if he were Beelzebub himself.

But rather than express the offence he had every right to express, in both a personal and professional capacity, Damjanović was clearly fascinated by the child's gesture.

"My word." He chuckled. "Over the years, my patients have reacted to me in many different ways, but I don't think anybody has ever made the sign of the cross over me before."

He placed his bag on the floor and asked to be directed to the bathroom.

"I will wash up, and then proceed with the examination."

While he was away, Dragan and Nevena fussed around Milica, pleading with her to behave. Her mother whispered in frantic prayer and made sure the child drank down some of the calming root extract that Sanja Babić had provided them with many months ago. Her father spoke in low, soothing tones as he stroked the girl's hair.

"Millie, this is important. You must remain calm and respectful. Remember what we told you about the school you'll be going to soon? Well, this doctor is like a teacher. You have to do everything he asks you to do. And please, please, try not to get upset."

But what had, in fact, worried them most in recent months, was her taciturnity. While fully capable of not only speaking, but often making thoughtful and considered observations for a girl of her age, Milica remained a child of astonishingly few words, especially when compared to other five-year-olds, who often torture their parents with incessant chatter and repetitive questions – why, what, how? Moreover, she could, at times, be strangely unresponsive, almost as if she had gone off into a trance-like state, the state Nevena had described in detail to Sanja Babić in the days leading up to the fateful examination, as if she was no longer in the room, certainly not in mind anyway.

And to her parents' immense consternation, this happened to be one such occasion.

When Damjanović returned, stripped down to his shirtsleeves and smelling of harsh antiseptic soap, it was as if he was examining a corpse. If he spoke to Milica directly, she didn't respond, look in his direction, nor give any indication that she was being addressed. She failed to comply to each one of his requests – "Please, open your mouth," "Say, '*Ah*'," "Turn to the side." Time and again, the parents had to intercede, to gently ease the girl's mouth open, to openly encourage her, or physically manoeuvre her body to the requested position themselves.

"We're terribly sorry, Doctor," said Dragan, not knowing whether to be pleased or wary of this development. "I think she's gone a bit shy. I don't think she's ever been in the presence of a man of your distinction before."

Whether he meant to resort to flattery or not, it failed to have the desired effect.

"Worrying." Damjanović stood and straightened. "Very worrying indeed." He turned to Nevena. "I will wash up again now. If it isn't too much trouble, I will partake of that cup of tea afterwards. But no pie. Heavy foods cause havoc with my digestive system."

*

"When was the last of the child's 'episodes'?" asked Damjanović. "And when I say 'episodes', I, of course, refer to her somewhat infamous screaming fits."

Dragan shared a quick, anxious glance with his wife. Ever since their visitor had taken a seat at the dining table for the requested cup of tea, he had, ironically, cut an even darker, more threatening figure, especially considering he was now in an informal setting.

"Screaming fits?" Dragan parroted, as if he had absolutely no idea what the Professor was talking about.

"That's correct, Mr. Stanković. The reason you originally made a request to have your daughter examined by a specialist in the field. The crying fits which have, so I've been led to believe, caused quite a stir in the local community."

"What?"

"Don't look so shocked." Damjanović smiled without a hint of warmth or genuine humour. "Word travels fast. But I am not here to discuss what may or may not have taken place in the past, no matter how recent. I'm here to discuss the findings of my preliminary examination and…"

"Preliminary examination?" Nevena interrupted nervously. "Whatever do you mean? As you can see, the child is perfectly fine now, if a little shy and withdrawn on account of a stranger being in the apartment."

"Yes," said Dragan. "She's over all that old nonsense; right calmed down, she has, these last few years. There was probably no need for you to have come all this way and – " Damjanović raised a hand, cutting him short.

"Please, allow me to explain. That way, we won't have any unfortunate misunderstandings later down the line. I have to be frank with you, Mr. and Mrs. Stanković. This case greatly concerns me. I advocate a more psychoanalytic approach than my peers, certainly in this country, anyway. In my medical opinion, this child needs to be closely monitored. Hysteria in the female, no matter how old, must be eradicated at the earliest possible moment. In fact, the 'woman question' has been at the forefront of the psychoanalytic debate for many years now.

"To clarify, to make my prognosis and the contents of the report I will send to the Medical Board crystal clear, I can only describe your daughter's 'religious mania' as a worrying indicator of future mental instability. The child is clearly highly strung, overwrought, veering from one extreme emotional state to the other. Take the incident I referenced a moment ago, when she interrupted a funeral procession with a screaming fit so intense, it stopped the mourners in their tracks. Compare that, if you will, with her behaviour before, during, and after my examination. She was docile to the point of imbecility. If I didn't know any better, if she hadn't made the sign of the cross over me the moment I walked into your home, I would've assumed that she'd sustained some kind of brain injury or been born a simpleton."

"But – but what does all of this mean?" asked Nevena, taking hold of the pretty patterned tablecloth and twisting and squeezing it like the throat of a mortal enemy.

"Nothing for you, as her parents, to be unduly alarmed about at this early stage. I will discuss my findings with my colleagues at the institute. Often, in unusual cases like this, it pays to get a second, third, and fourth opinion. For the time being, I encourage you to socialise the child. I understand that she is due to start preschool soon. Good. Mixing with other boys and girls could be just the thing that will help her avoid a future cataclysm, mental problems that she may never recover from."

*

In the days following Damjanović's visit, Dragan and Nevena talked about the ramifications almost non-stop (well, certainly first thing in the mornings, and on Dragan's return from the steelworks/tavern). They fretted, worried, and contemplated many worst-case scenarios.

"I can't make heads nor tails of it," said Dragan. "All that talk of 'hysteria' and the 'woman question' and 'socialising the child'. It were as if he were speaking a different ruddy language altogether."

"That wasn't what bothered me most. It was the part about closely monitoring Millie. Whatever did he mean by that? It's not like those medical people up at the big hospital are going to send someone all the way out here to spy on her, is it?"

"No, of course not. Most likely, he'll talk to someone at the school. You know, for an update on Millie's behaviour and whatnot. But like we've said many a time, that preschool might be just what the girl needs. If all goes well, she'll make some friends and come out of her shell."

"Let's hope so. I can't tell you how much Damjanović's visit has shaken me up. We were going along just fine until he darkened our door."

"I know, my darling. But don't let it worry you. Chances are, that report of his will be filed away by some clerk and forgotten about forever more."

*

Unbeknown to the Stankovićs – but perhaps that isn't quite the right way to put it, as Damjanović had clearly outlined his intentions, and actually namechecked the Medical Board during his visit – the Professor's report did make it to the desk of several high-ranking officials. To call it in-depth would have only told part of the story. In a weighty, seventy-five page document, Damjanović used Freudian and Jungian case studies to paint a picture of a 'quite extraordinarily disturbed young girl in the grips of a morbid religious fanaticism that could well precipitate severe mental health problems in later life'.

On Page 37, he wrote:

I suspect that the parents – two simple-minded but earnest working people – still hold onto the traditional religious beliefs. It would not surprise me in the least if they still prayed before every meal, and at night before they went to bed. Somehow – although the Freudian theories I referenced in my introductory comments suggest this is far from rare – the child has subconsciously picked up on these practices, perhaps through basic mimicry, which thus precipitated astonishingly violent crying and screaming fits, where the child went so far as to prostrate herself like an old believer before the cross in a church.

Despite the length of the report, and not to mention the dubious reasoning and abstruse psychoanalytical terminology and reference points, it was read (perhaps not in its entirety, granted) by the high-ranking officials it reached. Whether they took any great notice of the contents is a matter still open to debate. What cannot be disputed, however, is that Dragan and Nevena Stanković were now classified as 'persons of dubious ideological purity'.

More speculatively – and this rumour, if we can call it as such, only surfaced many years later, when Milica Stanković's name was known across the width and breadth of the country – an ambitious young functionary took a particular interest in Damjanović's report. This individual, Dušan Srna (who would go on to have a singularly impressive political career) was struck by the unusualness of the case, and the fact that a renowned specialist had been called out to a sleepy backwater town to perform a full examination of the child in the first place. In the margins of the report, he scribbled: *Waste of valuable resources that could've been redirected to matters of national NOT REGIONAL importance.* Regardless of his reservations, he never forgot about the 'five-year-old religious fanatic' from Velika Plana.

For the time being, the report was filed in a government office, and there it stayed for over a decade, until a desperate political situation put a young girl by the name of Milica Stanković and her somewhat unorthodox profession in a position of such importance, it would've seemed inconceivable when she came kicking and screaming into this world.

*

A few days after Damjanović's visit, Milica started preschool and began to mix with other children of her own age. Although worryingly passive when her mother washed and dressed her that morning, Milica didn't protest or exhibit the trepidation children naturally display on their first day at school. By definition (and most definitely in practice, of course), fresh, new experiences in life possess an element of the unknown, which can only ever unnerve. As they walked to the school, Nevena kept stealing glances at her daughter, to see whether she was concealing her emotions, whether she might be verging on one of her now-rare crying fits. But the girl displayed not even the remotest flicker of disquiet. She kept her eyes fixed firmly ahead and moved one foot after the other.

"Now, you needn't worry about a thing, my darling," said Nevena at the school gates. "Be a good girl and listen to your teachers, and who knows? You might make a friend or two by the end of the day."

But sadly, that didn't prove to be the case.

Throughout the entirety of her schooling (which was cut almost criminally short for reasons which will be explained in the fullness of time), Milica rarely interacted with any of her peers, let alone cultivated anything remotely resembling a friendship. All her teachers spoke of an odd, eccentric child completely uninterested in her studies. Granted, she paid full attention during class and took diligent notes. She knew the alphabet and her times tables as well as any child in her class, and wasn't afraid of standing up and reciting them, if requested. The girl could read and write to a more than passable standard. She just didn't seem to engage with any of her subjects. Nothing appealed to her – be it arithmetic or drawing, history or science. When she was a little older, she was often teased by the other children, called a 'freak' or a 'cry-baby', but she never appeared upset or unduly bothered by their taunts. She simply lowered her eyes, half-smiled, and made a gesture of meek entreaty, as if she felt sorry for her tormentors and their hateful, malformed impulses, gestures which left them baffled and affronted in equal measure:

"Why are you looking at me like that? We all know who you are. The religious freak who used to scream her head off from dusk to dawn."

Periodically – especially during the winter months – Milica was the target for the odd projectile, most notably snowballs. But again, rather than cower, or challenge whoever had been responsible, she simply walked away with her head lowered and that strange half-smile curling her lips.

"Yeah, walk away, Stanković. Your whole family are degenerates. Your old man's a roaring drunk, and you're possessed by the devil."

But we are, of course, referencing incidents which took place many years down the line.

To return to Milica's first day at school, it's easy to paint a picture of the scene. Little boys and girls clinging to their parents' hands at the school gates, looking lost and bewildered, if not slightly betrayed, as if their mothers and fathers were guilty of abandoning them to a cruel and unknown fate. There were as many tears as there were soft, practised words of reassurance. The only child who appeared unfazed by the situation was Milica Stanković. And, like her outpouring of anguish in front of the funeral procession all those years ago, it wasn't something that went unnoticed.

"Such a cold, distant child," said one mother.

"It were so unnatural, the way she acted," said another. "Like she were in some kind of trance."

"I don't think it's right to let her mix with normal children from good families," said a third. "The girl is mentally disturbed. She's not all there. It's plain for all to see."

When the children had finally been ushered into a classroom, the teacher asked each boy and girl to stand up in turn, and tell the other pupils their names. A ritual torment for immature minds in the grips of an icy panic and in such intimidating surroundings. When it came to her turn, Milica dutifully got to her feet and relayed her name, and that of her parents, in a clear, confident tone of voice.

"Milica Stanković. Daughter of Dragan and Nevena Stanković."

Then, with what the teacher took as a nervous bow, and with her hands clasped together in what looked like the prayer position, Milica duly retook her seat.

This set the tone for the early weeks and months of her schooling. If a teacher or fellow pupil spoke to her directly, she would be incredibly attentive. Like a light coming on in a darkened room, she would look at whoever had approached her, listen to what they had to say, and make an appropriate, if brief response. If left unmolested, however, Milica would (invariably) sit at a table on her own, head slightly lowered, and drift off into her own little world. Exactly what was going on in her head was the subject of much speculation.

"It's the oddest thing," remarked one teacher. "I stared at the girl for a good five minutes, and she didn't so much as flinch, blink, or take a breath. At one point, I thought she must've drifted off to sleep, and I had good mind to go over there and give her shoulder a jolly good shake. But then I noticed that her lips were moving, almost imperceptibly, that she was whispering something to herself, that she seemed to be deep in what I can only describe as prayer."

"I've noticed the very same thing," said another teacher. "It's a little unnerving. We all know the stories about her when she was a baby. But in fairness, she is far from a disruptive influence in the classroom. I don't think the other children pay much, if any, attention to her. I don't think they even know she's there half the time."

"Still," said the first teacher. "I think we should keep a close eye on her. After all, any display of religiosity should be reported to the appropriate authorities. Besides, it doesn't seem right for the girl to use the school as, for want of a better term, a place of worship. Like all the other children, she's here to learn."

But whenever the teachers checked Milica's work (usually when they observed her lost in her own little world of whispered prayer), they found neat, ordered columns of mathematical equations, or some attractive, albeit childish, cursive script; they found that she was working with the aforementioned diligence, and had not fallen behind the rest of the class. This both astonished and baffled them, as neither could remember seeing the girl with her head down and her pencil poised.

"I can't say her work is of a particularly high standard," said one teacher. "But it's certainly not the worst in her class."

"I agree," said another teacher. "It's as if she's doing just enough, the bare minimum, without really applying herself at all. And like I said before, it's not as if she gives me a moment's trouble in terms of her general behaviour."

"Agreed. Nevertheless, it might pay to have a word with the parents at some stage. Let them know exactly how their daughter is conducting herself during school hours."

*

Towards the end of Milica's first year at school, an incident took place which changed the teachers' opinion of her altogether. During morning break, a quite astonishingly violent altercation broke out between two of the boys. Astonishingly, because the diminutive combatants were not long out of the crib, and two more innocent, cherubic-faced children you could ever wish to see. How or why the disagreement transpired, the headteacher, or any of his colleagues never discovered. What couldn't be disputed, however, was the spitting, snarling, savage manner the two boys set about each other. Punch followed kick followed punch; heads clashed like rutting stags. They fell into a feisty clinch, only to break out of it almost immediately and circle around each other, as if looking for the perfect moment to launch a fresh assault.

By this time, a large crowd had gathered. Fascinated rather than appalled by the scene, they began to clap their hands with rhythmic gusto and shout words of encouragement:

"Go on, Uroš!"

"Whack him, Slaven!"

"Give him what for!"

Quite where they had picked up such primitive and incendiary language wasn't altogether clear. But, like the old healer Sanja Babić had rightly observed, children can be vicious creatures, especially when thrust together in this kind of environment. Like pack dogs, they feed off each other's negative, hostile energy.

But just as the two boys were about to pounce upon each other again, Milica Stanković intervened. She rushed in between the warring classmates, sunk down to her knees, and began to cry and beseech in wailing, despairing tones, writhing from side to side (not without an element of grace, it must be stated), her hands clasped together, her face a dark, beetroot-red hue, and with great big tears rolling down her cheeks. If nothing else, it had the desired effect of slowing the poisonous flow of energy pulsing through their veins. In truth, it looked as if they didn't know what to do next, what to make of such an unusual scene, something they had never witnessed before.

Such was the sheer force of Milica's outpouring, it wasn't long – barely a minute or so – before one of the teachers came rushing out of the main building.

"Whatever is going on?" she asked in confusion, looking from the little girl knelt on the concrete, prostrating herself in such a pitiable manner, to the two boys, bloodied of noses and with ripped and torn clothing.

When she received no answer to her question, she crouched beside Milica and tried to comfort and console her.

"Shush, shush, it's all right." She patted the girl's shoulder. "You need to calm down. Breathe. You need to get a grip on yourself."

Only she was far too…'upset' may be the wrong word to use; it was as if she had worked herself into such a state of wild, fervorous emotion, she was now in some kind of trance, with her eyes rolling back in her head. And no matter how long and determinedly the teacher shook her shoulder or gently slapped her face, she could not be shaken from that trance.

"My word," muttered the teacher. Lifting her head, she turned to the other children. "One of you go and fetch the nurse, will you? Tell her that we have an emergency situation."

By the time the nurse, a roly-poly septuagenarian suffering from alopecia in its advanced stages, had waddled out of the main building, Milica was much calmer. Rather than wail and writhe, she now lowered her head, clasped her hands together anew, and began to pray in a such a soft, melodious tone of voice, it couldn't help but move all those present. It was a contrary sight, like something from another world, a past world, that they had only read about in books, or heard descriptions of from parents and grandparents alike.

"I've got just the thing for this," said the nurse, breaking the spell somewhat of the vision of this little girl possessed by religious spirits.

From her apron, the nurse produced a jar of smelling salts. But when she placed them under Milica's nose, she neither flinched nor recoiled, despite breathing in and out heavily as she rocked back and forth and recited those whispered prayers.

"Erm, perhaps it would be best if we let the girl work this out of her system in her own time," said the teacher. "We might well do more harm than good if we try to push things."

Standing and straightening, she told the other pupils to return to the classroom.

"Open your textbooks to page fourteen. Your next lesson will commence shortly."

So disturbed were the teachers by Milica's behaviour, they decided to walk her back to the family apartment.

"Whatever has happened?" asked Nevena when she answered the door. "Millie, are you all right, my love?"

The little girl, almost completely recovered by now, if still red-eyed and slightly dishevelled, nodded her head.

Nevena looked up at the teacher. "Why have you brought her home?"

"There was an unpleasant scene in the playground. Two boys had an altercation."

"Altercation?"

"A fight. It got a little out of hand for lads of their age. And I'm afraid it upset Milica terribly. She had what I can only describe as some sort of fit, or seizure. It was, erm…quite disturbing for all concerned. We just couldn't seem to calm her down. I've never seen anything quite like it before."

Nevena's heart sank. It had been such a long time since her daughter had had one of her more extreme bouts of crying and screaming, both she and Dragan had thought they were a thing of the past, even if they always sensed that a mysterious, indefinable 'something special' lurked deep in the girl's heart and soul, just waiting to resurface.

"Oh, I see."

"It's probably best if Milica takes the rest of the week off. Let her rest up and get her strength back. I'm sure she'll feel all the better for it."

*

That year, the steelworks received one of the biggest industrial orders in its history. Overtime was mandatory for every worker. Scores of new men were taken on, both from the town and its environs, and from much further afield. Day and night, delivery trucks rumbled in and out of the complex. The main production line was a hive of activity. The furnaces raged. Always a hellishly hot environment, the increased productivity, not to mention the larger workforce made everything that little bit more challenging, demanding, frantic.

Each evening, when Dragan lifted his first tankard of ale from the counter at the tavern, he could feel the heavy toll the day had taken on his body. It felt as if he was lifting a lead weight.

"I tell you, Robert, steelwork is a young man's occupation."

"Never has a truer word been spoken, my friend. The time I worked in that big steel mill in Krakow were some of the hardest days of my life. Production, production, production. Don't get me wrong. I know all about the dignity of labour, an honest day's pay for an honest day's work. But sometimes in life, the more you give the bastards, the more they'll take."

*

During a particularly hectic shift, Dragan, for the first time in his professional life, succumbed to the demands of the job. As he leaned across a giant smelting pot to grab hold of a heavy steel chain dangling from a girder high up above – something he had done countless times before without incident – he lost his footing, and nearly tumbled head-first into the fiery pot of molten steel. For that split-second of terror, all he could think about was his daughter Milica, and how much he loved the child, and how much he wanted to watch her grow into a fine young woman. And it made him realise just how fleeting and precious life can be. How one misstep, one bad decision, could rob a person of the things they most cherished in this world.

Fortunately, his lapse went unnoticed by the other men, or worse, any of his supervisors. He managed to grab hold of a rail to support himself before it was too late.

But the incident shook Dragan to his core. For the rest of the day, he barely spoke a word to the colleagues he had had to work so hard to re-establish a connection with.

"What's wrong, Stanković?" asked Bubalo. "You've gone a funny ol' colour. White as a sheet. You not feeling too sharp or something?"

"Bah, I'm fine." He waved the words away, but far from convincingly. "I think I may've eaten something that didn't agree with me last night, that's all. I'll be right as rain tomorrow."

On his way home that evening, Dragan had to stop himself as he ploughed a familiar furrow towards the tavern. In fact, he had already reached the main entrance, and was about to push open the door.

"No, no," he whispered under his breath, and forcibly tore himself away from his intended destination. Even though his need was great, even though he could almost taste that first drink on his lips, remembered visions of the fiery abyss that had almost consumed him whole convinced him otherwise.

*

The worst thing that could've happened to Dragan regarding his newfound sobriety was to bump into his drinking partner Robert Savović in town, not a week after he had resolved to change his ways.

"Dragan, where on earth have you been hiding? I had a good mind to call 'round to your apartment to see if you were still living and breathing."

"I've, erm…been a bit under the weather. Food poisoning. And incredibly busy at the steelworks. Plus, we've had some problems with our little girl."

"My word. With such burdens on your shoulders, the tavern is the only place for you! Come. Share a tankard with me now. You can tell me all your troubles. A problem shared is a problem halved, so they say."

Dragan felt the powerful lure of the tavern and all it had come to represent for him. But still he resisted.

"I'm not sure I have time this evening, Robert. Like I said, my little girl has been out of sorts."

"Ach! I understand. I have children myself."

"You have children?"

Dragan couldn't help but express his surprise. Not once, over hundreds of drunken conversations, when it felt as if they had not only lamented the state of society and the sorry lot of the working man, but had told each other everything about themselves, had Savović mentioned that he was a father, too.

"Of course. I've told you many-a-time 'bout my son and daughter. Apples of my eye. Not that I get to see them all that much these days, as I'm on far from good terms with their mother. She's turned them against me in certain respects. But that doesn't mean I don't feel the same powerful stirring in my heart as you're feeling now for little Milica. I know what it's like to be a father, Dragan. Their pain is your pain.

"Now, come on. Tell me everything over a drink. You have my personal guarantee that you'll feel better for it."

*

"You see – ," Robert slipped an arm around Dragan's shoulder and drew him much closer, " – when a man has an experience like you had, nearly toppling into that great pot of molten metal, it does funny things to his head. Quite rightly, he sees it as a sign. The trick in life is in interpreting these signs correctly, and taking the appropriate action. Now, I know at heart that we're both God-fearing men. But you shouldn't necessarily see what happened to you as a bad or negative thing. You shouldn't blame yourself, or the way you're living your life."

"But, Robert, nothing like that has ever happened to me before. These days, in the mornings, especially if we've pushed the boat out the night before, I feel awful. My head's fuzzy, and I often get the shakes in my hands."

"Huh! That's easily cured with a drop of strong spirit. Nothing to worry 'bout. Think no more of it. I'm an old head. I've seen more than my fair share of this life. When you looked death in the face the other day, you were presented with an opportunity, not an ultimatum to change your ways."

"An opportunity?"

"Yes. It's time to make a radical change in your life, before it's too late."

"A change? I don't understand. I have everything I want."

"I know you do. That's exactly what I'm talking 'bout. You have assets you don't even know you've got. Now, listen, if things get too much for you at those steelworks, there might be another way for you to provide for your family. It may not be today, or tomorrow for that matter, but if anything were to go awry, you just come and speak to your old pal Robert Savović."

*

One Friday evening, around the time Dragan was expected back from the tavern (although this had become a shifting and unpredictable arrangement over the last few years), Nevena heard a light tapping at the front door.

"Oh," she said, on finding one of Milica's teachers standing in the hallway. "Miss Tadić. What a surprise."

Miss Tadić was a petite woman of around thirty-five years of age. Modest in appearance and manner, she was a popular figure in both the school and wider community. Known to be a fine and committed educator, she was the kind of teacher who strived to make a true connection with her pupils, who attempted to instil a love of learning in every child who came under her tutelage.

"Good evening, Mrs. Stanković. And apologies for calling 'round at this time of night. I hope it's not too much of an inconvenience. I was in the area and – and, well, something has been troubling me for some time now, something I wanted to discuss with you in person."

"Well, of course, do come in. I put Milica to bed half an hour ago. She usually waits up for her father but he's, erm…been called away on a family emergency."

"Oh dear. I do hope it's nothing serious."

"No, no, just one of those things. I'm expecting him back any minute, in fact."

Nevena ushered Miss Tadić into the main living area and offered her a cup of tea.

"Oh no," said the teacher. "I don't want to put you to any trouble. Besides, I would really like to say what I have to say before your husband returns. Not that it's anything I'm reluctant to share with him. I just think it would be best if we talked, woman to woman."

"Okay. If that's the case, then please sit down."

Both women took a seat at the dining table.

"As you can probably guess, I've come to speak to you about Milica. Quite simply, there's something about your daughter and, more specifically, her schoolwork, that baffles me. Not once, in all the time I've been teaching her, have I actually, physically, witnessed her doing any work."

"What?"

"Please, don't be alarmed. I'm not, for one single second, suggesting that your daughter is lazy, or falling behind with her studies. Far from it. Only when the other children have their heads buried in their books, reading a passage I instructed them to read, Milica invariably has her eyes closed and is deep in what I can only describe as whispered prayer. Yet, if I ask her a question related to the text she clearly hasn't been reading, she always provides the correct answer.

"Likewise, when I set a writing task for the children – and you must understand, I have a classroom of some forty students and can't constantly monitor any single pupil's activities – I rarely, if ever, see Milica so much as lift her pencil. But again, when I check her work, she has carried out the designated task to the letter. It's as if the words had magicked themselves upon the page.

"What I'm trying to say, Mrs. Stanković, is that I'm convinced your daughter is possessed of far superior intelligence to the rest of the children. She can apply herself to the bare minimum and still get more than satisfactory results. The question I keep asking myself – and that's the reason I called 'round this evening – is what would she be capable of if she really, truly did apply herself to her studies? Often in my teaching career, I've seen gifted pupils who, for whatever reason – be it trouble at home or some issues with other children, bullying, and the like – aren't fulfilling their vast potential. In many ways, I consider it my sacred duty to help unlock their talents.

"And I know there were some strange rumours surrounding your daughter, that she had some emotional or psychological problems when she was an infant. In all likelihood, that has had a profound effect on her personality today. There has been a lot of research into this area. Some children, most of whom are withdrawn, seem able to retain information much better than their peers. Their minds are less cluttered with the inconsequentialities of life in comparison to the more, for lack of a better word, popular pupils.

"For that reason, I would like to learn more about Milica's outside interests. For instance, do you read to her at night? Or does she, perhaps, like to read after school herself? Her vocabulary and use of language are highly advanced. And she is an articulate speaker, not that we hear too much from her in class, sadly."

Nevena didn't really know how to respond to Miss Tadić's questions. The only book Milica read, albeit voraciously, was a big, leather-bound bible that she had found in the bottom of a chest in the hallway.

"Well, yes, she does read a lot, most evenings, in fact. Just old books that are laying around the apartment. The classics, I suppose you'd call them. On the weekends we often go for walks into nature – the forest, down by the river. Millie loves to be outside. But she isn't a very outgoing person, in terms of other people. She likes her own company. Not that me and her father haven't tried to encourage her to mix, to make some friends – there's nothing we would like more, truth be told. It just doesn't seem to be something she's particularly interested in."

"I see." Miss Tadić slowly nodded her head; she looked thoughtful and distant for a moment. "It's just as I expected. Well, with your permission, Mrs. Stanković, I would like to try and reach out to Milica. I would like to give her some further reading material, novels which I think would be of great interest to her. If, indeed, reading is a fledgling passion of hers, then I would like to feed the fire, as it were. Books are such a great source of – " The front door swinging open and the sound of heavy padding feet cut her short.

A moment later, Dragan stumbled into the room. Red-faced and reeking of alcohol, he stood semi-swaying in the doorway, not realising, or perhaps unable to assimilate his surroundings through the boozy clouds fogging his brain, that they had a guest.

"Oh," he said, when the fact finally registered. "I didn't expect company." He squinted his eyes, leaned forward, and peered at the petite, neatly dressed woman sitting opposite his wife.

"Miss Tadić, one of Millie's teachers, called 'round," Nevena explained. "She thinks Millie is really intelligent and wants to give her a bit of extra schooling, some new books to read."

"What?" Instantly, stupidly, and wildly overemotional, he hooked a thumb over his shoulder in the direction of his daughter's bedroom. "That – that little girl through there is an angel on God's earth. She's pure, she is. She's better than all of us put together. She don't need no extra schooling or new books to read. It's us who need to learn from her, not the other way around."

*

A few months after Miss Tadić's visit, and Dragan's embarrassing drunken ramble, father and daughter were strolling through the forest in glorious spring sunshine. This had become a regular weekend activity. To put some extra money into the family coffers, Nevena had secured a part-time job at the local chemist shop. Invariably struggling with a wicked hangover, Dragan could think of nothing better to do on these Saturday mornings (bar having another skinful of strong liquor) than to be out in the fresh air, to walk, to get the blood flowing through his veins, to try and battle past the desperate after-effects of another epic drinking session with his friend and mentor Robert Savović.

True to her word, Miss Tadić had provided Milica with some of the finest works of world literature: books which, in truth, were a little advanced for a pupil of her age, but books which had nevertheless set the young girl alight. In her father's presence, Milica finally started to come out of her shell, showing a side of her character that no one – not even her mother – had ever seen before. With great enthusiasm, she told her father about the wonderful books she had read. In particular – and the religious parallels are impossible to ignore – she was drawn to the works of Leo Tolstoy. There was something about the way the great Russian novelist told a story that made a deep impression on Milica.

"And in the end, the poor woman throws herself in front of a train. It was one of the saddest things I've ever read, Daddy. Because Anna is a fine, generous, kind-hearted woman. Granted, she made mistakes in her life. But she should never have met such a tragic end. The people close to her should've recognised her goodness and kindness, and protected and forgiven her. That is what makes us worthy of God's love – that we can rise above our own personal feelings and show compassion, no matter if another person has hurt us terribly."

In time, the bond between them grew stronger and stronger. To the extent that Dragan gladly forsook any extra time he may have spent at the tavern with his drinking brethren, to the extent that he greatly looked forward to kissing his wife goodbye on a Saturday morning, happy in the knowledge that he would spend the rest of the day listening to his daughter's stories, her reflections on the book she was currently reading. In this respect, and in a curious, roundabout way he could never really explain to himself, Milica reminded him of none other than Robert Savović. Not that her stories were told in the coarse, colourful language of his drinking partner, but because they possessed an indefinable quality that it took Dragan months, if not years to identify – a love of life.

"But you see, Daddy, the young man was in a desperate situation. He was ill, terribly hungry, and not quite in his right mind. What he did was awful. No matter how unfortunate your circumstances, or what kind of lowly position you occupy, you should never hurt another human being. But after he kills the moneylender and her sister, he begins to understand the true meaning of what he has done, and how he must pay for his crimes and dedicate his life to something bigger than himself. Miss Tadić said that he goes on a 'journey of redemption'.

"And it made me think about those two boys who got into a fight at school when I was just a little girl. It made me feel incredibly sad. They were so young, and didn't really know what they were doing. If anything, they were acting on instinct, like the way a stray dog might snap and snarl if you accidentally step on its tail in the street. But now, many years later, I often see the two boys in question in town. They are firm friends, and have, to the best of my knowledge, been so ever since they punched and kicked each other in the playground that day. It's so strange. How people have to act badly towards each other – sometimes violently, even – before they realise that love and understanding, compassion and kindness, are what make them truly happy in life."

Dragan said little on their weekend excursions into the forest or down by the river. Perhaps he was a born listener, the kind of person who loved to be regaled with stories, rather than someone who felt compelled to tell any tales of his own. But that's not to say he wasn't moved by his daughter's words. Her level of comprehension, her deep understanding of life, and people and what motivates them, of their baser instincts, was nothing short of amazing. In his lifetime, Dragan had encountered all types of individuals. He had experienced his fair share of hardships and disappointments – none more so than during the years that he and Nevena had failed to conceive a child. He knew what it felt like to be angry and confused, humiliated and desperate. He knew that his daughter was expressing universal truths, things a girl of her age shouldn't possibly be able to appreciate, let alone articulate in such a profound manner. And it made him realise just how special his daughter was, how she was possessed of a spirit and intelligence that weren't quite of this world.

But what was perhaps most striking – and this was something he rejoiced and agonised over in equal measure – was just how different she was in his company than she was in anyone else's, including her mother's. In Nevena's presence, Milica was always restrained and slightly distant. If her mother showed her any affection, if she hugged or kissed her, she didn't seem particularly comfortable, or respond in the way a daughter should respond to her mother's embraces. It was almost as if she didn't feel worthy of that affection, that she felt she had to hold herself back from any earthly, human show of love, because her purpose in life was so much higher. Not that Nevena ever seemed to notice that anything was awry. Her love for Milica had always been pure and unconditional. There are some rare, beautiful souls in this life who want nothing in return for their love. They are happy to simply give of their affection. It has no price tag and makes no demands of the receiver. But that didn't make Dragan feel any better about the situation.

"She always seems so cheerful when you come back from your walks," Nevena remarked one Saturday evening. "You're gone for such a long time, hours and hours. Whatever do you talk about?"

In response, Dragan made a few neutral, general comments – far from the truth, but not so far from the truth to border upon an outright lie – that, nevertheless, satisfied his wife. But had he told her the true content of Milica's long, involved monologues, the passion with which she spoke about the books she had read, he knew it would've wounded Nevena beyond any notion of being lied to or misled, for the simple fact that she had never, ever heard her daughter talk like that. And it was this fear which kept not just the increasingly close relationship between father and daughter, but Milica's emerging personality as well, a complete secret from Nevena.

*

Tellingly, perhaps, it was on one of their cherished Saturday morning walks that an incident took place which led to a dramatic change in the Stankovićs' lives. For reasons not altogether clear to Dragan, they had decided to divert from their normal path and take a circuitous route through the town. In moments of reflection – both immediate and distant – he could never be quite sure if Milica had led the way, or even made a direct suggestion for them to take said route, a route almost bereft of areas of natural beauty or of any particular interest, as if she had foreseen what was about to take place, as if she had been given a sign from above.

Whatever the reason, father and daughter found themselves walking alongside the town's cemetery during a full burial service, at the very moment a coffin was being lowered into the ground. In what was an almost perfect reconstruction of the events that had taken place when Milica was no more than a baby in a pram, she was struck by one of her hysterical fits of despair. Breaking away from her father, she ran over to the mourners in a flood of tears. Dumbstruck, the men, women, and children in attendance (as stiff and emotionless as the mourners all those years ago) didn't quite know what to make of this young girl lamenting their dearly departed's demise. Presuming that she must be a relative of some kind, a few of the older members of the party stepped forward and tried to comfort Milica.

"Don't upset yourself, my girl. He led a good life."

"Yes, calm you down. Everybody has to pass away sometime. And Alexandre was a fine man who will be remembered for years to come."

"That's right. He touched the hearts and minds of so many people."

But Milica would not be soothed, pacified, or quieted to even the remotest degree. In fact, their kind, reassuring words only increased her distress, as if the mere thought of the man's fine moral character and notable achievements made the sadness of his death even harder to bear, even though he was a complete stranger to her. Choking on her upset, she collapsed to the ground, close to the very edge of the open grave, and pounded her fists against the grass and wailed and beseeched and writhed around in such a heartfelt and despairing manner, it couldn't help but affect the mourners themselves – people, it must be said, who had far more legitimate claims to express their sorrow at the man's passing. And again, the bereaved were so moved by Milica's performance (and I don't think it amiss to describe it as such at this point in our story) that they too began to cry, sob, and embrace each other in a manner befitting the sombre occasion.

"He was a great man."

"I can't believe he's gone."

"He'll be sorely missed."

In a fugue-like despair of his own – for he was immediately aware of the potential ramifications – Dragan cursed himself for not running after Milica and dragging her away from the mourners. But there was something about the way the day itself had unfolded, as if preordained, that held him back.

It was a truly remarkable scene. How one young girl had had such a powerful effect on all those around her. It was as if she had tapped into their innermost feelings, thoughts, souls – the tender expressive apparatus that make us truly human, things people had been forced to lock away and repress, things they had been told showed a weakness and sentimentality that had no place in modern society. Within the space of a handful of minutes, Milica had reduced a large group of vacant, blank-faced individuals into one big heaving mass of sorrowful despair. They were now comforting each other, crying on shoulders, heartily blowing noses into cotton handkerchiefs, or huddled close together, sharing warm, whispered reminiscences about the deceased. But what struck Dragan more than anything else – and yet again, this mirrored the transformative effect baby Milica had had on the funeral party many years ago – was the distinct warmth now emanating from the mourners, so palpable and pervasive that it brought a tear to his eye. If he didn't know before – and perhaps he didn't, not really – the true power of Milica's 'gift' had just been revealed to him.

As all those gathered began to recover themselves, one old man – white of hair, slight of build, but not without a certain poise and elegance about his person – approached Dragan.

67

"Alexandre must've made a great impression on your daughter. It gladdens my heart to know that his work is being read by the younger generation."

Dragan blinked in confusion. He had absolutely no idea who the deceased was, or what his work represented.

"Of course," the old man went on, evidently oblivious to the puzzled look on Dragan's face, "he suffered terribly over the last twenty or so years. Writings of that nature were not so much frowned upon by the new regime but banned outright. And I am by no means making any judgements that could, erm…be considered compromising, you no doubt understand me. But things change very quickly in this life. What is frowned upon today may well be embraced tomorrow."

It was only later, as he and Milica (strangely tranquil, in that trance-like state which had baffled both teachers and medical professionals alike in recent years) walked home, that Dragan recalled a glimpse he had got of the deceased's headstone: *Alexandre Mihajlović. A Religious Thinker and Renowned Philosopher.* And it was only then something struck him. It was only then that he asked himself a perplexing yet nonetheless important question. Had, as he previously speculated, their change of route that day been quite as coincidental as it first appeared? Milica's room, after all, was full of books, tomes so weighty the mere sight of them intimidated Dragan more than the biggest and burliest of fighting men (and he had encountered many, both in the steelworks and tavern). It would not be beyond the realms of belief, therefore, to suggest that Milica had read Mihajlović's work, and dearly wanted to pay her respects to a man she genuinely admired.

*

It had indeed been a portentous day for the Stanković family. Like before, news of the extraordinary scene at the cemetery quickly spread across the town. And it most certainly reached the ears of a certain Robert Savović.

But let us not get ahead ourselves. We have one more dramatic scene to describe before the man himself enters our story again in any significant way. For the time being we only have a few brief, yet nonetheless relevant observations to make about his friendship with Dragan Stanković or – perhaps more correctly, about friendships in general.

While it may be too sweeping of a generalisation to say that all influence is bad, some people undoubtedly wield far too much power over others. Likewise, it is strange how much credence we, as human beings, give to the words of those people who have that influence and wield that power. Even though many a sensible individual would've taken any word that came out of Robert Savović's mouth with a whole shaker of salt, not just a pinch, Dragan Stanković had always accepted his advice in regards to drinking as gospel truth. Now, in the mornings, when he woke up with a throbbing headache, dry mouth, delicate stomach, and what were by now almost certainly delirium tremens, he sneaked off to the bathroom and had a few glugs of strong spirit (a bottle of which he had concealed behind the cistern). Like all chronic drinkers, Dragan had become both crafty and paranoid to the extreme.

"Whatever are you doing in there, Dragan?" Nevena hammered on the door impatiently. "You'll be late for work."

"Just on the toilet, my love. I'll be out in a jiffy."

And, happy that he'd allayed both her suspicions and the knocks upon the door, he had another long, glorious swig of his 'magic potion' as he now called it (such miraculous restorative powers did it possess) to celebrate.

Only there is a rank complacency that comes with imbibing strong spirits. Even if the imbibers imagine themselves to be superhuman, blessed with incredible strength and enough wily intelligence to outwit the most celebrated of modern thinkers, they are, invariably, shambling, rambling half-people whose predilection is almost tattooed across their foreheads, rather than being concealed behind the façade they think their fiery elixir has constructed around them. And this was becoming more and more apparent with Dragan Stanković. For months, if not years, the other men at the steelworks had noticed his gradual decline, both physical and mental.

"You can smell it on his breath."

"He's a shadow of the man he were before."

"That Stanković is an accident waiting to happen," were just a few of the observations that had been circulating for some time now.

How word of Dragan's raggedy condition and somewhat ponderous, if not sloppy, working practises hadn't reached the higher-ups at the steelworks was a mystery unto itself. Perhaps the men felt they would be violating a sacred code if they turned informant against one of their own. Or perhaps they realised that it was only a matter of time before Dragan's own actions betrayed him.

And they were right.

For reasons he never really understood (although he had taken to concealing a small hipflask in the inside pocket of his overalls), Dragan – and this could well have been as much by force of habit as a desperate need to satisfy his ever-stronger alcoholic cravings – had the audacity to take the same flask from his pocket one morning, in full view of not only his co-workers, but Mihailo Pančev himself, and have not one, but two liberal guzzles of the potent contents contained therein. In terms of brazenness, a man could not have made a more revealing statement regarding the depths to which he had fallen.

Pančev rushed over.

"Stanković! What on earth do you think you're doing, man? Drinking on the job! For pity's sake, this is a highly dangerous environment. You're putting your life and those of your colleagues at risk. Get to my office right now."

When Dragan sat down in Pančev's office, he was so bleary-eyed and incoherent, and looked so much older and wearier, that it truly shocked his line manager. Over a significant period – the months and years in which Dragan's drinking had come to the notice of his colleagues – Pančev had only ever really had passing, fleeting contact with Dragan, what consisted of a comradely greeting each morning or a standard goodbye at the end of each shift. He hadn't been in the man's presence, certainly not up close enough to scrutinize his appearance – the cloudy, bloodshot eyes, puffy face, and shambling gait – nor smell the sour, alcoholic fumes that no amount of toothpaste or strong mints could ever conceal. And it was this grotesque transformation that made Pančev act so decisively. In the years he'd worked side by side with Dragan Stanković, he had always known him to be a quiet, modest, hardworking man, someone you could rely on in times of crisis. The mumbling, shifting-in-his-seat drunkard who sat before him now bore little-to-no resemblance to the man he had respected for so many years.

"I have no idea what has happened to you, Stanković. But drunkenness on the main production line is unacceptable. In other circumstances, I would suspend you on half-pay for a period of one week and tell you to sober yourself up. But I can tell, just by taking one look at you, that it would take far longer than seven days to dry you out. As such, I suspend you indefinitely. You have a wife and young daughter to provide for. Go and get some help. Go and see Dr. Ivanović."

*

Rather than heed Pančev's well-meaning advice, Dragan – somehow affronted by the treatment he had received, despite the fact he had clearly been the one at serious fault – headed straight to the tavern to drown his sorrows. And we need not speculate as to the first person he saw when he pushed open the door – one Robert Savović.

"You're kidding me!" he cried, when Dragan relayed the news of his suspension. "They've got a nerve, them bosses. I mean, how many years loyal service have you given to those steelworks? Twenty? Twenty-five? And what's a tiny nip of the good stuff just to focus a man's mind and steady his hand in the bigger scheme of things, eh? I tell you, when I was working in those steelworks out in Poland, us men used to pass a bottle of spirit 'round as we worked. It were common practise back then. And never once did we have no accidents or mishaps or ever miss our work quota.

"No. Make no mistake, Dragan. You've been unfairly treated. Let me get you a tankard of ale, and a drop of something stronger to chase it down with."

And thus commenced a drinking session that, even by the standards of Robert Savović and Dragan Stanković, was epic in both proportion and duration. With each subsequent round, Savović offered not only his full sympathy, but made Dragan feel as he had been the victim of a great injustice, to the point where he became infected with a towering sense of resentment, and vowed never to set foot in the steelworks again.

"Those bosses have had their pound of flesh off'a me. Mark my words. It's time I struck out on my own. It ain't healthy for a man to live like a mouse."

"Never has a truer word been spoken, my friend. Now, come on, drink up. We must have one more round before we can even think about returning to our homes."

*

When Dragan stumbled in through the front door late that evening, Nevena was as much appalled as afraid by the sight of him. Barely able to stand, mumbling vicious-sounding curses and bitter oaths under his breath, words so out of character for a man of his usually mild temperament, he knocked one of her favourite porcelain figurines off the mantelpiece, sending it smashing to the floor, before finally managing to slump down in an armchair.

"Dragan, whatever has happened? Why have you got yourself into such a state?"

By this point, however, he was some way past coherence. In the handful of minutes before he fell into a profound alcoholic slumber, something akin to a full-blown medical coma, all he could do was hiss more vicious-sounding curses and bitter oaths, and jab an accusatory finger in the air.

"Don't worry, Mother," said Milica, who appeared completely unconcerned by her father's condition. "I will watch over him while he sleeps, and make sure that he's all right. And when he wakes up, I shall heat up some broth. That way, he will have something warm inside him."

Nevena's first inclination was to refuse and send her daughter straight to her room. She didn't want the girl to see her father in this state. But there was such conviction in Milica's voice, she found herself nodding her head and thanking her daughter for her consideration.

"I'll go to bed now, then, Millie. It's getting late. Make sure he doesn't try and get up, or topple out of the chair and do himself any harm."

In the early hours of the morning, when Dragan eventually stirred from his slumber, he was so full of alcoholic remorse that he, much to his shame and consternation, shed tears in front of his daughter. Milica, true to her word, brought a bowl of wholesome beef soup through from the kitchen, and spooned the contents into his mouth in the way a parent would feed an infant child.

"Slowly," she said. "There's no rush. Take your time. You don't have to be at work today, after all."

Dragan gave a slight start, mid-soup slurp. "How did you know that?"

"You were talking in your sleep. Please, don't worry about a thing. It's not your fault, but mine. I'm the reason why you fell out of favour with the people at the steelworks."

"You? Why no, my darling. It was —"

"Please, Father, I'm not stupid. I've heard all the stories that have been circulating around town. I know how many problems I have caused you and mother. I hope you don't resent me for making your life so difficult."

"Resent you? Of course I don't. Whatever gave you such a silly idea? You're my own flesh and blood. My only child. I love you more than anything in the whole wide world. And I'm the only one to blame for losing my job. It's the ruddy drink. I can't believe I've let it get a-hold of me like this. I've got to stop. I've got to knock it on the head, once and for all. I've got to get back on the straight and narrow."

"No, Father, that isn't true. You should drink. It makes you happy. It's good for you; it brings you closer to God."

Dragan shot his daughter a quick, questioning glance. The rusty, drink-addled cogs in his head began to turn. Had he heard correctly? Had his daughter, the young girl with such a powerful spirituality, a connection to the Lord, actually encouraged him to continue drinking? And if so, could he argue with, what was, from a certain point of view, the word of the Almighty Himself?

"For now," said Milica, "you must rest. Mother is worried. You need to speak to her and explain the situation. But please, don't worry. I know that everything will be all right. I know that you will come up with a solution to our problems as a family."

*

"When a man suffers at the hands of authority," said Robert Savović, with one of his arms draped around Dragan's shoulders, "as you have suffered, it causes him to drastically reassess his life."

"Exactly, that's just what I were saying to my Nevena this morning. What's done is done. There's no point crying over spilt milk. We've got to move on."

"Never has a truer word been spoken, Dragan. In times of crisis, a family has to pool their collective resources. You're a highly skilled tradesman. Your wife has been making herself very useful at the chemist shop, so I hear. And then there's that daughter of yours."

"Milica?"

"Yes," said Savović. "Her unique gifts could make men with vision, men like you and I, a pretty penny."

"However do you mean? She's just a girl. I wouldn't dream of putting her out to work."

"No, no – ," Savović raised his free hand, palm upturned in mock surrender of the point, " – you misunderstand me. I'm not talking about work, per se, something more in the…entertainment line, if you catch my drift."

"No. No, I don't." Dragan rose up from the counter, feeling suddenly affronted.

"Calm yourself, my friend. I will explain everything in due course. But first, let me tell you a little story. Something which might help put things in the proper context.

"Now, you remember when I mentioned the time I spent in Germany? Well, there were these two young lads I heard 'bout, both of whom wanted to be cobblers. As it so happened, there was a master shoemaker in the area, a fella who was getting a bit long in the tooth and who wanted to pass his knowledge on to the younger generation. Hence, he took these two lads on as apprentices. For the best part of six years, Boy A and Boy B – that's what we'll call 'em, for sake of argument – lived and worked with the old man, the master cobbler. Each morning, they got up, ate a modest breakfast, and spent the rest of the day in the workshop, learning the shoemaking trade. Eager to get on in life, to perfect their art, as it were, the boys were good listeners and hard workers. Anytime the old man imparted a bit of wisdom, they hung from his every word, taking in every last detail. They went above and beyond, would stay in the workshop long after the working day had ended, honing their skills, the techniques their master had painstakingly showcased. And it was this dedication, the way they devoted every waking hour to becoming master tradesmen themselves, that gave their teacher a new lease on life, that saw him live out a few more years than anybody would have thought possible before he took on his two apprentices.

"Those six years passed quickly. A and B were now the most highly skilled and sought-after shoemakers in the entire region. Each day, the workshop was a hive of activity. The great and the good, men and women of the highest office and repute, the moneyed elite would all call in for fittings, or to deliver old shoes for repairs. Steadily, A and B's stock rose. Business could not have been better. The footwear they produced could not have been of higher quality, comfort, or durability. And the old man – he was still alive at the time – oversaw all of this, night and day, week after week.

"In time he signed over the premises to the boys. But he couldn't go on forever. One evening at the height of an unusually hot summer, he suffered a mild yet significant stroke, which brought him to the very foot of death's door. Before he passed away, tho', he called the two boys to his bedside and told them how proud he was of their achievements, how their talents now eclipsed his own, and how he wanted them to always go on working together – that no matter what direction life would take them, they had trained side by side, that people would always need shoes, and that there were more than enough feet in a region this size to support two tradesmen of their skill and dedication.

"He died an hour later.

"But times change, Dragan. You know that better than anyone else on this earth. The town grew at an exponential rate. Progress dictated. Factories were built. Heavy machinery was imported. The town developed into a commercial mecca. Instead of selling their wares from the back of the old man's workshop, the two cobblers now had a hired pitch on the market square, and sold their fine, leather handcrafted shoes from separate stalls, to capture the biggest share of custom. It wasn't long before the town square itself was completely transformed, the ramshackle wooden shops torn down and replaced with sturdy brick, rows and rows of ample-spaced business premises for sale or rent.

"Now, with wives and young families of their own, the two shoemakers eventually decided to go their separate ways. Feeling no animosity towards each other whatsoever, they both invested in modest business premises on opposite sides of the now thriving town (just as they had occupied market stalls in their younger days). Such was the swell in population, they knew their master's deathbed assessment had been correct, that the area was more than capable of supporting two shoemakers, that citizens would always need an abundant supply of the finest footwear.

"Many more years passed. Both businesses flourished. The shoemakers became very rich men indeed. They had an unspoken agreement to never undercut each other. They lived in perfect harmony, producing exactly the same models of footwear, of the same impeccable quality. So consistent, so precise, the townsfolk could never quite separate them, could never quite tell who was the more highly skilled tradesman. On occasion, arguments would break out between friends or work colleagues. A man would roll up his trouser leg to show off a shiny handstitched brogue or hobnailed working boot he had just purchased from either A or B. In turn, said friend or colleague would roll up *his* trouser leg and show off *his* newly purchased footwear by way of comparison. After much debate regarding the quality of the leather, stitching, comfort, fit, they would invariably concede that there was nothing to choose between the two shoes, that one cobbler was just as gifted as the other.

"But each man (now well into his middle years, approaching the autumn of his life, so to speak) secretly felt that he was the better tradesman, the superior shoemaker. Not that they shared that conviction with anyone else, not even their closest family and friends. It became a kind of vanity, something they savoured late at night before they drifted off to sleep, something they felt the other man tacitly accepted. With rose-tinted relish, they recalled their master's words, occasions when he had bestowed specific praise upon them, occasions their work had particularly pleased him. Perhaps both were guilty of embellishing these scenes (perhaps even inventing them completely – the passage of time can muddy a mind full of conceited thoughts), creating counterfeit memories where the other boy had been slighted, and put firmly in his place in the hierarchy. But whenever the two men met in the street by chance, they couldn't have been more friendly, cordial, sharing a warm embrace and asking about each other's family. At the back of their minds, however, each harboured a distinct superiority, convinced that he was the better tradesman, but terrified that the opposite may, in fact, be the case.

"So when A was officially awarded the title of Master Tradesman and B was overlooked, it filled B with resentment, fuelling a hatred which had lain dormant for years. No matter how many people, customers, family, and friends expressed their astonishment (some even went so far as to suggest that underhanded means had been involved), he couldn't contain his anger. Feeling as if he had been betrayed by the whole town, he reduced the prices of all his shoes, the entire range stocked in his shop. In response, A felt that he had to do likewise. This went on for several weeks until a vicious price war broke out, wiith both businesses offering their shoes at a rate which didn't even cover the costs of producing them in the first place.

"Late one night, the big plate-glass window in A's shop was smashed with a brick. 'Kids', said the local police constable, 'we're seeing more and more of it these days. Now the factories have closed down, now you can easily jump on a train to the city, the town has been left behind. The children are bored. Most can't find work. And this is the result. Sorry to say, Mr A Master Tradesman, but it looks like you're the victim of a wider social malaise.'

"And he was right. Life in town had become much harder. With the introduction of cheap overseas imports, the heavier industries had slowly gone out of business. The factories the townsfolk depended upon for their livelihoods had shut down. Unemployment, drunkenness, and crime were rife. The entire region suffered. The smaller shops struggled to survive. But that didn't stop A from venting his spleen, circulating his suspicions, and laying the blame for his smashed window firmly at B's door. Jealousy was the motivating factor, he told many a respected member of the community, knowing full well that his story would get back to B. 'He could never accept that I was the better tradesman, that I enjoyed the favour of our master far more than he, that I was always the chosen one.'

"Naturally, this scathing rebuke made him even more enraged. Not just because of the secret fears he had always harboured, but because B knew that he was indeed guilty of the original criminal offence – the smashing of the window – and that he had, for petty and vindictive reasons, broken their age-old unspoken agreement regarding their pricing policy. 'No,' he told the same respected members of the community (them, and any others willing to listen), 'A was only given that award because he'd ingratiated himself with regional dignitaries. Each week he was up at the freemason's tavern buying committee members endless drinks. His award was bought through bribery, literally lubricating the wheels of commerce.'

"When this in turn reached A, he was beside himself with rage and wounded pride. Because he, just like B when hearing those well-founded accusations regarding the act of vandalism, knew there was more than grain of truth in B's statement. In recent years he had frequented the tavern far more often than at any other time in his life. He had tried to curry favour with those of influence in town, cosying up to them, always offering discounted footwear (more or less giving his beautifully handcrafted shoes away for free), always being the first man at the bar, buying all and sundry a glass or two of premium liquor. In many ways he had become a clown to these people, a yes-man, a buffoon. In many ways he had prostituted himself to the revered members of the community in the hope of receiving the cherished title of Master Tradesman, in hope of finally usurping his former friend and colleague.

"And there's nothing worse in this life than someone seeing right through the flimsy façade of respectability you've tried to create to cover your baser motivations, when they see you for exactly what you are.

"To appease this horrible sense of shame and self-reproach, A took the foolhardy and almost suicidal step, from a business point of view, of swapping all his shop's display model shoes over from right foot to left. An unprecedented, highly controversial, and spiteful move, because A and B manufactured the exact same type of shoes. They had, after all, been trained by the same man. For that reason, shoplifters (and remember, the town, now in decline, had become rife with thievery of all kinds) could now help themselves to a right shoe on display outside A's shop, dash across town, and match it with a display shoe outside B's shop – of which there were unsupervised racks upon unsupervised racks.

"Another unspoken rule had been unceremoniously broken. Since the first shoe shop opened its doors, the display model shoes were seen as worthless, of no use to anyone, because unless you suffered the misfortune of having lost a leg or foot, right or left, one shoe was no good without the other, its rightful twin.

"When the more kleptomaniacally-minded townsfolk became aware of this development, they exploited it for their own benefit. It heralded a mini-crimewave which threatened to bankrupt both businesses. One gang would steal one shoe from A's establishment whilst another gang would steal the corresponding shoe from B's, making a matching pair. In smoky taverns, dozens of shoes were now being bartered, mixed and matched, until a whole black market of stolen shoes flourished, until even half-respectable members of the community were walking around in illegally procured shoes crafted by the hands of two different tradesmen, yet that were indistinguishable from right foot to left.

"At the height of their dispute, one town councillor attempted to intercede. He went to visit each shoemaker in turn. He tried to make them see sense, to revert back to their old sensible business practices, in both pricing policy and which shoe they displayed outside their shops. But these were stubborn men, who each refused to accept that they were responsible for creating the situation in the first place, who refused to even discuss the matter, refused to back down, even if it meant that they would go went out of business. 'With bribery of local officials being common practise,' said B, 'with certain businessmen paying off those in the know to receive coveted awards, I'd have thought the widespread thieving of shoes was the least of your concerns.'

'But I'm *the* Master Tradesman,' A contended. 'Surely my status alone should afford me protection from a petty saboteur intent on encouraging the town to descend into anarchy'."

Savović fell silent, reached for his glass, and took a great swallow of his ale.

"And do you know why I've told you this story, Dragan?"

He shook his head.

"Because I was the original street urchin who went from shop A to shop B pinching those shoes. I was the one in those taverns matching the right-footed shoe with the left. I was the one who turned the whole situation to my advantage. And while those two stupid old fools argued the toss, I filled my pockets. It's called opportunity. And that's what you've been presented with in the form of your daughter's incredible gift. And it's an opportunity I'd like to help you and your family make the most of."

Part Two

In the beginning, Robert Savović's tactics were somewhat amateurish and rudimentary. Each day, he scanned the death announcements in the regional newspaper. Noting down the names of the deceased's family members, he attempted to contact the bereaved by telephone. Naturally, in the circumstances, he received one harsh rebuff after another. In most cases, the people he contacted couldn't quite comprehend what kind of service he was offering them.

"A professional mourner?"

It was only as he became bolder, as he polished his salesman's patter – 'You owe it to your late husband's memory to put provisions in place that ensure the true nature of the devastation you feel upon his passing is expressed at the funeral in an appropriate manner' – that he generated even a modicum of interest.

"We have achieved spectacular results in the past," he openly lied to one potential client. "On such occasions, loved ones are afraid to show their emotions. That's where we come in. Our professional mourner will display such sadness at the passing of your grandmother, that everyone present will react in kind. We guarantee that there will not be a dry eye in the house, and that the funeral will be a celebration of your departed's life and truly show how much love and respect you had for her."

But still, not one of the families followed up on their initial interest and booked Milica's services. Moreover, Dragan's enthusiasm for the proposal had started to waver.

"I don't know if I like the idea of all of this. These people are grieving. They don't want no one calling 'em up and offering such a peculiar ruddy service."

"Granted," Savović replied. "It's a delicate operation, but what you must understand, my friend, is that we are satisfying a very real demand in the market. You've seen with your own eyes what has happened to people over the last ten, twenty years. They've become like robots. They don't know how to express their emotions no more. They need encouragement, visual aids, if you like, to tease them out of their shells. Peculiar our service might be, but its relevancy and importance cannot be denied. Mark my words. As soon as we get up and running, as soon as we've made a name for ourselves, the money will start rolling in."

When Dragan sat Milica down, explained the situation, and asked how she felt about any potential involvement, her reply left him even more confused and uncertain.

"I will do whatever I can to help the family."

"I know that. You're a good girl. But you're not really answering my question. This 'gift' of yours, is it something you can control? Is it something you can summon up at will, or does there have to be special circumstances or what have you?"

"Father, please, you don't have to worry about me. If God wills it, we shall enjoy great success in whatever we set out to do in life."

"But you understand what's expected of you?"

"Of course. And I will play my part to the full, and do my very best not to disappoint you."

*

Their breakthrough came a few weeks after Savović's proposal in the tavern. In conversation with a fellow former convict, Savović had learned of the death of a high-ranking official's wife. By all accounts, the man in question (a certain Predrag Dedić) was devastated by the loss of his partner of over fifty years. To mark the occasion, he had been putting all kinds of elaborate, not to mention costly arrangements in place – a funeral procession through the centre of town, the finest marble headstone, a lavish wake at the civic hall (a huge venue usually reserved for classical concerts and political rallies). But in private – and how Savović's associate came by this information was questionable to say the least – Dedić was seriously concerned about the potential success of the event. His late wife, Maria, was a particularly unpopular woman. Known to be a vicious gossip and singularly cold-hearted and conniving creature, she had, on more than one occasion, used her husband's influence to avenge herself for any number of petty perceived slights. In one extreme case, she persuaded Dedić to put parking restrictions outside the local bakery, all because the baker's wife had failed to return her greeting at a social event. The fact that the poor woman was so partially-sighted that she was registered blind, failed to dampen Mrs Dedić's sense of outrage. The result: a forty-five percent drop in sales. For that, and any number of similar reasons, her husband was worried that there may not be any genuine outpouring of emotion for his beloved wife's passing.

Contriving a chance meeting – although contrivance is perhaps an unsuitable word in the circumstances, considering he waited outside Dedić's office for five hours straight – Savović played out his role of concerned, compassionate citizen to perfection, before adeptly launching into full salesman mode.

"I just wanted to offer my heartfelt condolences for your loss," he said, having borderline accosted Dedić as soon as the bewhiskered old man stepped into the corridor. "I know it's no consolation, but your late wife was well-known for her charitable work, and did so much good in the local community, that I know she will be sorely missed."

"Thank you," said Dedić, in that dim distant way those recently bereaved tend to react, as their minds are somewhere else altogether. "I appreciate your kind words at this most difficult of times."

"That said – ," here, Savović paused for a moment longer than was necessary (a strictly tactical and ultimately successful move) " – it always pays to put provisions in place to ensure that the day goes off precisely in the manner you had envisaged. What I mean to say is, there is nothing worse than a poignant occasion without the appropriate degree of poignancy. It would certainly be tragic if, for instance, the sense of that occasion held people back from expressing their true emotions, their sense of loss, grief, bewilderment at the baffling nature of our own mortality, how the best amongst us are taken far too soon."

On hearing those words, what very much constituted his own secret fears expressed out loud, Dedić roused from the haze of his distant distraction.

"Yes, of course, it is a worry. Most citizens are in awe of people in my position – people who occupy a high station in social life, that is."

"Never has a truer word been spoken, sir. Therefore, I would suggest you make certain arrangements to ensure that that isn't the case."

"How do you mean?"

"That I happen to know of a service that will guarantee the success of your sad event."

"What service?"

"A professional mourner is what you need, sir. Make no mistake. And I know the ideal young lady to help lament your wife's passing in the perfect way."

*

On the day of the funeral, the most revered, influential, and decorated members of the local community were all in attendance. And, as Dedić had feared, there was such a lack of sincerity in the eyes of everyone who came over to shake his hand, or pat his back and offer words of commiseration, it angered, hurt, humiliated, and insulted him in equal measure. It felt like the graveside was populated by granite and stone statues rather than flesh and blood human beings. Moreover, there was a distinctly chilly and unpleasant undertone to the proceedings, as if these people hadn't gathered to pay their respects, but rather to verify for themselves that the deceased was really, truly dead. On more than one occasion, Dedić could've sworn that he heard a whispered comment, an unpleasant word or two about his wife's character. If the professional services he had paid so handsomely for had not arrived at the timeliest of moments – when the coffin was about to be lowered into the ground – the councillor may very well have joined her in death, such was the intense pounding of his heart and the blood throbbing in his temples.

In terms of pure theatricality, drama, and pathos, Milica's entrance onto this barren, stilted scene could not have been more perfectly choreographed. Dragan's fears as to whether his daughter would be able to summon up the requisite power of emotion proved completely unfounded. Pushing her way through the crowd of mourners gathered at the graveside, the young girl threw herself to the ground in front of the coffin in a fit of sobs so gut-wrenchingly violent, it visibly shook every person present. Rising to her knees, her hands clasped tightly together, she wailed and sobbed and lamented and cried, "Why, why, why?" over and over again. She moaned, groaned, and writhed as if in intense physical, not just spiritual, pain. In response – and this display was so wildly demonstrative it was impossible for any person not to react (they would've really had to have been granite and stone statues not to have been moved in any way) – the whole congregation began to sob, if not break out in floods of tears themselves.

Sensing that this was his cue, the councillor dropped to his knees right beside Milica, and began to cry and beat a frail old man's fist against his chest, to tear at his wispy white hair, and repeat his wife's name in a throaty, wheezing whisper that his grief (both genuine and contrived) would never quite let him articulate in full.

"Mari…Mari…Mari…"

From his vantage point, concealed in some bushes fifteen or twenty feet away, Dragan – as moved as everyone else present – noticed something in Milica which stirred memories of those early days just after she was born, when both he and Nevena could've sworn that she broke off from one of her crying fits, if only momentarily, to appraise her parents, to see if it had garnered the reaction she had hoped for. Now, in this veritable maelstrom of collective grief, he witnessed the same phenomenon. Milica suddenly stopped bewailing and lamenting, and stole a glance at all those present, just to see if they, just like her mother and father all those years ago, had been affected by her performance in the way she wanted them to be.

"Just look at her go." Savović nudged Dragan's elbow, dismissing those memories and, indeed, the sight of Milica's momentary pause from his mind. "That girl of yours is a sight to behold, a real force of nature. If we play this right, my friend, we'll be set for life."

*

The day after the funeral – the grandest the region had seen for quite some time – Dedić used his immense influence to ensure that the event was front-page news. With more than a little creative licence, he didn't merely vet but more or less dictated word-for-word the contents of the report:

Yesterday afternoon, there were hugely emotional scenes at the funeral of Maria Dedić, wife of esteemed councillor Predrag Dedić. At one point in proceedings, one of the Dedićs' nieces broke down in such a wild outpouring of grief, it reduced every single mourner to floods of tears. A fitting tribute to a wonderful woman who will be greatly missed by everyone who knew her.

And even though it soon became common knowledge that the councillor had hired professional services to make it appear as if his wife was far more revered than she actually was, he remained wholly unbothered, not concerned in the slightest. For the day to have been such a sombre yet successful occasion, surpassing even his own wildest imaginings – and the fact it had been reported in the press for posterity – were more than enough to satisfy the man himself, and secure the professional mourning service a generous bonus.

But it meant so much more than just one-off remuneration for Robert Savović and Dragan Stanković. No matter how many days they went off on a wild drinking spree to celebrate their success. No matter how little money was left over after said spree. Both men knew that this was just the beginning of a very lucrative business partnership. Then as now, word of mouth is an incredibly powerful tool. For all his tireless (and ultimately fruitless) preliminary work, making phone calls, regurgitating his spiel to people so grief-stricken they could barely respond, that one chance conversation with a former prison inmate transformed their lives forever more. Never again did Savović have to peruse the death notices in the local paper or pick up a telephone. Now, customers (or 'clients', as he liked to call them) approached him, en masse.

"Are you the chap who organises them professional mourning services?"

"That young girl, the one who appeared at old lady Dedić's funeral, is she available late next week?"

"I just want to send my Filip off in the right way. Only my family isn't the closest. But if your girl was to perform her services, I reckon it would be more than enough to bring us close together again."

*

A fortnight after the Dedić funeral, when the two fledgling businessmen had finally managed to sober up, they confirmed three more bookings for the upcoming week. With a little tactical finagling – Milica would have to miss a full day of schooling – and persistent persuading – Nevena wasn't very happy about the idea of her daughter missing any classes – they set out on a thirty-kilometre journey to Knez Selo, a small village of around eight or nine hundred souls.

"Funny ol' booking, if you ask me," Dragan observed, as Savović manoeuvred a borrowed van – a rusty, semi-dilapidated vehicle with a tubercular engine and screechy fan belt – over some rutted country lanes. "Back of beyond. How on earth did they hear 'bout Millie and everything she can do for 'em?"

"Word travels fast, my friend. Besides, who are we to argue? A fee has been agreed and will be paid on arrival. In addition, I managed to negotiate a few refreshments. Namely, all the rakija we can drink."

"Rakija, you say?"

"Some of the most potent in the region, so I'm told. It's sure to be a fine occasion for all concerned."

"Well, let's just hope they have the necessary finances to pay up. Last time I passed through these here parts, all I remember seeing were a few tatty old shacks and a rundown church."

And it was this phenomenon that surprised the two men most in the early days of their entrepreneurship – the number of ordinary, everyday people, those without that much money, who contacted them. Far from the most affordable of services – from the outset, Savović felt that they should pitch themselves at the 'high-end of the market' – it seemed strange that people who struggled to put food on their tables were willing to make such a relatively extravagant outlay.

The reasons why, however, were revealed on that very visit to Knez Selo, during what constituted only their second-ever booking. When they pulled up alongside the cemetery, it was plain to see that the raggedly-dressed mourners were split into two distinct factions. More tellingly still, that those factions bore the utmost hostility towards each other. To say the atmosphere was prickly when Savović, Dragan, and Milica disembarked from the van would've been a vast and unquantifiable understatement. From opposite sides of the fresh hole dug in the ground, men, women, and even children eyed each other with visible disdain.

"I'd wager a bet that this is a family at war," Savović whispered to Dragan. "I'd wager a bet that that's the reason they hired our services. One side wants to outdo the other and stake a claim to an inheritance."

And that proved to be very much the case.

Immediately after the funeral and all that Milica had contributed to proceedings, Savović learned that the deceased, the beloved brother of an elderly spinster with pots of money, had pledged to leave his own not-insubstantial fortune to his 'less fortunate' kith and kin. Only he died before drawing up an official will, and the ultimate dissemination of his estate was to be decided by his sister. Resorting to any means necessary, the Jovetić faction (as they were called) had contacted the professional mourning service with the sole intention of outshining the Ilić faction, and currying favour with the old spinster who held their fate in her hands.

When the coffin was about to be lowered into the ground, and Milica made her suitably dramatic entrance – crying, wailing, sobbing, prostrating herself to the heavens above – the Ilić clan sensed exactly what was afoot – namely, foul play, that Milica was, for want of a better word, an imposter. To counter what many would consider underhanded means in securing the legacy, the matriarchal figure on the Ilić side of the family began to cry and sob and drop to her knees before the grave in the exact same way as the young girl who had just burst upon the scene so unexpectedly.

"Oh, my dear Uncle Sladen. Why has God taken you from us so soon?"

In a counter-counter offensive, the men on the Jovetić side of the grave dropped to their knees and burst out in uncontrollable but clearly counterfeit tears (these were big burly men who worked in the fields, men with little or no education, men who, even though they felt it incumbent upon themselves to perform in this way, were woeful actors of the very worst stamp). Not to be outdone, the men of the Ilić faction did likewise. Now, Milica was marooned in the middle of the warring families trying to out-cry, out-sob, and out-bewail each other. But it didn't end there. The women on each side joined in, only in a far more hysterical thus totally unconvincing manner. The children quickly followed suit. If a child on one side of the family divide let out a feigned cry of despair, a child on the other side let out an even louder, if identically feigned cry of their own.

"Uncle Sladen, we love you. You were our favourite uncle. Why did this have to happen?"

"Uncle Sladen, we miss you. If only we could see you one last time."

Leaning up against the van, guzzling away at what amounted to an unlimited supply of the strongest of strong liquor, Savović and Dragan couldn't quite work out if what appeared to be taking place in front of them was actually happening, or if the rakija in Knez Selo had potent hallucinogenic properties.

"This is very odd behaviour, Robert. Very odd indeed."

"Never has a truer word been spoken. Money, I'm afraid, Dragan, brings out the very worst in people."

How or when this pantomime of the absurd would have ended had not the old woman herself intervened was impossible to predict, as neither side looked ready to back down any time soon.

"Stop it this instant!" She waved her walking stick in the air. "You idiots. The money was always going to be shared out on an equal basis. All my dear brother Sladen wanted was for everyone in the family to get along again, just like we used to in the old days. It was his dying wish. But after today, I can see that is far from the case. For that reason, I refuse to hand over a single dinar until you change your ways."

*

"I'll tell you what, Dragan – ," Savović made a clumsy drunken grab for his friend's elbow as they stumbled over towards the van, " – that was a real eye-opener, I can tell you."

"How do you mean?"

"Think about it. Most families can't stand the sight of each other, right? When an old 'un croaks it, like this here Sladen chap today, they're at each other's throats to get the lion's share of the legacy. If we do our due diligence, we could quite easily bump up our fee, or perhaps even come to some arrangement with the client themselves."

"What? Take a cut of the will, you mean? A percentage?"

"Exactly. And if the stakes are high, we might go so far to offer our services on a no-win, no-fee basis."

*

Later that week, at a funeral in Novi Sad, they encountered a similar set of circumstances. One group of relatives had secured the services of a professional mourner to outdo rivals to a legacy. And while this was a far more subdued affair in comparison to the phony emotional battlefield in Knez Selo, the animosity on display was almost painful to behold, the way members of the same family would deploy any tactics, no matter how sly or underhanded, to secure financial remuneration over their rivals. But rather than try and intervene when Milica interrupted proceedings with her trademark outpouring of graveside emotion, the other side of the family reserved their outrage for the moments immediately after the funeral had ended.

Through no fault of her own, Milica became, if not embroiled in, then certainly at the centre of a bitter, furious debate.

"Who is this girl?" A pug-nosed old man jabbed a finger in Milica's direction. "I've never seen her before in my life."

"Why, she's the niece of my first cousin, Roberta. She often used to visit during the summer and got very close to grandmother."

"Bah! Horse shit," spluttered a younger, but identically pug-nosed man on what was clearly the other side of the family divide. "That girl there is a professional mourner. Your lot brought her in from the city. I've been reading all 'bout it in the papers."

This triggered an even more bitter and furious debate. Not just over the validity of Milica's identity and whether she had a special place in the heart of the deceased, but whether or not any such profession even existed.

"I've never heard so much nonsense in my entire life – a professional mourning service! There's no such thing. You're just sour 'cause our side of the family showed how much more Grandmother meant to us than your lot did."

"How dare you!" cried a woman's voice from deep within what was now a chaotic melee. "I nursed and looked after that woman, day and night, for over five year after she had that fall. I bathed and dressed her. I cleaned her up after she'd soiled herself. That's a damn sight more than your family ever did. And it takes a hell of a lot more than a few crocodile tears to prove otherwise."

"What are you talking 'bout?" A stout, red-faced woman pushed her way through a tight clinch of bodies. "It were me who nursed the old girl. You were nowhere to be seen when she couldn't control her bodily functions no more. It were me that were elbow deep in shit and piss. Besides, you lot of thieving bastards were over that cottage before her body were even cold, helping yourself to anything of any value. Not for sentimental reasons, mind. No. I seen some of her best porcelain in a market stall the other day. Bloody scavengers, you are, mercenaries."

"Lies!" cried the same woman as before. "Everything we took from that cottage were given us by Grannie. In the weeks before she died, she told me exactly what she wanted me to have after she were gone. Simple as that."

"A likely story. But don't you for one minute think you're getting your hands on that cottage. By birthright, it's mine. And I've got all the proper legal paperwork to prove it."

*

On the way back to Velika Plana, with Savović and Dragan sitting in the front of the van, passing a bottle of rakija back and forth, Milica posed a somewhat awkward and philosophical question.

"Father, why are people so greedy?"

Dragan, at that moment counting through a great wad of well-thumbed banknotes, didn't quite know how to answer his daughter.

"Erm, it's hard to say, my darling. It's only natural for folk to want a better life for 'emselves, I s'pose. But where families are concerned, things can get a little nasty and out of hand."

"But why can't they just share things out, fairly, like the old woman said at the funeral in Knez Selo?"

Savović interceded. "Listen, Milica, I know you won't want to hear this, but in my experience, people aren't particularly good, noble, or worthy creatures. Years ago, in the seaport of

Odessa, I saw twin brothers fight over a chicken bone. Not 'cause they wanted it, just so the other one couldn't have it. And unfortunately, over the last few days, you've seen examples of that, you've seen the very worst of humanity."

"I don't believe that for one minute," said Milica. "At heart, people are good. Only some have been led down the wrong path and need a helping hand to see the light again."

*

It was a very different and incredibly tragic story at their final performance of the week. When they arrived at a cemetery in Sopot, they found it almost deserted, bar for a lone figure who stood before a hole in the ground with a great pile of soil gathered beside it. For a horrible moment, Savović feared that they might have gone to the wrong destination.

"Strange." He brought the old van to a juddering halt. "I'm certain we're at the right place. I know this part of the world like the back of my hand. I used to chew bread for the ducks of a rich fella who lived just across the way there."

Both Dragan and Milica couldn't help but chuckle at the surreal image he had just conjured.

"What?" Savović feigned perplexity. "It's true. The duck is a very discerning eater. He won't swallow his bread down unless it's chewed just right." He pushed opened the door. "I'll just have a quick word with that old girl over by the grave. Maybe she can shed some light on all of this."

He returned a few minutes later with an uncharacteristically stern, almost troubled look upon his face.

"We're in the right place. Only we won't be having to deal with no crowds of backstabbing family members trying to get one over on each other today, I can tell you."

"How d'you mean?" asked Dragan.

"That Mrs Čubrić over there is the sole and chief mourner. She's all on her own."

"What?"

"It's true." Savović turned to Milica. "Is this okay with you? I mean, it might be a little awkward, different from what you're used to."

"Of course. It's God's will. I consider it an honour to share Mrs Čubrić's grief, and help her with her burden."

In what turned out to be an almost excruciatingly poignant spectacle, Milica approached Mrs Čubrić and exchanged a few brief words before embracing her. For a good hour, maybe longer, the old woman and the young girl knelt before the grave in silent prayer, their shoulders pressed tightly together. Even when some light, drizzly rain started to fall and the wind began to whip up the dead leaves that had fallen from the trees, they could not be parted.

"This is another rum ol' situation – ," Savović passed a bottle of spirit to his friend and business partner, " – I had no idea she meant it would only be her when she told me it would be a small, intimate gathering."

"This last week has been full of surprises, Robert. If nothing else, our new business venture is certainly an interesting one."

"Never has a truer word been spoken." Savović took the bottle back from Dragan and had a liberal swallow from the neck. "It's sad, though, to have but one person see you off to the other side. Now and then, I visualise my own funeral in my head and wonder who will and won't be in attendance. Naturally, for a man who's travelled far and wide, word of my inevitable demise won't reach some of my former friends and associates, people who may well want to raise a glass to my memory. But I hope I've made a lasting impression on some good, kindly souls who won't abandon me to the same fate as poor old Mr Čubrić. I don't mind telling you, the very thought terrifies me."

Dragan felt suddenly emotional. He had never heard his drinking partner talk with such sentimentality before. It made him think about his own funeral, and the people that would gather at his graveside.

"Death is an odd concept, Dragan, 'specially for those who feel so alive it's as if they're an essential part of the ebb and flow, the moon, the stars, the sun, the ocean. Maybe that's why we drink – to keep living that life rather than ponder what comes after."

*

"No," said Milica, as Mrs Čubrić took a wad of banknotes out of her money belt. "We will not accept any payment."

"But, Milica," said Savović, stepping (a little unsteadily, it must be said) forward, "we had an agreement in place. And there are basic expenses to take into account – fuel for the vehicle, our food and, erm…drinks. We have to eat, after all. It would be –"

"No," Milica repeated. "There will be plenty of opportunities for you to make money in the coming weeks and months. Like I said before, it was a great privilege to be with Mrs Čubrić today. No money should change hands."

Savović adopted several other lines of reasoning, some more persuasive than others, but Milica would not be swayed, even when he, not so much lost his temper (he was an experienced negotiator who knew that any loss of control was fatal to achieving one's swindling goals), but rather pressed a little harder, lessening his demands.

"Just enough to cover the expenses I mentioned earlier, then?" He reached out as if to snatch the money from Mrs Čubrić's very palm. "No more, no less. I can't say any fairer than that."

"Millie said no." Dragan placed a hand on Savović's shoulder. "Without her, we have no business. We have to respect that."

*

Meanwhile, Nevena had to content herself with third-party accounts of her daughter's exploits in the region. With increasing regularity, customers would visit the chemist shop and relay stories they had heard from relatives and friends in Knez Selo, Novi Sad, and Sopot, stories which delighted Nevena. While sceptical about Milica's participation in what she saw as a dubious, exploitative enterprise – for people of her generation, funerals, and the grieving process in general were as sacred as they were private – she couldn't help but flush with pride when a customer mentioned Milica's worthy actions.

"She does a lot of good, that child of yours. Nobody likes to lose someone close to 'em, but if you don't send 'em off in the proper way, it can leave a strange, empty feeling inside."

"And she wouldn't hear of taking a single dinar off that poor ol' widow in Sopot, even though she spent the best part of half a day comforting her, and helping her come to terms with her loss."

"There's a lot to be said for it – this professional mourning business. These days, I think we're all guilty of bottling things up. It ain't healthy. We need to get it out of our systems. If not, it'll make us ill."

This was so different to how the townsfolk had reacted to Milica's crying fits when she was just a baby. During the family's lowest point, Nevena didn't think they would enjoy the goodwill of the local community ever again. Now it felt as they had been rehabilitated solely due to Milica's 'gift'.

"She is special, after all," Nevena said to herself. "And now everybody knows it."

*

As Robert Savović had rightly predicted, now that the business had received a number of glowing endorsements, the bookings started to pour in. Day and night, he fielded queries from interested parties. It got to the stage where he, ever the opportunist, had the temerity to suggest that the bereaved family alter the time or date of the funeral to accommodate the professional mourning services he provided.

"Well, if you could reschedule to, say three o'clock in the afternoon, it would allow us to attend another service in the area in the morning."

And such were his skills of persuasion and undoubted personal charm, he, in the vast majority of cases, managed to talk the interested party into doing just that – rescheduling the entire funeral.

"You won't regret it. Our services are unique. We guarantee that your sad day will be a day to remember."

Over the next six months, they travelled the width and breadth of the country in that rattling old van (which, somehow, stood up to the rigours of the miles clocked, despite sounding as if it was about to breakdown at any moment). At each service, Milica truly excelled herself. Her performances, her expressions of raw grief and despair were such, they never failed to reduce the mourners to fits of sobs, to, ultimately, bring everyone together to give their dearly departed a fitting send-off. So much so, those most affected routinely offered Milica additional monies (sometimes far from insubstantial sums).

"Please, take this, my lovely. You've not only helped us pay proper respects to my late mother, but helped me patch up my differences with my sister. Before today, we hadn't spoken a word without anger for over twelve years."

"I want to give you a little something extra. Today was so special. To share my grief, to have a good ol' cry and get rid of all the sadness, side-by-side with those closest to me, has done us all a power of good."

"This is for you. You deserve it. The service you provided for my family today has helped us all get over the loss of our uncle."

But, of course, Milica never kept any of the money for herself. Nor did she hand it over to Robert Savović or her father. She slipped the banknotes into her pocket and, on return to the family apartment, stashed them away in a box she kept concealed under her bed. Whenever she had a few hours to herself, she would count out the money and take it to Father Miroslav, to go towards the upkeep of the church.

"Bless you, my child," he would say to her. "I knew as soon as I held you in my arms when you were just a baby that you were an angel on God's earth."

And then, she would jump into the back of the van and travel to another funeral. One day they might be in Subotica, the next, Negotin, the day after that, Niš. Back and forth, one service after another, one set of mourners after another. If they travelled too far afield, they would either find cheap lodgings for the night, or sleep in the van at the side of the road. With each performance, her reputation grew. People in Velika Plana started to acknowledge her in the street, as if she were a celebrity, a star of stage or screen. Her father and Robert Savović were always in the highest of high spirits now. Their two primary functions, aside from transporting the professional mourner from A to B, were to get roaring drunk each day, and count the money that was coming their way in such great handfuls each night.

"This is the life, Robert. Work hard, play hard, as they say."

"Never has a truer word been spoken. I told you, my friend. We've filled a gap in the market. We've struck while the iron was hot and now, we're reaping the rewards."

To celebrate a particularly lucrative booking, the two business partners (wildly inebriated at the time) decided to get themselves fitted out with new suits.

"It's a legitimate business expense, Dragan. Now that we're heading up a highly successful enterprise, we must look the part. We might even have to rent some office space in Velika Plana. The sky's the limit."

But when they offered to buy Milica a new wardrobe full of clothes, even something to perhaps enhance her performances, she politely declined.

"What? Not even a nice new frock for special occasions?"

"No. I don't need anything, thank you. My old clothes are perfectly adequate, and have served me well up to this point."

And now, looking like middle-aged dandies, resplendent in well-cut suits made of the finest cloth, they continued on what very much felt like a never-ending tour of the country. They ran out of excuses to tell Milica's teachers at the school, and simply removed her from full-time education altogether.

"But the girl must finish her studies," Nevena had argued. "It's not right or fair to take her out of school. You must think of her future."

"This is her future, darling." And Dragan produced a wad of banknotes so thick, all of Nevena's reservations melted away.

Early each morning, Robert Savović would pull up outside the apartment building and honk the van's horn. And a minute or two later, Dragan and Milica would appear and they would set off on a journey to yet another funeral.

"You look a little out of sorts," Savović would invariably remark to his business partner, whether he actually appeared worse for the wear or not. "You better have a nip of this to put you right." At which point, he would hand him a bottle of strong spirit. "What makes you bad makes you better."

And only after both men had had a little drink – and not before – would the rattling old van pull away from the kerb.

During the services themselves – or more correctly, once Milica had made her dramatic entrance onto the scene – Dragan would often study his daughter intently. In this regard, the copious amounts of alcohol he and Robert Savović consumed sharpened his senses, rather than dulled them. Aside from the heartfelt despair she routinely displayed to such powerful effect, it was the way each of her performances was slightly different to the last – or indeed the performance that immediately followed it – that stood out the most. It was as if Milica intuitively picked up on the nature of her surroundings, the dynamic of those gathered at the graveside, who she should focus her energy upon. Be it the exact spot where she collapsed in front of the coffin, the more subtly choreographed gestures, or the modulation and timing of her cries and appeals to the heavens above. Everything – or so it seemed to Dragan – had a purpose and was perfectly executed. No movement, gesture, nor sob was wasted or unnecessary. There was a distinctive grace and rhythm to each of her performances now, something akin to a prima ballerina or gifted soprano.

When Robert Savović leaned close and said, not for the first time, "That girl of yours is a real artist," Dragan couldn't help but agree.

Milica was not only pure of spirit, and closer to God than any person he had ever encountered before – including the priests and other holy men who had dominated his childhood years – but she really was an artist, and a performer of the highest order.

"We must look after her, Robert. If any of those big city folk were to see what she's truly capable of, they'd try and take her away from us. Mark my words. It'd be disaster for all concerned."

*

Late one morning, while en route to the tavern for a 'business meeting' with Robert Savović, Dragan bumped into Mihailo Pančev from the steelworks. At first, he almost walked straight past the man, despite the fact he had stopped in the middle of the busy thoroughfare and was addressing him by his first name.

"Dragan, where on earth have you been? And what on earth are you wearing?" He eyed his suit and shiny Italian leather shoes with a mixture of suspicion and contempt. "We've been trying to get hold of you. Your tribunal is set for tomorrow afternoon. If successful, you can return to work."

"Return to work?" Dragan tried to repress a chuckle, but failed quite spectacularly.

"Why yes. I personally vouched for your good character and exemplary past conduct. I told the executive committee that the unfortunate incident last year was an aberration, something that would never, ever happen again."

"Right, well, thank you for your kindness and consideration. It's nice to know that nigh on a quarter of a century of working above and beyond the call of duty has not gone unnoticed. But to be perfectly honest with you, I've started up my own business venture, and doubt I'll ever be returning to the steelworks now."

"Business venture? Whatever do you mean? Not that nonsense with your daughter, surely? There's no future in it. Besides, you're a steelworker, through and through. You were born to be on the main production line."

"I used to think the same way myself, but events over the last few months, most notably, my suspension, have changed my outlook on life. Now, I feel much more comfortable working for myself. And as you can see – ," he made an open-armed gesture, showing off the fine-cut lines of his tailored suit, " – I'm doing very nicely and can't really see no point in me turning up to no tribunal to plead my case, 'specially as I don't need the job no more."

It was only then, as that suspicious, contemptuous look deepened across Pančev's heavily lined face, that Dragan really scrutinised him at closer quarters. Of around the same age, he was – in comparison to the Dragan of today in all his finery, his ruddy cheeks aglow from drinking premium spirits and eating the finest of food – a scrawny, sickly-looking individual who had been completely worn out by life. His skin had that blank, pasty pallor specific to those who spend most of their time shut away inside a factory. He looked malnourished, jumpy, anxious, as if fear of missing his daily work quotas kept him up tossing and turning every night.

"Well, that's entirely up to you," Pančev said. "But some very important people will be in attendance. I therefore advise you to put in an appearance. It won't look good on your record otherwise."

Dragan could never remember how the conversation ended, or how he left things with Pančev regarding whether he would attend the tribunal or not. But the more he thought about it, the more the idea appealed to him, the idea of standing in front of a room full of Party bigwigs and making a scene, the more he revelled in the thought of not only telling them a few home-truths regarding the plight of working men in general, and how criminally overworked and underpaid they were, but telling them exactly what they could do with their job.

"Don't waste your time on 'em, Dragan," Savović counselled over a tankard of ale. "Granted, telling them to shove that job where the sun don't shine will give you a hell of lot of satisfaction, but if I were you, I'd wipe my hands clean of the whole rotten business. Think of the poor bastards who aren't as lucky as you."

"I know, I know. And I agree – up to a point. Only something has rankled with me ever since they nigh on gave me my marching orders. For over twenty-five years, I never put a foot wrong. If we ever had to work overtime, or at weekends to meet our quota, I never made a single word of complaint. I just got on with things and worked harder than I'd ever worked before. Countless times, I trudged home from the steelworks, collapsed in an armchair from sheer exhaustion, and slept until the next morning, until my next shift was about to start. No dinner, no sustenance to help see me through. It was inhuman, what I went through for those bosses, week after week, year after year. And I think they need to know exactly what goes on behind the scenes, exactly what sacrifices loyal, hard-working men like me make on a daily basis."

"I understand, Dragan. But let me tell you a story 'bout a chap I met in a labour camp when I were just a young man of two-and-twenty. Once upon a time, before his arrest, he were a big soccer star, a striker, one of the best in Europe, in fact. Now, if I were to tell you that he were younger than even me, you'll get an inkling of just how tragic his story truly were. How or why he found himself in the camps were a bit of a mystery. By all accounts, he offended or upset a person of influence at some function or other, and the rest, as they say, is history. Anyway, every day, he were the first one up in our barracks. At the quarry where we worked, he toiled harder and longer than any other inmate. For the three years I knew him, he worked like two men. Never did he moan or groan about his predicament. He just got on with things as best he could.

"In all, he served seven years in the camps. And while he looked to have come through his ordeal in reasonably good shape, physically, and while he were still only in his mid- to late twenties when he were released, those years of incarceration, a poor diet, and backbreaking work had taken their toll. When he tried to play soccer again, he knew he weren't the same player as before. He'd lost that yard of pace which got him away from defenders. He weren't as strong as he used to be – he could no longer bully centre-halves. He didn't have the

113

same sort of stamina, no matter how hard he trained, or how many miles he ran to try and get back into shape."

"What did he do?"

"What could he do, other than give up the game he loved and try something different? What I'm trying to say is, life leaves its mark on you. Even if you do everything that's expected of you, just like my man in the camp, just like you in the steelworks for all those years, even if you work yourself into the ground, it doesn't mean you're going to get your just deserts. Life ain't like that. It picks you up and plonks you down and tells you to get on with things. A sporting career is short at the best of times. Even a rainbow is a fluke of nature, let alone the pot of gold at the end of it. My former inmate's best years, his prime years, were spent cracking open rocks with a pickaxe. What a waste! He should've been playing in World Cups and European Championships. Instead, he were in the back of beyond slaving away with murderers and child molesters."

"What happened to him in the end?"

"He drank himself to death 'fore he were thirty. When he realised he couldn't play at the top level no more, he gave up on life completely. In actual fact, I came across him again a few year 'fore he died. He were on the streets, begging for a handful of coins to get himself another drink. Pitiful sight, don't bear thinking 'bout, really. He weren't lucky enough to be given a second chance.

"That's why I told you his story. A year or two ago, I bet you could never have envisaged anything other than serving out your working life in those steelworks. Only now, you've gotten a glimpse of a far better existence. Unlike him, you've been given a second chance, and you've grabbed it with both hands. So why worry 'bout the things you've left behind, eh? Look forward, and don't give them bosses the satisfaction of talking down to you one last time."

*

While Dragan and Robert Savović were leaning on the counter at the tavern, Milica's teacher, Miss Tadić , was riding the elevator up to the fourth floor of the Stanković's apartment building. When the contraption had conveyed her to her intended destination, she disembarked and knocked on Dragan and Nevena's front door.

"Oh, hello, Miss Tadić," said Nevena, upon answering. "What a surprise. Please, come in. I'm afraid Milica has just popped out to the store, though."

"It's not Milica I came to see, but you."

"Really?" Nevena flashed an awkward smile. "Well, if that's the case, do take a seat in the living room. I've just made some tea."

It would be ridiculous to suggest that Nevena had no idea why the teacher had called 'round in the middle of the afternoon. She knew that Milica's attendance this term had been woeful to say the least. She knew that news of her professional mourning exploits in the region were common knowledge, and that the many excuses she herself had used to explain those absences now looked spurious to the point of insulting.

"I'll come straight to the point," said Miss Tadić. "I'm seriously concerned about Milica's progress. As you well know, she's missed a lot of schooling over the last twelve to eighteen months. She is now so far behind the other pupils, in terms of the curriculum, our one and only course of action is to hold her back for a year."

"Hold her back?"

"Yes. It's such a pity. Ever since she started to read so widely, she's really excelled. I've seen it happen before – how the written word can give so much to a young person. The great works of literature broaden the mind. And Milica has been so receptive. I had such high hopes for her development. The standard of her writing, and how well she expresses herself, made me think that she might have a career in literature herself. That, or perhaps enter the teaching profession.

"It saddens me to hear that your husband has been whisking her up and down the country to 'perform' at funerals, of all things. And I have to be frank. If Milica doesn't return to full-time education soon, I sincerely fear for her future. Young people get nowhere in life these days if they don't have excellent academic qualifications.

"That's why I came here today to plead my case. I don't think it's fair for your husband to take Milica out of school at such a critical time and force her to participate in his business venture."

"Well, that's not strictly true." Nevena, despite her own reservations regarding the professional mourning service, felt she had to defend her husband. "From an early age – from the moment she were born, in fact – Milica has had a calling in life, a gift. I don't really know how best to explain it. But she's always been able to feel another person's pain so acutely, it's as if she's suffering herself. She hasn't been forced into doing anything. She's doing what she's doing because she wants to help people."

Miss Tadić placed her teacup on the saucer on the table.

"Look, Mrs. Stanković, I think we both know that Milica would be much better off in the classroom, rather than galivanting around the region with her father and his somewhat dubious associate. When she returns from the store, please sit her down and explain the situation. Tell her that she doesn't have to give up on her education if she doesn't want to. It would be such a shame if so much potential were to go to waste."

*

As it transpired, Milica hadn't gone to the store to buy sweet treats for her mother, after all. She had gone to visit Father Miroslav, on the other side of town. A few months ago, the priest had been diagnosed with an inoperable brain tumour, for which there was no effective treatment available, let alone any hope of a recovery. In later years, Milica would describe this scene in great detail – the old man's poky rooms, how gaunt and emaciated the priest himself had become in such a short period. But more than anything, she recalled the lucid nature of his words and how much they comforted her at a time when so many things were unclear and muddled in her head.

"Ah, Milica, my child, I've been laying in this bed for the best part of a week now. And while sleep doesn't come easy, it is you who occupies my dreams. I knew, without a shadow of a doubt, that I would see you one last time before I pass on to the other side. Come." He beckoned her over to a chair beside the bed. "Sit down. Tell me what is on your mind. I have been hearing such wonderful things about you. You truly are spreading God's word far and wide."

Milica sat down, but it took a few moments before she felt comfortable enough to speak.

"I don't quite know why I came here, Father. This afternoon, I felt a powerful compulsion to visit you. It pains me to see you in so much discomfort, and to know that you are not long for this world."

"Bah! Don't let that trouble your mind. I am truly going to a better place. But something tells me that you are at odds with yourself, child. Why, I must ask you? You are doing what God put you on this earth to do. You are helping people in times of great need. You are giving them strength and consolation when they are at their lowest point."

"I know that, Father, and I feel truly blessed to be able to help. It gives me so much pleasure. Only – "

"Only what?"

"Only I worry about the financial side of things, that my father and his partner are taking advantage of people."

"You are facing a moral dilemma, you mean?"

She nodded.

"You know something, Milica, this new breed of men, they have a terrible saying: 'the ends justify the means'. What an awful concept! No more than a way of excusing the terrible violence and cruelty they have perpetrated, ever since the Party seized power. Now, not to sound hypocritical, but if the last twenty years have taught me anything, it's that modern life is all about compromises. If it were not for your father and his business partner, you would not be in a position to visit different parts of the region and interact with those poor grieving souls. Hence, I do not think you should have any moral reservations, or question the goodness of what you are doing."

"But some of the people, the mourners at the funerals, are just as greedy and conniving. They literally hire our services to try and make a favourable impression on a relative, in an attempt to secure a larger part of a legacy. All of which has left me feeling terribly disillusioned, as if I am participating in a grand deception."

"It is not for you to judge, Milica. If your conscience pains you to distraction, you must think about all the good you are doing. The old widow in Sopot, for example. Yes. Do not look so surprised. I heard all about your kindly deed, how you refused to charge the woman for your services. You have it in your power to do the right thing at the right time. Never lose sight of that. One day – and I feel this with complete certainty – you will have to make a decision which affects not just one person or one family, but the entire nation. Then, you will have to listen to your heart and conscience, in just the same way you did in Sopot."

*

In the early hours of the morning, the phone started to ring at the tavern. Long after Dragan Stanković had departed, Robert Savović continued drinking steadily until the herald of a new day. Through a thick fog of strong alcohol, he somehow managed to both comprehend that the phone call was for him and make his way over to the booth by the main door.

"Robert Savović?"

"That it izz," he slurred. "An' who do I have the pleasure of talking to?"

"You don't know us, but we know you very well indeed. Now listen, and listen good. You have set up a very lucrative business for yourself. People in high places have started to take notice. That girl, your star attraction, your cash cow, is a valuable asset. Our associates are interested in her development, and are prepared to make you an offer."

"An offer? No, no. We won't be considering any offers or entering into any negotiations. The girl stays with us."

"But you haven't heard our proposal yet, Mr. Savović…"

*

While Robert Savović slept off last night's excesses in the backroom at the tavern, Dragan Stanković was entering Mihailo Pančev's office at the steelworks. In his best suit of clothes, and with three-quarters of a bottle of strong spirit inside him, Dragan felt a steely resolve that was not altogether misplaced, despite the fact he was, to all intents and purposes, quite emphatically drunk. So motivated was he to have his say, to tell the higher-ups at the steelworks exactly what he thought of them, it overrode any notion of intoxication slurring his words, of becoming muddled and making a fool of himself. When asked to confirm his name, address, and duration of employment at the steelworks, he answered clearly and confidently, if not with a bristly contempt that didn't escape the notice of the four men who made up the panel that would ultimately decide upon his future.

"It is alleged, Mr. Stanković," said the spokesperson, Gregor Horvat, a high-ranking official of seventy or so years of age, "that you were drinking strong alcohol on the main production line. Do you deny that this incident took place?"

"No, sir, I do not. It was wrong of me to do so, and I deeply regret that it happened. But I feel it were the culmination of the many wrongs perpetrated against me. Primarily, that after over twenty years of loyal service, I was demoted and put to work with the junior employees for the simple fact that I had problems with my first-born child – something which had absolutely nothing to do with my duties at the steelworks."

"Problems with your child?" In evident bemusement, Horvat looked right and left, as if appealing for assistance from his colleagues, or from Pančev, who was seated in the far corner of the room.

"That's correct, sir. My daughter was prone to crying fits which disturbed the neighbours. I was told by Mr. Pančev there that if I didn't do something about it, I could even lose my home. It were a very disheartening period. Like most of the men here, I'd dedicated my whole life to the steelworks. I worked tirelessly to fulfil our quotas. Never did we fall behind when I were on the main production line. If we needed to work late or over the weekend, I never once complained. I just worked harder to ensure we were amongst the most productive and efficient steelworks in the region."

"Yes, I can see that, Mr. Stanković," said Horvat. "Your service record is exemplary."

"Thank you, sir. It gladdens my heart to know that my efforts have been officially acknowledged. But I would like to take this opportunity to speak out about the treatment of the

121

workers in general. Granted, our wages aren't great. Most of us struggle to make ends meet, 'specially if we have families to feed. But the bosses here, the supervisors and what have you, treat us like cattle. There's no respect or comradely conduct. They just like to crack the whip to make 'emselves feel important, when it's us lads who are putting in the hard miles to make sure we keep up with our monthly targets. For that reason, I could never see myself coming back here ever again."

"Hold on, Mr. Stanković, are you saying that you have no intention of returning to your duties?"

"That's right, sir. After the treatment I received, I wouldn't come back to work here if you doubled, or even trebled, my wages. I know all about the dignity of labour, of getting by from the sweat off my brow, but it has to be a two-way process. Mutual respect. If not, you're going back to the dark ages. I was a steelworker, not a galley slave."

"But if that's the case, then what are we doing here?"

"It beats me, sir. I just wanted to have my say."

"And you have spoken well, Mr. Stanković. We will most certainly look into the management style adopted at this facility. For the official record, you were to be offered a return to your post today, on the same terms and conditions as before. Men of your calibre and long service history are hard to find these days. We will be very sorry to see you go."

*

"I did it, Robert!" Dragan wheeled into the tavern with all the furious oscillating dynamic of a spinning top. "I got up in front of the top brass and told 'em what for. You should've seen me. I really stood my ground. I even got 'em to promise to look into the way the workers at the steelworks are treated."

"That's fine and dandy, Dragan. I'm pleased for you, even if I weren't too keen on you going through with it. Here." Robert gestured to the barkeep. "Let me get you a tankard of ale and a little chaser to celebrate."

"No, no, let *me* get these. Drinks all 'round. I feel like really pushing the boat out today."

"Ha! I like your style. And I have good news. Just half an hour ago, I received a visit from none other than the personal secretary of the late Colonel Cvetković."

"What, the old boy who died the other day, the most decorated military man in the region?"

"The very same. They want Milica to perform at his funeral tomorrow. By all accounts, the man was an absolute tyrant. A violent drunkard of all things, who used to beat not only his own family, wife and children, black and blue, but the domestic staff as well. And in terms of his military career, things were much the same. He was universally despised for the way he conducted himself, the way he would court martial a soldier for looking at him the wrong way.

"This is big, Dragan, bigger than the Dedić funeral even. It could really, truly put us on the map, and make us a pretty penny in the process."

Why Savović failed to mention the late-night telephone call will become apparent in the fullness of time. For now, it is enough to suggest that it wasn't the only thing he was keeping from his business partner.

*

Unbeknown to the vast majority of the population, the nation's great leader had not been in the best of health recently. An ageing man, he had nevertheless cultivated an aura of invincibility, of being fit and active beyond his years. Every day, the papers and television news reported extensively on his activities, his visits to new hospitals or schools, or large construction projects. They showed pictures of him riding on horseback, swimming in a river, or attending major sporting events. What citizens didn't realise was that some of these news reels or photographs were years, if not decades, old. And, in actual fact, the old man had been plagued by any number of ailments, ranging from a series of minor heart attacks, and mini-strokes, to an early Parkinson's disease diagnosis.

"I seriously doubt he will see the year out," his personal secretary confided to Dušan Srna. "When I took the daily correspondence to his bed chamber yesterday, he didn't recognise me, he didn't know who I was, or what I was doing there."

In the intervening years, Srna's rise through the ranks, from ambitious functionary to the head of his own department, had been nothing short of spectacular. The still-young man had risen to a position of power and influence. More importantly, he had the confidence and ear of members of the leader's inner circle.

"I don't want to be unduly pessimistic," the secretary went on, "but the matter of accession cannot be ignored. At present, I don't think, in the thirty-six years he has been in power, that his popularity has ever been lower amongst not just the common people, but his own closest allies. Yes. Make no mistake. The vultures are circling."

"It's a complicated business, of that there is no doubt," said Srna. "But in high stakes politics, one has to be pragmatic, and use certain situations to one's benefit."

"How do you mean?"

"That, in the awful eventuality of the old man dying, we could use, in particular, the media to manipulate the general public. We could reshape and repackage his legacy. Often, when a notable figure dies, people look back with rose-tinted spectacles. If we were to stage a massive state funeral, and turn it into both the saddest day the nation has ever known *and* a celebration of the man's life and achievements, it would give us a huge amount of political goodwill. To the extent that the Party could choose whoever they wanted to take his place."

"But like I said, the leader's stock has never been lower. For the first time, people are openly questioning his policies. There have been strikes and protests in the towns and cities, not to mention open hostility in the countryside. If he were to die tomorrow, I fear there could be an uprising rather than an outpouring of heartfelt emotion over his passing."

"Leave that to me. I'm certain I can engineer the kind of event that will live long in the memory. In fact, I know just the person to help us create the perfect send-off, to make the people see just how much their leader meant to them."

*

On the morning of Colonel Cvetković's funeral, there was much commotion in the Stanković household. The night previous, Dragan had drunk far more than his fill again. This he attributed to nerves, the anxiety he felt on the eve of their biggest performance to date. As a result of his excesses, he awoke to a throbbing headache, blurred vision (at one point, he nudged Nevena in the ribs and in floods of tears told her that he feared he had gone blind overnight), a stomach so delicate he found it hard to breathe without feeling nauseous, and a mouth so dry, his lips felt like sandpaper when he tried to moisten them with his tongue. Knowing that any kind of recovery was on a knife-edge, he had his wife heat up some beef soup – the only thing he felt confident of holding down without vomiting – and periodically visited the bathroom (and his secret bottle of spirit hidden behind the cistern). In between tentative sips of the 'magic potion' and a spoonful or two of broth, he slowly started to feel a little better.

"That broth has done the trick," he said, feeling not the beef soup in actual fact, but the fresh alcohol starting to work its way around his bloodstream with reassuring effectiveness. "I feel like a new man, ready to tackle whatever the day has in store for us. Now, where's Millie? Is she all set and ready to go?"

In contrast to her father, Milica had been perfectly calm all morning. She woke at the usual time, a few hours before they were due to leave, ate a boiled egg and drank a cup of tea, washed, dressed, and lay out on her bed reading while Dragan was stumbling, fumbling, drinking, and spooning incredibly small amounts of beef soup into his mouth, in the hope it would enable him to not just function properly, but leave the apartment, full-stop.

"I'm in my room, Father," she shouted through the door to him. "Robert should be here in fifteen minutes. You need to get washed and dressed. I have left a suit and tie out on your bed for you."

"You're an angel. Thank you. I'll be quick, don't you worry."

Even though this was the biggest event Milica had ever performed at – on their way to the cemetery, they saw hundreds of mourners lining the streets – it nevertheless had an almost identical physical dynamic to the other, smaller funerals they had attended. The people who had turned out to pay their respects in such great numbers – many of whom had been cajoled, if not openly forced to attend by their military superiors or heads of ministries and assorted governmental departments – had the same empty, emotionless look upon their faces. Never was this more apparent than when they entered the cemetery itself. The colonel's close family, friends, and colleagues stood by the graveside, displaying not a flicker of emotion. They looked like images in a photograph, rather than living, breathing human beings participating in a real-life, real-time event.

"My word," said Robert Savović, as he discreetly parked the van behind the chapel of rest. "I don't like the looks of this crowd. All them medals and decorations on show. And they look so grumpy, angry almost, I don't like our chances of winning 'em over."

Yet, the most radical of transformations took place when Milica came sobbing and wailing upon the scene. Whether the power of her introduction was heightened by the ten-gun military salute that immediately preceded it, or whether it was just the open-wound rawness of the emotion she displayed, the way she collapsed to her knees by the graveside and prostrated herself before the coffin, was impossible to say with any certainty. Within a mere handful of seconds, the other mourners were deeply and visibly moved. Those who had appeared so detached and dispassionate before found themselves stifling sobs, or turning to a loved one for a comforting embrace. Even the more senior military officers in attendance lowered their heads and brushed tears from the sides of their faces. In what constituted a lightning re-evaluation of the deceased's character, those who were having trouble controlling their emotions now spoke of the man with genuine, if begrudging fondness, something which would've seemed impossible a few minutes ago.

"He was a hard man, but fair. Everything he did was in the service of his country."

"I never really understood why he was so angry all the time. But he was possessed of an incredible military mind."

"He said many harsh, cruel things to me over the years. But now I realise it was for my own good. He wanted me to be strong and resilient. As much as it hurt at the time, he made me the man I am today."

The atmosphere around the graveside changed completely. The people who knew the colonel best began to share more reminiscences of the man. Admittedly, not all of these were good or happy memories. But now he had passed away, now he no longer ruled over them with such a tyrannical fist, they saw the funny side of his outbursts, his fits of rage, and they cried tears of joy, not upset. Further back, as far as the street outside the boundary of the cemetery wall, the common people who had either been drafted in to attend by local government officials or who had come out of mere curiosity for the pomp and ceremony of the occasion, were deeply moved by the collective show of emotion displayed by their social superiors. Even though many had no idea who was being buried here today, they still burst into floods of tears, hid their faces in their hands, or hugged the person standing next to them.

"It's so sad. He looks like he were such a great man."

"I can't help meself (sniff, sob). You can't beat a good funeral."

"I reckon he must've been a fine military leader. You can tell how much the soldiers he commanded respected him."

And it was all true – at least for appearance's sake (and that was exactly why the family had reached out to Robert Savović in the first place). They wanted, even if they still felt the utmost animosity towards their late husband, father, uncle, commanding officer, and so on, to create the impression that he was loved and respected. They wanted, if only for one day, for him to be the person they dearly wished he was when he was alive. And whether that was belated and futile didn't really matter in the bigger scheme of things, for it was a worthy and noble gesture, even if it wasn't something the colonel himself deserved.

"I know I've said it before – ," Savović took a deep swallow from a bottle of spirit and then handed it to Dragan, "– but your Milica really is a consummate performer. Did you see the way she planted herself right in front of that widow, and sort of pitched and tossed like a ship on choppy waters, while appealing to the heavens above? It certainly broke through the wife's frosty exterior. I mean, look at these people – ," he made an expansive gesture with one hand, taking in the hundreds of mourners sobbing uncontrollably, " – it's as if your girl has got their hearts on a string."

Dragan, a highly sensitive man himself, someone who was always deeply affected by Milica's performances, how she could reduce all those around her to shivering wrecks of emotion, took a swallow of spirit just as, if not deeper than that of his friend and business partner. At that moment, he felt something akin to a premonition. Despite the undoubted success of the day, he had a horrible feeling that he would never see Milica perform like this ever again.

"Maybe we're holding her back," Savović said. "Maybe she's destined for a life on the stage, or in the movie business."

"Yes, maybe she is. After all, nobody knows what the future holds."

"Never has a truer word been spoken. But let's not get all philosophical or melancholy, old friend. Pass me back that bottle. A performance like this calls for a celebration. If this life has taught me anything, it's to enjoy the good times when they come your way – which, as you know better than anyone else on this earth, can be more seldom than often. For that reason, I reckon we should have ourselves a little holiday."

"A holiday?"

"Yes, why not? Me, you, Milica, and Nevena can drive out to the seaside for a few days. Rest, relax, have a few drinks on the beach, put a bit of colour back in our cheeks. What do you say?"

"Well, yes, I agree. It sounds like a fine idea. We've never had much by the way of holidays."

"Grand. Leave it to me. I'll make all the arrangements. If I were to wager a bet, I fancy we stand a good chance of receiving a generous additional gratuity from the old widow and her family. The bereavement dividend. Ha!" He took another liberal swig from the neck of the bottle. "Yes. Make no mistake, Dragan, if we hadn't before, we have now well and truly put ourselves on the map."

*

While Milica was performing at the most significant event of her short, yet spectacular professional mourning career, and Savović and her father were busy making vacation plans, Nevena had a surprise visitor to the apartment. While preparing a pie for supper, rolling out pastry dusted in flour on the counter, she heard what could easily have been described as a hammering on the door.

"My word," she muttered to herself. "Whoever could that be?"

When she opened the front door, she found Sanja Babić standing in the hallway. Clearly agitated, the old woman shifted her weight from one foot to the other and twined the string of beads dangling from her neck around her fingers.

"I've had an awful premonition," she said, in lieu of any kind of standard greeting. "Your daughter is in grave danger. Dark clouds are forming on the horizon."

"Danger? Dark clouds? Whatever are you talking about? Millie is out with her father and his business partner. No harm could come to her."

"You're not listening to me." Sanja pushed past Nevena and entered the apartment. "I saw it all in a vision," she said over her shoulder. "Never has my third eye been anything other than an accurate predictor of future events."

Nevena followed after her unexpected guest.

"I don't understand. Who or what would want to harm my daughter?"

The old woman, who had taken to pacing up and down the front room and muttering under her breath, came to an abrupt halt.

"Word of Milica's gift has travelled far and wide. It has reached the ears of dubious persons of questionable moral character. They know that an individual possessed of such unique spiritual power could be of huge financial benefit to them."

"Sanja, you're worrying me now. What do these people have in mind?"

"That I don't know – not exactly. I can only warn you, and tell you to beware. In the not-too-distant future, attempts will be made to take Milica from you. And if that happens, you may not see the girl ever again."

*

Despite his assurances, Robert Savović was unable (or perhaps 'unwilling' is a more suitable word) to put their holiday plans into place. The morning after the Cvetković funeral, he received three more booking requests: a former police chief who had died of natural causes; the infant son of a famous musician who had tragically drowned in a swimming pool; and a revered Party scribe, the victim of an automobile accident (a woman who was rumoured to have penned the words of some of the leader's most stirring speeches). All of which were well-paid, high-profile assignments.

"It's been madness," he said, having dashed straight over to the Stankovićhs' apartment. "We'll have to put our vacation plans on hold for a week or two. More pressingly, we need to hire a secretary, someone who can take bookings and keep our records up-to-date. And I can think of no finer person for the job than your good lady wife."

"Me?" said Nevena.

"Why, of course. You could easily fit it in around your work at the chemist shop. What's more, it would make us a real family business. And it goes without saying that you would be well-remunerated for your efforts."

And thus, Nevena became heavily involved with the running of the professional mourning enterprise. Deploying his somewhat mysterious administrative skills, Savović had all calls relating to the business redirected to the chemist's phone line. A kindly, understanding man, the proprietor, Mr. Vidić, offered no objection to Nevena fielding a steady stream of calls throughout her working day when, by rights, she should've been serving customers, or recording inventory or stocking the shelves with the various medicaments on offer.

"I'm terribly sorry, Mr. Vidić," she apologised on more than one occasion. "I had no idea I would receive so many phone calls."

"Not at all. I hear your daughter is performing a valuable service to the local community and beyond. Tell her to keep up the good work. I know first-hand how hard it can be to lose a loved one. When my wife passed away, long before her time, I kept all my emotions bottled up, and didn't feel as if I ever properly mourned for her. If I'd have been encouraged to get everything out of my system, it would've saved me a lot of pain and sleepless nights over the years, I can tell you."

*

The week that followed was the most lucrative in the professional mourning business's short history. At each funeral service, Milica's astonishingly powerful outpourings of graveside emotion had an equally powerful effect on the mourners gathered to pay their respects. In particular, the close family and friends of the drowned child were finally able to get the collective grief out of their systems. In a truly heart-wrenching scene, they dropped to their knees beside Milica and cried and sobbed, lamented and despaired, held and comforted each other for what constituted close to two hours. And when they had finally cried and sobbed themselves out, Milica went over to each one of them in turn, made the sign of the cross, and told them to never lose their faith in God, no matter how cruel or inexplicable His actions may seem at times.

"A parent should never have to bury their own child," the father of the deceased, a musician who had penned a catchy chart-topping hit several years ago, said to Dragan after the service. "I don't think it's something we will ever get over. But today, your daughter helped us so much. When I read about what she had done for other families in the paper, I just knew I had to have her here today."

To show his appreciation – and whether his grief was such that it affected his judgement – he handed Dragan and Savović a sum of money so large (far in excess of the fee they had agreed over the telephone), they could barely believe their eyes.

"Take it. I sincerely hope that your daughter continues to help people just like us. What she does is of immeasurable importance."

*

In light of Milica's success and growing renown, the impact she was having on local people, it was inevitable that the regional press would take an interest in the professional mourning service. One afternoon, around half an hour after Robert Savović had surfaced from his slumber in the backroom of the tavern, which more-or-less served as both his living quarters and office now, a local journalist approached him at the bar.

"Are you Mr. Robert Savović of the professional mourning service?"

Through beady and bloodshot eyes, Savović looked this slightly scrawny, resoundingly average-looking man of thirty or so years up and down.

"That depends on who's asking," he said evasively, worried that the man may be associated with the local government – namely the tax department.

"Matija Dimitrijević, senior reporter with the regional newspaper. I was wondering if we could arrange to do an interview with Milica Stanković. We at the paper feel her story is of great interest to people in the area."

"Interview, eh?" Affecting an equal measure of distraction and disinterest, Savović cracked a raw egg into his tankard of ale and tossed the shell over his shoulder. "Well, to be perfectly honest, the girl is a little on the shy side, and not really interested in speaking to any journalists. Besides, as a matter of company policy, we always charge a small fee for any kind of public appearance."

"But, Mr. Savović, an interview is hardly a public appearance. And think of the exposure. Any article we write about your services will be positive in nature – you have my personal guarantee of that. We just want to know a little more about how and why all of this came about, what inspired you to start up such a unique business in the first place."

"I understand. And you're not the first journalist to have approached us."

This was a lie – barefaced and blasé – but told with such casual conviction, Dimitrijević had no reason to doubt its validity.

"I see. Well, perhaps we could come to some sort of arrangement, then. Although highly irregular, if you guaranteed us an exclusive interview, I think I may be able to persuade my superiors at the paper to offer you a small one-off payment."

"And perhaps a percentage of sales?"

"What? No, that's out of the question. I can't see them ever agreeing to that."

"Never say never, my man. Why don't you go back to the paper and put my proposal to whomever has the authority to make a decision. If they agree, we can do an interview this very day. If they say no, then we can shake hands, no hard feelings, and I'll negotiate with another publication for an exclusive."

Later that afternoon, Dimitrijević and the paper's photographer called 'round to the Stankovićs' apartment to conduct the interview. Within an hour of leaving the tavern, the reporter had managed to persuade his superiors to not only provide the requested payment (a not-insubstantial sum of money), but offer Savović a generous five percent cut of revenue for the edition of the paper the interview featured in.

"Thank you for agreeing to talk to us, Milica," said Dimitrijević, once seated around the family's dining table. "And please, don't be nervous. See this as no more than an informal chat between two old friends. I, like so many people in the region, am fascinated by the services you provide. When did you first realise you had such an unusual gift?"

Even though she had been briefed in advance, it was clear that Milica felt uncomfortable answering questions of both a direct and spiritual nature. Not that she was rude or abrupt during the interview, or failed to provide an answer to any of those questions. It was just her manner – and Dragan, as always, studied his daughter particularly intently – that betrayed her nerves and anxiety.

"Ever since I was a young child, I've been drawn to adversity and sadness. If I saw someone crying in the street, it was as if I could not only feel their pain, but desperately needed to comfort them."

"You like to help people, you mean?"

"More than anything."

"And it's my understanding that this compulsion to do good saw you comfort mourners at a funeral in town."

"That's correct. For me, a funeral is a sacred and hugely important event. None of us truly understands why we are here, or what our true purpose is in life. When a loved one dies, it can only increase that sense of confusion and uncertainty. It pains me to see people in such distress, or worse, trying to repress their emotions, that I feel an uncontrollable outpouring of emotion myself."

"So, your performances – if we can call them as such – are genuine rather than staged?"

Milica nodded her head.

"Amazing! And presumably, this is what inspired you to offer your services as a professional mourner?"

"I can't really answer that question. At present, I feel as if I am doing good deeds, that I am actively helping people when they are at their lowest point. I don't really see it as a service – more a calling, or vocation."

"But the very people you are helping have heard about your exploits and have sought out your services, have they not?"

Milica nodded once again.

"And do you ever get nervous prior to performing? For example, there were hundreds, if not thousands of people in attendance at Colonel Cvetković's funeral. Surely, that couldn't have escaped your notice, and must've felt a little intimidating?"

"No. I don't get nervous or feel in any way apprehensive. It would be disrespectful not just to the deceased, but to the bereaved at the graveside to be subject to such vain emotions when they are dealing with the ultimate of all life's most baffling mysteries."

"Great answer," Dimitrijević said almost to himself, as he frantically scribbled into his notebook. "In preparation for this interview, I spoke to several people who have attended the funerals at which you have performed. Nearly all of them commented on your 'trance-like state'. Is that an accurate way to describe it? Do you enter a trance when you perform?"

"I'm not sure, really. I just feel closer to a higher power."

"God, you mean?"

"Hang on, you," Dragan interceded. "We agreed to make no direct reference to religion, didn't we?"

"Yes, of course," said Dimitrijević. "It just felt like a natural question to ask, in the context of the previous answer. Let me rephrase that…"

The interview continued in much the same vein – Dimitrijević reeled off twenty or more questions relating to the professional mourning service, Milica's thoughts and feelings towards the people she helped come to terms with their loss, and what hopes and dreams she had for the future.

"I can't really say with any certainty," she said in reply to his final question. "As long as I am needed, I will try my best to be of service to people. Like everyone else, I am guided by my conscience, and a sense of what is right and wrong. If tomorrow, I feel like I am no longer performing good and worthy acts, I will have no other option than to stop what I am currently doing and direct my energy elsewhere."

"Right, I see. I guess every endeavour, no matter how worthy, has to end sometime."

"I didn't say it would end, just that I would channel my resources in a different way. I am what I am. Nothing will change that."

True to his word, Dimitrijević's interview had an incredibly positive slant. From the first sentence to the last, he eulogised Milica Stanković's impact on the local community. With careful, guarded (and skilful, it must be said) use of language, he circumnavigated the prickly and controversial issues of religion and spirituality by stating that any act which brings comfort to citizens at their lowest point following the death of a loved one can only be a good and worthy thing. No mention was made of any moral considerations, nor any allusions to taking advantage of vulnerable people for financial gain – accusations which could easily have been levelled at a professional mourning service, and with some justification. Nor did he dig too deeply into Milica's past, her reputation for being a child possessed by dark forces, a child who may well have been seen as mentally unstable, if not defective in some way.

And all to great effect.

Not only was it the highest-selling edition in the paper's history (netting the professional mourning business a tidy sum in the process) but it most certainly came to the attention of persons as yet unknown who had been taking an increasing interest in Milica Stanković in recent months.

But what perhaps made the biggest impression on the readers was the striking photograph of Milica that accompanied the article. Even though it was in black and white, the picture captured the young girl at her most contemplative and disarming-looking. In some circles, people thought she appeared positively angelic. In others, her appearance was likened to that of the mad monk, Rasputin. Be it the light or the camera angle or the fact she was wearing a plain round-necked house dress that resembled a nun's habit, there was something about her eyes – so benign and singularly unspectacular in the flesh – that gave her an otherworldly appearance which fascinated the general public, making Milica an even more talked-about and divisive figure.

"I always knew there were something not quite right about that girl. Look at her eyes. Like the devil's own."

"She looks like she ain't quite right in the head, if you ask me. And some of them quotes! – 'bout feeling close to a higher power and balling her eyes out at stranger's funerals being her vocation."

"I blame the father. Being permanently sozzled has made that there daughter of his all mixed up in the head. It's no environment for a young girl to grow up in."

*

In the days that followed, the phone at the chemist shop rang almost non-stop. It got to the stage where Nevena – in between apologising profusely to Mr. Vidić for the constant disruption – started to feel completely overwhelmed. She wasn't sure if she had double-booked some dates, or recorded the location and contact details of the caller with the requisite degree of accuracy to check. In the end, she felt she had no other option than to telephone Robert Savović at the tavern, and inform him of the deluge of calls.

"I see. Well, not to worry. It's better than nobody showing any interest, eh? Tell you what I'll do. I'll pop 'round to see you tonight. We can have a look at the bookings and draw up a proper schedule."

That evening, Robert Savović did indeed call 'round to the Stankovićs' apartment. Ever charming and ebullient – and the fact he was clearly semi-intoxicated certainly contributed to his good mood – he displayed not the slightest hint of exasperation when Nevena presented him with her barely legible notes, what constituted a list of scribbled names, addresses, dates, and contact telephone numbers.

"You've done a grand job, Nevena, you really have. We'll just copy these out in block capitals on another sheet of paper. If a date or what have you is a little unclear, we can try and contact the interested party in question first thing in the morning."

With a patience almost as astonishing as the steadiness of his hand, he somehow drew up a clear and comprehensive schedule, including all the particulars he had just mentioned.

"Well, I never," he said, as he got to the final few entries. "This name here, Nevena." He pointed to a childish scrawl which even the most competent of handwriting experts would've had difficulty deciphering. "Does that say Luka Marković? Because if it does, it could be one of the biggest bookings we've ever had. His family is amongst the most revered in the country and absolutely minted."

"Yes, yes it is," she replied. "I remember thinking that the personal secretary, or whoever called sounded awfully well-spoken over the telephone."

"And it looks like it's for the day after tomorrow. Amazing. If we start mixing with the likes of the Marković clan, we'll be set for life."

"I'm terribly sorry, Robert," said Milica, who had been quietly reading a book in one of the armchairs by the electric fire, "but there is no possible way I can attend a funeral on that date."

"Why ever not?"

"Because I have a previous engagement."

Confused, Savović leaned over the dining table and began to interrogate the new schedule he had drawn up from Nevena's hodgepodge scribblings.

"No, you're mistaken, my girl. We don't have any other bookings for that particular day."

"I wasn't referring to any bookings. I was referring to the funeral of Father Miroslav."

"Father who?"

"He was a former priest," Dragan explained. "And was very kind to us when Milica was just a baby." He turned to his daughter. "I had no idea he'd been sick, my darling."

"Yes. Quite recently, he was diagnosed with a brain tumour, and only given a few months to live. In the circumstances, I know that you will understand why I have to pay my respects to him. Without his help, I doubt I would've been able to control my 'gift'. I doubt we would've been able to start up a professional mourning business at all."

"It's true, Robert. In life sometimes, you simply have to do the right thing, no matter how much it may cost you financially. Millie must go and say a proper goodbye to the priest."

In contrast to his previous behaviour, when faced with Nevena's gross administrative incompetence, Savović failed to completely mask his disappointment and anger.

"But this is Luka Marković, Dragan. Folk don't say no to people of that calibre. It just ain't done."

"I'm sorry, Robert. We must respect Millie's wishes on this one."

*

The day after next was gloomy and overcast, although a brisk wind kept the rain from falling over the town of Velika Plana until late into the evening. In the same simple, round-necked housedress that she had worn for her newspaper interview, Milica made her way to the cemetery a few minutes before the service was scheduled to begin. Like the funeral in Sopot, there was only one other mourner at the Father's graveside – his loyal housekeeper of over fifty years. A morose, taciturn woman at the best of times, she barely acknowledged Milica's arrival, or exchanged anything more significant than a nod or grunt instead of words she seemed incapable or unwilling to speak. Regardless, Milica felt a sense of solidarity and kinship with this stoic domestic, who had clearly led the most spartan of existences in the priest's austere household. Never more so than when some volunteer workers from town, ably assisted by the gravediggers, brought the coffin over to the open hole in the ground, and the old woman dropped to her knees and began to pray before the graveside.

144

In contrast to her performances, Milica acted with the utmost restraint, and side by side with the aged housekeeper, she prayed for the soul of the priest who had shown such an interest in her ever since she was a baby.

When the coffin was finally lowered into the ground, and the gravediggers began to cover the casket with a fresh pile of soil, Milica took a great wad of money from her purse – money which had been pressed into her hand at various funerals she had performed at with such distinction, money which she had kept secret from her father and Robert Savović.

"Here." She handed the bundle of banknotes to the old housekeeper. "Take this to help tide you over. I know Father Miroslav suffered terribly, that he was persecuted and denied the right to practise his religion. He would've wanted you to have this money to make a fresh start somewhere else."

While reluctant, if not visibly offended by the gesture, the old woman finally relented.

"Thank you, child." She took the money and concealed it under her mourning clothes. "He often talked about you, you know? You were a source of great comfort to him in his final days. Every now and then, he sent me into town to find out any news about you. In many ways, it gave him a reason to live when he must've been in the most unbearable pain. Carry on his good work. It were his most ardent wish for you to spread the word of God."

Later, as Milica trudged back through the town, she couldn't help but despair at the priest's sad, lonely departure from this world. She knew how revered he had been in the past. If anybody in the region ever had any problems, the priest would be the first person they consulted. If any misfortune befell a family, be it a sick child or a poor harvest, they would ask Father Miroslav to pray for them. And whether or not religion was merely a delusion, an invention of man, it was a worthy delusion, one that brought comfort to people in times of need.

Caught up in these dark, depressing thoughts, Milica didn't realise – certainly not for a good thirty seconds or more – that the two children shouting on the opposite side of the street were, in fact, addressing her.

"You're Dragan Stanković's daughter, aren't you?"

"That's right." She came to a stop and looked these two dirty-faced urchins up and down. Scruffy, but far from poorly dressed, they looked as if they'd been rolling around in the mud all morning.

"You're the girl everyone is talking about," said the other boy. "Can we have your autograph?"

"Please." His friend began to search his pockets for a pencil and a scrap of paper. "You're right famous you are, had your picture in the newspaper and everything. I reckon your signature will be worth a pretty penny in a few years."

Whether it was the emotion of the day finally catching up with her, Milica found herself bursting into floods of tears. Not the kind of tears she was now famed for, but softer, gentler yet no less heartfelt and genuine tears. Never, at any time over the last few months, had she ever given a single thought to any personal gain or recognition for the work she had done. The one and only consideration was to comfort people and help them get over their pain, even if it was just for a few hours. Now, she realised that her performances had elevated her to a position in the town she didn't want to occupy, and she wasn't sure how she felt about that, or whether she could ever reconcile her new image with the purity of the deeds she so desperately wanted to undertake.

*

When Milica returned home, she told her parents that she would no longer perform at any funerals.

"As much as I want to help the family financially, I can no longer justify my participation in such an enterprise."

"What?" Dragan shot up from his chair by the electric fire. "No. You're all upset about Father Miroslav. You're not thinking straight. And I know Robert can be a little insensitive at times, but his heart is in the right place. Besides, there are people relying on you to help them get over the pain of losing a loved one."

"I'm sorry, Father, but my decision is final." She walked towards her bedroom. "I will go to my room and rest now. It's been a long and tiring day."

"Millie, please don't be hasty," he shouted after her. "Sleep on it. You might see things differently in the morning."

Dragan was beside himself with worry. He had become so accustomed to the steady stream of income, the likes of which he had never known before, the lifestyle, the travelling, the almost constant drunkenness, that he didn't want to even contemplate what awaited him if the professional mourning business really was no more. He felt he simply had to contact Robert Savović to discuss the matter.

"She said what? Don't worry. I'll call 'round this instant. I'm sure I can persuade her to reconsider her options."

Within the space of five minutes, Savović was knocking on the Stanković's door. In an attempt to alleviate the crisis, he called Milica through to the main living area and attempted each and every devious and underhanded means of emotional blackmail to get her to change her mind.

"If you don't help these people, they're likely to follow their loved ones into the grave. That's how important your services have become. You've seen how they bottle up their feelings. What you provide helps them become warm, sensitive human beings again, real people subject to real emotions."

But no matter how hard he tried, no matter what bleak, despairing phrasing or imagery he conjured, painting a picture of such grief and despair, the kind only Milica herself could assuage, she would not be swayed.

"I've turned into something I despise," she told him. "I don't want to be a performing monkey. And I don't want to exploit vulnerable people anymore, or play a leading role in a family swindle, where money-grubbing relatives are squabbling over an inheritance."

"Granted, you've seen some unsavoury things, but that's human nature, I'm afraid. What you must focus on are the positive aspects. The poor old widow in Sopot, for example."

"But the bad experiences far outweigh the good. I want – no, let me rephrase that – I *need* to channel my energies elsewhere."

"Good. Great. I'm all for it. Let me know what you have in mind. Let's bounce some ideas around. With your unique talents and my business acumen, the world is our oyster."

"No, you misunderstand me. And I don't want to be rude, or come across as ungrateful for all the time and effort you've put in to make the business such a success, but you're part of the problem."

"Me?"

"Yes, Robert. From the outset, I knew you were more interested in making money than helping people at their time of need. In my naivety, I thought that the positive aspects, as you called them, justified the more calculated side of things. But now I realise they don't. If any endeavour in life is to be considered truly good, it must be pure, noble, and worthy, without any self-interest or petty gain involved."

Despite the unequivocal nature of her words, Savović continued to plead, to argue, to try and make her change her mind. He repeated previous points, he said the same things over and over again, using slightly different terminology, or twisting the meaning of his words in an attempt to make them sound more compelling. He tried to make her feel guilty for deserting people, for letting them down, for failing to fulfil her contractual obligations (even though she had not once signed a single piece of paper). At one point, he got so heated up, Dragan had to intercede.

"That's enough, Robert. Millie has made up her mind. I don't think any amount of talking is going to change that now." He turned to his daughter. "Why don't you go to bed, darling? Don't worry 'bout a thing. If you don't want to carry on, you don't have to. We'll manage to get by somehow."

*

In the aftermath of what had turned into a quite unpleasant scene – both Dragan and Nevena had been appalled by Savović's bullying tactics – the two men sat around the dining table and proceeded to consume a bottle and a half of strong spirits. Mellowed by the alcohol, Savović, in particular, seemed to reconcile himself to the situation, that the easy money that had been rolling in for so many months was about to become a thing of the past.

"Okay, Dragan. It's a crying shame, though. Any number of unexplored opportunities have presented themselves in the wake of that newspaper interview. But I'm nothing if not compassionate at heart. Tell you what, first thing tomorrow morning, the four of us will set off on that holiday, eh? A few days by the seaside is just what we need. Clear our heads, recharge our batteries. What do you say?"

This was a surprising concession from a man who was so angry and frustrated a short time ago that he looked very close to losing all control of himself.

"A holiday? Yes, that's exactly we need. We've been travelling up and down the country almost non-stop for months on end now. But, Robert, I must speak frankly. If you think that Millie will have a big change of heart, you're only setting yourself up for a major disappointment. My daughter doesn't say things for the sake of it. She doesn't play games or seek attention. If she's come to such a big decision, she wouldn't have done so lightly."

"Understood. And please accept my sincerest apologies for losing my temper earlier. It just came as a bit of a shock, that's all." He picked up his glass and drained the contents in one easy swallow. "Here. Pass me that bottle. I shall have one more drink and then be on my way."

*

Meanwhile, in the capital city, Dušan Srna was putting important contingency plans into place, should the calamitous event of the leader's death befall the nation. Principally, he had requested that Professor Dejan Damjanović pay him a visit at his office.

"Thank you for coming to see me, Professor," said Srna. "It's much appreciated. Please, do take a seat."

Now in both the twilight of his career and the autumn of his life, the physician still cut an impressive figure, even if his hair was more snow-white than gunmetal grey, and the lines on his face of a heavier and deeper nature than before.

"No trouble at all. I had a consultation in the city earlier this morning."

"Excellent." Srna flashed a grateful smile delivered solely to put the much older man at ease. "What I'm about to ask you may sound rather odd, though. But it is my understanding that you once examined a young girl in the town of Velika Plana, who had been subject to fits of extreme upset – put simply, she couldn't stop crying. Of course, quite some time has passed since then, but do you recall that particular visit?"

"Yes, I remember it very well. A most curious case. Hysteria in an infant, or young girl as she was when I eventually examined her, is as rare as it is worrying. I could see nothing but problems on the horizon. If left unchecked, mental

151

instability of that nature could have devastating effects in later life."

"But you never saw the child again?"

"Sadly I did not – for it was certainly an interesting phenomenon. Periodically, I received reports from the school authorities regarding her progress, from the teachers who worked with her on a day-to-day basis. After a somewhat uncomfortable period of adjustment, she settled down into a more normal routine. She became, to an extent, socialised. And while a slightly odd and distant character, she was far from a disruptive influence. Over the course of time, my professional career went in a very different direction. By that I mean, I was charged with undertaking important research work in the field, and never had the opportunity to follow up with the Stanković girl."

"I see. But were you aware that she is now using her 'talents' in a professional capacity?"

Damjanović tilted his head to the side and raised a bushy old man's eyebrow, indicating that he most certainly had not been party to this information.

"By all accounts, she's been hired to attend dozens of funerals in the local region to help the mourners express their grief – with spectacular results, I might add. At present, I have it on very good authority that her services are in high demand."

"How irregular," said Damjanović. "I was, of course, briefed about her crying fits as a baby, but I had no idea it was something she could harness for financial gain. More to the point, I got the distinct impression that the girl had a strong religious fixation. How an enterprise of this nature sits with that, from a moral standpoint, is dubious to say the least."

"Well, we're led to believe it may have been born out of necessity rather than choice. The father, a drunkard of some repute, lost his job at the local steelworks."

"That makes sense," said Damjanović. "During my visit to their home, I noticed a strong family bond. Still, it's a fascinating development, the likes of which I've not come across before."

"So you'd be interested in working with the girl again?"

"How do you mean, exactly?"

"That we, as a nation, may well need her unique services in the not-too-distant future. For that reason, I would like to have her interned at a nearby facility. If you were to authorise the necessary paperwork, you could carry out further research into her condition, and we could have her on hand should the worst come to pass." Srna got to his feet, whether merely for effect, or to indicate that the meeting was drawing to a close, he probably didn't even know himself at that moment in time. "You would be doing the country a great service, Professor. In desperate times, we often have to resort to desperate measures."

*

The very next day, in the same decrepit van that had transported them to so many funerals in different parts of the region, the four travellers embarked upon their long journey out to the coast. In almost suspiciously high spirits – although the strong drink he imbibed for the entire seven-hour drive was more than enough to justify his surprisingly melodious singing, whooping and hollering, raucous laughter, and almost non-stop chatter – Savović conveyed them along vast stretches of motorway, up precarious, zig-zagging mountain roads, and rutted country lanes in his own irrepressible, daredevil style. Most noticeably of all – and this is perhaps where the element of suspicion was applicable – he was particularly attentive to Milica. Every few kilometres, he would ask her if she was all right, if she was enjoying the scenery, or if she wanted to stop for a rest, a drink, a bite to eat (Nevena had packed up a veritable feast into a picnic basket).

"If there's anything you need, my girl, just you ask. This is your trip. You've expended a hell of a lot of mental energy over the last few months. You need to rest and relax. And we're going to the perfect place to do just that."

Pleasant enough sentiments, but everyone present – Savović included – knew that each word was loaded with as much double-meaning as it was insincerity. Despite Dragan's stark warning regarding the firm, unwavering nature of his daughter's decision, Savović clearly harboured hopes of changing her mind. His constant allusions to the restorative benefits of a holiday, how the tranquil calm of a seaside location had been known to rejuvenate the spirit were testament to the fact. Regardless, the three passengers couldn't help but be entertained by the man's impressive baritone, and the range of songs he knew by heart (everything from stirring Irish rebel songs to soaring arias from the world's most famous operas), his long, meandering stories, and endless observations and reminiscences whenever they passed a town or village or stretch of river that stirred particularly strong memories with him.

"See that there hillock off to your right?" He, in somewhat fumbling fashion, jabbed the bottle he held in his free hand in its general direction. "I once saw a man consume twenty-two freshly-baked apple pies in an eating contest on that very spot. Never seen the likes of it before or since. He were like a machine, a human dustbin. But do you know what were even more impressive than the number of pies he actually ate? He didn't leave so much as a single crumb. He ate every last morsel, every last grain of sugar on top of each pie. Whereas the other fellas, who'd not eaten half of what he had, had made a hell of a mess. Most of what they claimed to have tossed down their necks were strewn across the table in great big clumps of pastry and half-chewed apple. Make no mistake, that man were an artist, someone who took pride in his work. Last I heard, he'd headed over to America, where overconsumption of that nature is like a national sport."

At every stop, after Savović had emptied his bladder in the loudest, most voluminous, and unabashed fashion imaginable, he would shake his trouser leg, demolish the pastries, sandwiches, and sweet treats that Nevena had prepared (with the exact same gluttonous aplomb as the apple pie eater he had described to the family earlier), and grab another bottle of spirit from the back of the van.

"I don't know why they make so much a fuss 'bout all this drink-driving nonsense. If anything, a few nips of the good stuff sharpens a man's mind. If anything, I'm a far more responsive driver, my reactions are quicker. Did you see the way I avoided that cow in the middle of the road earlier, Dragan? Like a world champion rally driver, eh?"

"But, Robert, that wasn't a cow but a snow goose."

155

Savović paused mid-glug from the fresh bottle of spirit. "Goose, you say? Ai, it were a funny ol' shape for a cow, I s'pose. Still, you can't deny my driving skills in avoiding it."

"But you ploughed right through the poor thing, Robert, splattering it across the highway."

"Bah, I just clipped it. Here." He handed the bottle to Dragan. "Have a little drink. We better get back on the road. We're making good time. With any luck, we'll be there around mid-afternoon."

*

There was more general disbelief, and not wholly comprehensible drunken bravado when they finally arrived at their destination. Having somehow managed to manoeuvre the rotting old van up a steep and winding set of coastal paths, Savović pulled up outside a luxurious villa cut into a stone cliff-face, and overlooking a crystalline stretch of sun-streaked ocean.

"There must be some mistake, Robert." Nevena was the first to voice her concerns.

"Not a bit of it. I made all my mistakes when I were but a youngster." He threw the driver's side door open and clambered a little unsteadily out of the aged, yet in perfect and illustratable fairness, vehicle. "Take a look at our abode for the next few days."

"You've got to be kidding me." Dragan clambered out of the passenger-side with similar shaky-legged uncertainty. "This place is incredible. How on earth did you manage to wangle us a stay at a palace like this?"

"Let's just say an old friend owed me a favour." Savović winked, stretched his arms, rolled his neck, and jogged on the spot, like an athlete limbering up moments before competing in a big sporting event. "As you know as well as anyone on this earth, Dragan, I've hit the kerb more than once in my time. As has everyone who came from nothing and made a good life for 'emselves. By definition, therefore, I've rubbed shoulders with some rum ol' characters."

"Say no more," said Dragan, strangely pacified by what could easily have been classified as a vague, if not evasive answer.

"And if you think the exterior is impressive, just you wait until you see what it looks like inside."

Contrary to the dubious nature of his more outlandish claims, Savović, if anything, had downplayed the striking opulence of the villa's interior: shiny marble floors, crystal chandeliers, handcrafted leather furniture, a billiard room, what looked like fine art hanging from the walls, a large country-style kitchen, and some French doors leading to a swimming pool which looked out over that same stretch of crystalline, sun-streaked ocean.

"I'm speechless, I'm in heaven," beamed Nevena, who had never seen such luxury before. "I daren't touch anything. I daren't sit down. I don't feel worthy of being in such wonderful surroundings."

"Nonsense," said Savović. "There ain't no one in this world better than anyone else. You're my guest, as I'm a guest of my associates. You feel free to touch what you want and sit where you want. If you fancy a bite to eat or a drop of wine from the cellar, you just open the refrigerator or skip down those steps to the basement. Make yourself at home." He turned and looked at Milica, who was lingering uncertainly in the main hallway. "Hey, don't be shy. Come on in. What do you think of the place?"

"It's beautiful, Robert. Thank you for bringing us here."

"Don't mention it." He clapped his hands together. "Right, let's assemble ourselves a little feast, some refreshments, a bite to eat, and a few glasses of the good stuff. I can't tell you how much I've been looking forward to a proper drink."

"But we put away the best part of three bottles of spirits on the road," said Dragan.

"That doesn't count. It isn't the same as relaxing with your feet up, is it? Now, follow me, my friend. We have carte blanche access to not just the cellar, but an extensive drinks cabinet in the drawing room. Girls – ," he turned to Nevena and Milica, " – we shall convene around the swimming pool in twenty minutes."

As if it was indeed his own home, Savović plundered the attractive mahogany drinks cabinet, handing Dragan one refined and ludicrously expensive-looking bottle of spirit after another, and then proceeded to empty the fridge of an extensive array of fresh produce (clearly their arrival had been fully expected and well-provisioned for) – a whole roast chicken, salads and pâtés, cheeses and cold cuts of meat, caviar, and a host of picked delicacies.

"This is the life, eh, Dragan? Pity it all has to come to an end soon."

"How'd you mean?" he asked, although, even in his half-intoxicated state and wearied by the long journey, he knew exactly what Savović was hinting at.

"Now we are no longer in business, the finer things in life might not come our way again for quite some time."

"Robert, we've been through all of this. Millie has made her decision."

"I know, I know." Savović took a step closer to Dragan, drawing him into what could easily have passed off – certainly to anyone who may have stumbled upon them at that moment in time – as a conspiratorial huddle. "But with your permission, I'd like to talk to the girl one last time. If you don't think it's a good idea, I wouldn't dream of going against your wishes. Only something tells me that the death of that old priest back in Velika Plana has upset her so much, she's made a rash decision. Put simply, I don't believe she's thinking straight at the present time."

Dragan's face creased. "Oh, I don't know, Robert. I wouldn't –"

"Just a quick word. I won't lose my temper like I did yesterday. I'll just take her aside and ask her if this is what she really, truly wants to do."

While reluctant – Dragan hated the idea of putting Milica through any kind of ordeal, of pressuring her, or placing her in an awkward or uncomfortable position – he finally relented.

"Okay, Robert. You can talk to her again. But be warned. Milica, as I'm sure you're aware, isn't like other people. She won't be swayed by a nice holiday, a fine house, and a big slice of cake. Deep in her own heart, she knows she's been put on this earth for a purpose. Perhaps we all do to a lesser or greater extent. Whether it's to tend a flock of sheep in the mountains, slave away in a factory, or sip champagne in the sun. It may not be today, or tomorrow, or even this year, but that girl will find her way in life, to be what she was born to be."

Having reached a tentative agreement of sorts, the two men took all the food and drink out to the pool area. There they found Nevena and Milica stretched out on sun loungers, sheltered from the still-fierce late afternoon sun by brilliant-white parasols.

"Ah, I see you ladies have made yourselves comfortable already." Savović let out a throaty chuckle. "Look. Our hosts have done us proud. Tuck in. You must be ravenous. I know I am. I could eat a horse, tail an' all!"

*

For the rest of the afternoon and the early evening (they really had made impressive time), they swam, sunbathed, snoozed, ate heartily, and (Savović and Dragan exclusively) drank heavily. During the hottest part of the day, while Nevena and her husband snored with a not-unpleasant staccato rhythm, like parts of a classical orchestra tuning up before a gala performance, Savović, glass full to the brim, came and sat next to Milica, who, up to that point, had been absorbed in a book about the life of Saint Augustine.

"Ah, Saint Augustine, the most interesting of the great Christian thinkers. A true humanist, if ever there was one."

Milica put her book aside and looked at Savović with, not so much thoughtful or questioning eyes, but a weariness that should at least have made him pause for thought, if not refrain from broaching the subject they both knew he was about to broach.

"I often think about the true meaning of religion, the pure teachings of Jesus Christ, do to others as you would have them do to you, love thy neighbour, turn the other cheek. It makes you wonder how we as people ended up taking the wrong path in life, when we had such simple guidelines to follow. But by the same token, you can understand why some folk wanted to restructure our society. 'Cause you can't really argue with sayings like 'the greatest good for the greatest number'. That's why I wanted to come over and have another little chat with you about throwing in the professional mourning business. Like I said before, it don't make no sense. It don't –"

"Robert, there's no point in you continuing. I've told you. There's not even the slightest possibility that I will perform for you at another funeral. I made you a tidy sum of money in a relatively short period of time. You will, I'm afraid, have to be satisfied with that."

Even though Savović had anticipated such a reaction, he was a man used to getting his own way, a man who fully understood the power of his persuasive skills, the way he had, in the past, not only been able to talk himself out of untold perilous situations, but been able to manipulate and control people, cajoling them, often with no more than a kind word, to do his bidding, even at major detriment to themselves or their loved ones. To have been met with such an emphatic rebuttal put him on the defensive, a position he had rarely if ever occupied before.

161

"But what are you going to do? Think 'bout your family. Your poor ol' father is in no state, physically, to go back to the steelworks. And your mother, despite working all hours God sends, earns a pittance at that chemist shop in town. Surely you can find it in your heart to put in a few more performances. Surely you can do the right thing by your parents."

Milica shook her head. "I don't know why I believe this with such conviction, Robert, but my parents will be just fine. Life isn't supposed to be easy. If we knew nothing of suffering, we wouldn't learn about the higher, purer nature of our existence, and who and what we should really serve.

"More to the point, I think we both knew that our association would be brief. You have lived, and will go on to live a very different life to me. You are an entertaining man, of that there is no doubt – I can see why my father enjoys your company so much – but what you ultimately represent, I could only ever revile. So I implore you to accept my decision."

"And that's your final word?"

"Yes."

"Well, don't say I didn't try." He stood and straightened, being careful not to spill a single drop of his drink, even though his glass was still full to the utmost brim. "The thing is, Milica, there is a lot of truth in them old secular sayings, the clichés, I s'pose you'd call 'em – 'better the devil you know', 'the grass isn't always greener', and suchlike. Life is a nasty business, all right. I guess people have to find out the hard way."

"What do you mean by that, exactly? It sounds like a warning."

"No, no, my lovely. I'm just generalising, making an observation on what I've learnt by bitter life experience. I'll leave you to your book now. If there's anything you need, just you holler, okay?"

*

Later, Savović seemed particularly intent on getting both Dragan and Nevena incredibly tipsy. From the depths of the refrigerator, he produced a perfectly chilled magnum of champagne. With great ceremony, he poured them each a glass, and made a series of solemn, heartfelt toasts to eternal friendship, love, laughter – even poetry got a mention, as did Dionysus and Epicurus, gods of wine and the kind of hedonistic lifestyle Savović himself had lived, and would continue to live, until the day he died.

"Like I said before, unfortunately, all good things come to an end. We have to make decisions in life, some harder than others. But one thing is for sure, no matter what paths we tread in the future, we will always have good memories of each other to temper any bad experiences we may have the misfortune to encounter."

"Never has a truer word been spoken," said Dragan, borrowing one of his drinking partner's favourite sayings.

"Ha! You're not wrong there, my friend. Come. Drink up. I think there just might be another big bottle of bubbly in the refrigerator."

When Dragan and Nevena had finally stumbled to their bedroom (and by this time, Milica had long-since said her goodnights), Savović sat alone at the kitchen table, bathed in the half-light of a half-moon, lost in a complex web of darkest thought. Every now and then – and with increased regularity as dawn approached – he picked up a bottle at random (and the table was strewn with all kinds of weird and wonderful alcoholic delights) and poured himself a great unregulated measure of whatever said receptacle contained. Suddenly stiffening, as if in receipt of a mild electric shock, he pushed the chair back with his legs and shot up to his feet.

"Okay," he muttered to himself. "There's no other way."

Walking purposefully through to the drawing room (a feat in itself considering the current state of his blood alcohol levels), he entered stealthily, and carefully closed the door behind him. On the attractive walnut writing desk was a telephone. Taking a folded-up piece of paper from his pocket, he picked up the receiver and dialled the number clearly printed out in stark black ink. It rang twice before a gruff voice answered with a simple hello.

"It's me. They're all fast asleep. You can come for the girl now."

*

Next morning – or more correctly, just before noon, so late had the rest of the household slept in – Nevena found Milica's room empty, the floor a mess of twisted bedsheets, and one of the windows wide open, the thin muslin drapes fluttering on the light coastal breeze drifting in off the sea. All of which – and anyone who had stumbled upon the scene would've come to the same conclusion, not just an experienced detective – indicated that something seriously amiss had happened, that Milica had been taken against her will.

"Dragan! Come quickly! Something has happened to Millie!"

*

In the hours that followed, during which the local police questioned the parents of the missing girl, and their family friend and business partner, Robert Savović, and conducted a thorough search of the villa, the grounds, and the surrounding beach, everything became so chaotic and muddled, neither Dragan nor Nevena could quite work out what was going on.

"And you didn't have an argument with your daughter?" asked Detective Inspector Milošević, the officer heading the investigation.

"No, not at all," Dragan replied. "We'd only just got here. We were all in good spirits. We'd spent the afternoon by the pool, swimming and sunbathing. The last time I spoke to Milica, she said she were going to read for a little while in her room before she went to sleep."

But even as he said those words, Dragan couldn't help but recall his conversation with Robert Savović, how he had requested permission to talk to Milica alone, to try and persuade her to change her mind regarding the professional mourning business.

"Besides," said Dragan, trying to dismiss such unhelpful and distressing speculation from his mind, "you can clearly see that there's been some kind of struggle here, with the sheets all over the floor and the window wide open."

"On the face of it, yes, I agree," said Milošević. "But in my experience – and I apologise if this sounds cynical, or casts any

165

aspersions on your daughter's character – if the physical evidence found at a crime scene appears a little too signposted as to what allegedly took place, then it may well have been staged to make it look that way."

"What? You think Milica wanted to fake her own abduction? Don't be so ridiculous. Why on earth would she do that?"

Milošević shrugged. "Beats me. But at this early stage of the investigation, we're ruling nothing out. Unfortunately, due to the remote nature of this property, there are no neighbours or local businesses we can question for information or a potential sighting of your daughter."

"Officer," Savović interceded. "Sorry to interrupt. I don't know if this will be of any help to your investigation, but young Milica had, quite recently, became a well-known figure in the region in which we live. She was a performer of sorts, and last week, she had her picture in the local newspaper. I know it sounds a little fanciful, something you might read about in a detective novel, but her star was on the rise. People all over the country had started to take notice."

Tactically, in terms of redirecting the guilt away from himself, this was a masterstroke on Savović's behalf. Moreover, it was, to all intents and purposes, true.

"You don't think this has got something to do with the business, do you?" asked Dragan, his mind racing with all kinds of fresh terror and new, more complex worries.

"I'm not sure, Dragan. But you know how much interest there had been in Milica in recent weeks. I mean, we had Luka

Marković's people contact us. And it doesn't get any bigger than that."

"Okay, we'll look into things," said Milošević. "For the time being, I suggest you remain here at the villa. From what you told me earlier, you had planned on staying for another day or two, anyway."

"That's correct, officer," Savović confirmed. "We'll stick close to the phone at all times. Only please, do your utmost to find the girl. I don't know if I'd be able to forgive myself if she came to any harm."

*

To break off from the scene at the villa, with the distraught parents worried out of their minds, we return now to the capital city and a certain Dušan Srna.

Like a lot of ambitious young men, Srna had dedicated himself to government service. Unlike many of his contemporaries, though, Srna didn't merely work hard and ingratiate himself with the right kinds of people. He was, as the saying goes, playing the long game. Over the course of many years, he watched, he listened, and he waited. He became conversant with every procedure, policy, and protocol. He knew how the hierarchical bureaucratic structure operated, down to the last memo and fully-typed report. He knew who held the levers of power and who wielded little or no influence whatsoever. Naturally, like any sensible functionary with an eye on advancing through the ranks, he aligned himself accordingly.

At the time he re-enters our story, Srna, as previously intimated, had ascended to a position of power and influence himself. He had replaced the superiors he once admired so much, the men who had held those levers of power. Known to be a man of action (his underlings had nicknamed him the 'pit-bull'), whenever a serious problem arose, no matter what department, or province, for that matter, Srna was invariably the first official contacted. Not that his aggressive tactics were to everybody's taste, yet, begrudgingly, he commanded universal respect from all those who came into contact with him on a professional basis.

In terms of his personal life, however, Srna was considered somewhat of an enigma. The abrupt, unapproachable persona he had cultivated made it all but impossible for colleagues to find out much, if anything, about the man when he wasn't at the Ministry. Rumours, of course, abounded, ranging from questions about his sexuality to whether he still lived at home with his mother. Neither of which, it should be stated for the record, had any foundation. Srna, quite simply, was a workaholic, a man who, even if he stayed late at the office, left with files bundled under his arm to study at home.

On one such evening, when Srna had stayed behind to write a report long after his colleagues had departed, he heard two polite knocks on his office door.

"Enter."

The door opened, and in walked his personal secretary, Adam Popović.

"Sorry to bother you so late, sir. I was just passing and saw your light on."

"No need to apologise, Popović. I trust you have an update of some kind to deliver."

"Yes, that's right. I have all the paperwork you requested from the Ministry of Health. Professor Damjanović has signed the necessary documents, and provided a quite lengthy additional report." Popović held up a thick, two-to-three-hundred-page dossier. "I've only had time to skim through it. But on the evidence of what I've read so far, I'm not sure it's particularly relevant to the matter at hand."

"Never mind. Just be sure to keep it with the case notes. If any remotely challenging questions are asked about this decidedly unorthodox operation, we can dangle the good Professor's report under the interested party's nose as a…justification of sorts. Let them try and make sense of it. But I take it that wasn't the main reason why you wanted to see me."

"No, sir. Something rather odd has happened to the subject herself – Milica Stanković, that is."

"Odd? How do you mean?"

"Well, it would appear that she's gone missing while holidaying with her parents."

"You've got to be joking."

"I'm afraid not. I've spoken to the militia in the area. Even though the investigation is in its very early stages, it looks as if the girl was abducted."

"Abducted?"

"That's correct. The local police are working on the assumption that a criminal organisation keen to exploit her special 'gift' is responsible."

"Damn!" Srna banged his fist against the desk. "This is a disaster." He glared at Popović, as if he were somehow responsible for the whole catastrophe. "Now, listen and listen well. Contact the military immediately. Our very best men must be sent out to locate that girl and bring her to the capital *unharmed*, do you understand me? This is a matter of utmost importance to the future prosperity of the nation."

*

Back at the villa, in the two days following Milica's disappearance, the police had made no progress with the investigation whatsoever. Despite televised appeals and newspaper articles featuring her photograph, no one came forward with any information. No clues or potential leads were uncovered. There were no sightings of a girl fitting her description in the area and, far more worryingly from a police perspective, the kidnappers made no attempt to contact the authorities, demanding a ransom for her safe release.

"In the circumstances," said Milošević, "it's probably best if you returned home now. If we make a breakthrough, I promise you'll be the first to know."

Left with no other option, they set off for Velika Plana. In stark contrast to the outward journey, no stories were told, no jokes cracked, no places of interest or outstanding natural beauty identified, no alcohol was consumed. In the back seat, almost statue-like in her despair, Nevena sat with her head lowered and her arms folded across her chest. Likewise, Dragan sat motionless in the passenger-side seat, staring out of the window. Reining in his natural garrulity – and maybe this had as much to do with guilt as respect for the situation – Robert Savović barely uttered a word for the whole seven-hour journey himself, bar informing the passengers of an imminent stop for fuel, and an opportunity to relieve themselves and purchase some refreshments.

"We can have a bite to eat and a coffee, and maybe rest up for a little while."

"No, Robert," said Dragan. "I think we'd just like to get home as quickly as possible. We don't want to miss a phone call from the police."

"Understood, old friend. I'll fill the tank in a jiffy, and we can be on our way again."

Over two sleepless nights at the villa, the true gravity of the situation had well and truly sunk in. For hours, Dragan and Nevena had speculated, theorised, drove themselves half-mad looking at the disappearance of their daughter from every conceivable angle. Most of all, they returned to Robert Savović's theory, the tactical masterstroke he had slyly inserted into the conversation with the investigating officer.

"I know it sounds far-fetched, but it's the only feasible explanation," said Dragan. "I reckon word of how much money we were making reached the ears of some big-time criminal organisation. God knows there's enough of 'em around. And it were no secret that Luka Marković's people had contacted us recently."

"I don't know what to think anymore. The only thing I'm certain of is that Milica would never have run off on her own. There's no way she would've turned her room upside-down to deceive everybody. It's just not in her nature"

"No, of course not. She's a good girl. She'd never do nothing to worry us."

"Agreed. The thing that troubles me most, though, is how all of this has coincided with Millie not wanting to perform at the funerals anymore. It's too coincidental, suspicious."

"I've been thinking along the same lines myself. Only I can't work out what the connection could be. Granted, Robert was hugely disappointed when Millie told us she were done with the business. He asked if he could speak to her again, to try and get her to change her mind. I think we both know that's why he arranged the holiday, the luxury villa, and all the top-quality food and drink. But aside from ourselves, he's the one person with the least to gain from Millie disappearing like that."

*

Upon their arrival back in Velika Plana, Dragan and Nevena found, amongst other, more standard correspondence on the doormat (outstanding bills being the most prevalent), a letter with an official government stamp on the envelope.

"I wonder what this could be about?" Dragan tore open the envelope. "You're not going to believe this. It's a letter from that Professor who came out to examine Millie. Damjanović."

"But that were an age ago."

"I know. But it says here that they want her to travel to the capital to undergo a series of 'extensive tests'. It says that her participation is 'mandatory' and of 'huge importance'. Whatever are we going to tell them?"

This unexpected request, on top of the emotional turmoil she had suffered ever since Milica disappeared, was too much for Nevena. Like a condemned building, subject to a controlled demolition, she collapsed into her husband's arms and burst into floods of tears.

"Oh, come you here, my darling…that's it, get it all out of your system. You'll feel all the better for it. Trust me."

"But, Dragan," she managed through her sobs, "whatever are we going to do? How on earth are we going to find Millie and bring her back home? I can't bear the idea of her being scared, on her own, being held against her will…or worse."

"Please, Nevena, don't torture yourself like this. I promise that we'll find her. I'll talk to Robert first thing in the morning. I'll see how our finances stand. Maybe we could put up a reward, a big cash sum for information leading to her safe return. That might be what this is all about – money. If we can get enough exposure, Millie could be back home 'fore the week is out."

Part Three

The events surrounding Milica Stanković's disappearance have been a topic of intense speculation for many years. Naturally, for a young girl who had just attained a level of fame in the region of her birth, the rumours that circulated amongst local people, once they had learned of the abduction, were rife, colourful, and often not too far from the truth. The less sympathetic townsfolk saw this as just another example of Milica's erratic, freakish nature.

"She were never right in the head that one. It don't surprise me that she's run off."

Others showed far more concern and compassion. "I do hope they find her safe and sound. She's done a lot of good in this community in recent months. It would be a tragedy if any harm were to come to her."

It was only a select few, however, perhaps those who recognised the financial implications, that the Colonel Cvetkovićs or Luka Markovićhs of this world paid handsomely for the most select of services, whose take on recent events was unnervingly accurate. "That girl has been kidnapped. I reckon they'll take her overseas, out to the West, and have her perform for the capitalists. That's where the real money is at."

Even though we may never know the true version of events, not in their entirety, there is a serviceable narrative that we can follow, a filling in of the gaps that wouldn't be veering into the realm of pure fantasy:

Having looked deep into the girl's eyes, and realised that her mind would not be changed in relation to the professional mourning business, Robert Savović had done what any canny businessman in an impossible situation would've done – he cut his losses. He had, after all, received what we can only assume was a generous offer to relinquish control over Milica's affairs. Whether he would've proceeded with his back-up plan had he managed to persuade the girl to reconsider her stance, we cannot answer with any certainty. Although the fact that he transported her to a prearranged rendezvous point is perhaps indicative of his state of mind in that regard.

In terms of the actual abduction itself, we need only say that the state of the bedroom as Nevena discovered it – the twisted sheets, open window, signs of a struggle, and general disarray – were most certainly genuine. Persons as yet unknown, but soon to be identified, had somehow gained entry to the villa. After a brief yet determined struggle (the aforementioned disarray is testament to that), Milica was likely rendered unconscious (chloroform being the obvious suspect), carried from the property, and deposited into the back of a vehicle. Where she was taken is another question that cannot be answered with any certainty. All she could remember, and all she relayed when she was finally reunited with her parents, was waking up in a luxurious hotel room, in what, as she would soon discover, was a penthouse suite, equipped with every conceivable amenity, from a jacuzzi bath to a huge television set to a modern fitted kitchen and sauna room.

Now, we must introduce those responsible.

The perpetrators of the act, the Jakšić brothers (Radovan and Vlado), were indeed part of the underground criminal fraternity. In fact, they were two of the most feared men in the entire region. Having made a considerable fortune pedalling black market goods, the brothers had, over a ten-to-fifteen-year period, diversified their various operations. They smuggled everything from guns to drugs to illegal workers.

Well-connected, on a global, not just European, scale, they had attempted, to a certain degree, to legitimise their business interests. They now had controlling shares in many hotels, bars, and restaurants, some of which were even frequented by high-ranking government officials. In keeping with their black-marketing roots, they offered generous gratuities to persons of influence – in some circles, these payments and gifts may well have been called bribes. Consequently, they were afforded the kind of preferential treatment not usually afforded to men of their ilk.

While difficult to interpret the true motivations of the criminal mind, the Jakšić brothers' attempts to gain respectability in society are perhaps both telling and instructive. Unlike many of their contemporaries, Radovan and Vlado cultivated very different personas, both in the way they dressed (fine tailored suits) and the way they conducted themselves in public (with a degree of decorum and restraint). Despite their fearsome reputation (for they were not only responsible for pedalling stolen goods, arms, drugs, people, and suchlike, but both had bloodied their hands with dozens of murders over the years), the brothers were well-spoken, polite, displaying what could quite easily be described as refined manners. Whilst striving to be accepted, rather than feared and shunned by respectable citizens, the Jakšić brothers, in a further diversification attempt, now presented themselves to the outside world as impresarios, lovers of the arts, with a roster of talented performers affiliated with their 'agency'.

Always on the lookout for new artistes, it was only a matter of time before their attention was drawn to a certain young performer from the town of Velika Plana. But while you may be able to take the career criminal out of criminal circles, you can't take the criminal soul out of the criminal themselves. When they read about Milica's extraordinary performances in the local press, Radovan and Vlado saw an incredible business opportunity ripe for exploitation. Moreover, the brothers – and this is far from unique in the criminal underworld, where the perpetrators of grisly, blood-curdling deeds crave forgiveness from a power even higher than themselves – were devoutly religious men. They attended church every Sunday and said a silent prayer before they went to bed at night. Hence, they were fascinated by the Milica Stanković phenomenon. They felt that if they were able to exclusively manage her affairs, they could cleanse their own consciences, and repent of their past sins in the process.

By the same token, they knew that obtaining her services would be far from a straightforward affair. When they initially reached out to her current manager, Robert Savović, they immediately knew they were dealing with a worldly, wise businessman who knew her true worth on the open market – if we can place professional mourning in such a category. Accordingly, their more devious and underhanded instincts began to resurface. Over many a late-night discussion, they pondered their options – intimidation, threats, a vicious beating (broken limbs were bandied about on more than one occasion), or the simple murder of Savović and kidnapping of the girl. Imagine their surprise, therefore, just as they were putting their nefarious plans into place, when they received a phone call from the very same Robert Savović, the man they had all but decided to kill in the coming days.

"I think we can come to an arrangement about Milica Stanković, after all. Even if she doesn't know it herself yet, the girl needs to spread her wings. If you're still interested in acquiring her services, I'd be willing to do a deal. That said, in light of her recent newspaper interview, and the exponential rise in interest in her as a performer, it would have to be for a significantly higher fee than we originally discussed."

As money was no real object to the brothers, they – after the kind of extensive haggling both parties felt duty-bound to conduct – agreed on a price, and made arrangements for Milica to be transported to the Jakšićs' holiday home on the coast.

The rest of the story, up to the point of the abduction, has already been set out in these pages.

*

When Milica awoke in the penthouse suite of a luxury hotel, she found the two brothers seated on either side of the bed. Big, hulking men, they were impeccably dressed and sipping tea from dainty china cups, which looked somewhat at odds with their size and stature.

"Ah, dear Milica, you're awake," said Radovan, with a slight, almost effeminate lisp. "Please, don't be alarmed. You're in no danger. Unquestionably, my brother and I have done a terrible thing, taking you away from your family like that. But we've done it for all the right reasons."

"Radovan speaks the truth," said Vlado, placing his cup on its saucer and resting both in his lap – delicate, considered gestures which, again, belied his hulking physique, meaty hands, and chewed-up prize pugilist's nose. "We want to help you help more people in the way you've helped them previously. You know yourself, deep down, that you need to cast your net much wider than the region of your birth. Working with us, you can have truly international reach."

Taking turns, the brothers outlined their vision for Milica's future. They spoke of travelling into Western Europe, of a string of high-profile bookings ("People of influence, royalty even, have contacted us. They have loved ones not long for this world, and want to secure your unique services at their funerals"). Even though death could be as sudden as any potentially fatal illness could be prolonged and painful, the brothers were confident of securing a number of lucrative contracts. There was such assurance in their manner and words, they didn't even stop to ask if she had any objections, or verify whether she was willing to participate or not, as if everything had been agreed upon beforehand. But what perhaps made the biggest impression on Milica was the way they talked about their spirituality and deep religious convictions. Making no secret of their past indiscretions, while, granted, not elaborating upon the many grave acts they had perpetrated, the brothers spoke about the redemption of the human soul, and how they wanted to do God's work now.

"Starting with you, we want to spread the word of the Almighty far and wide. We want people to know that they are not alone at the time of their greatest need."

Strangely, and Milica could never explain this to herself, let alone anyone else she confided in long after the events in question had passed, she offered up no complaint or resistance to their plans. She didn't – as she most certainly had to Robert Savović – refuse to participate, telling them that her professional mourning days were over. Whenever she was pressed for an answer, however, she could only respond honestly, that, from the outset, she felt a genuine bond of affection towards the brothers. She saw them as fallen angels trying to make amends for the terrible things they had done.

Furthermore, she felt certain that this was the path that God Himself had chosen for her, regardless of the fact that these two mortal men had plotted and schemed, and eventually abducted her from the villa on the coast.

"Tonight, we fly to Vienna," said Radovan. "A highly regarded composer, a classical musician of worldwide repute has just passed away. His body of work is legendary. He represents the very pinnacle of achievement in his field, even if the man himself was not of the highest moral character."

"How do you mean?" asked Milica.

"Let's just say he had…vile sexual proclivities and leave it at that. Due to his reputation, his many indiscretions were kept out of the public eye. But that didn't stop the rumours from circulating. The Austrian government, however, has decided to give one of their most famous sons a state funeral. The only problem being the man's family, and half the nation, hold him in the utmost contempt."

"That's where you come in, Milica," said Vlado. "If we can combine the power of the man's music – the plan is to make the event a celebration of his most popular pieces of work – and the power of your performance, we are sure to put on a spectacle befitting of his genius. We are all human. We all have our weaknesses and faults, some more serious than others. But if we refuse to forgive someone for the wrongs they have committed, is it not a greater sin than the sin itself?"

His words greatly moved Milica, for they contained an important and inviolable truth. During anybody's journey through life, it was natural to err and make mistakes. To progress as a person, one must, of course, learn from their errors. But if they receive no understanding, compassion, or empathy from other people, only censure and disregard, it will be almost impossible for them to grow as a person.

"Now, if you're not too sleepy, I would suggest you bathe and get dressed. We can then have some breakfast and make our way to the airport. No rush. We have plenty of time."

Everything had been planned out to the last detail. When Milica returned from the bathroom, she found a stylish trouser suit laid out on the bed that was the perfect fit for her. Breakfast was served on the sun-drenched balcony and consisted of an array of eggs – scrambled, poached, fried, boiled – smoked salmon, bacon and sausages, and a selection of cold meats, cheeses, cereals, yoghurts, and freshly squeezed juices.

"If you would like the chef to prepare you something else," said Vlado, "all you have to do is ask."

"No, this is perfectly fine," she replied. "I tend to eat very little in the mornings."

"You live a sparse existence, you mean?" asked Radovan.

"That's correct. I don't want to take more than I need to sustain myself."

Nodding thoughtfully, both brothers proceeded to put only a single slice of toast and a small serving of scrambled eggs onto their plates, mirroring Milica's frugal portion, even though they were big men who no doubt had appetites to match their statures.

"Don't worry," said Vlado. "We will ensure that this food doesn't go to waste. We will have our driver deliver it to the local homeless shelter."

"What a wonderful idea," Milica commended him, pleased not just with their kindness and consideration, but the fact that, even then, in the very early stages of their relationship, she could exert a positive influence over the brothers.

*

After breakfast, the brothers escorted Milica to a shiny black limousine. Once they were all safely seated inside, the chauffeur pulled away from the kerb and they began their journey to the airport. From a plush leather seat, she watched buildings larger than she had ever seen before flash past the window, images she tried to lock away in her mind for future reference. But no matter how far and wide she travelled, and how many big cities she visited, she never discovered exactly where she had been taken following her abduction from the villa on the coast.

"Here." Radovan handed her a passport. "This is not strictly legitimate, you understand. But for the purposes of our project, it will be more than sufficient."

Milica opened the passport and flicked through the pages, until coming to a photograph of herself that she had not only never seen before, but couldn't remember ever being taken.

"Your new name is Maria Mitrović. But don't be in any way apprehensive. You will not be harassed by passport control. The documentation is perfectly valid."

Novelty, doing exciting things you have never done before, can be of great appeal, especially to the young and impressionable mind. And while Milica was very different from other girls of the age of fifteen, in that she wasn't impressed by material objects, lavish shows of wealth, money, and what it can do for a person in life, she couldn't help but be awed when she stepped into an aeroplane for the very first time. For someone of her background, the whole concept of airflight was almost preposterous.

"Just sit and relax." Vlado squeezed her hand. "In two hours, maybe less, we will be at our destination."

The flight itself, the somewhat discomforting ascent and equally unnerving landing, produced a series of serene, soaring sensations in Milica. More than anything, she felt closer to God (and not just in a literal sense, cruising at thirty-five thousand feet), but safe and secure in the knowledge that she was doing the right thing, that it was her duty to perform for the brothers like she had never performed before.

For that reason alone, she felt completely nerveless and focused when they arrived at the magnificent cathedral in the centre of the Austrian capital. The crowds lining the streets, what must have constituted tens of thousands of people, barely registered with her. Deep down, she felt a great volcanic stirring of emotion, a sadness for all the tragedies of the world: all the stillborn children; all the brave soldiers killed or maimed in senseless wars; all those ravaged or taken from this world far too soon through indiscriminate yet devasting diseases; the starving, downtrodden, and destitute; those born with crippling or disfiguring afflictions; the handicapped, deaf, dumb, and blind – all rose up before her, highlighting just how cruel and unjust this world can be.

When she was ushered into the cathedral through a side door, just as a priest was reciting the last few words of the funeral oration, and one of the deceased composer's finest works began to soar through the airwaves via concealed speakers, all of that emotion, all of that pain overwhelmed her to such an extent that she couldn't help but rush over to the open casket, throw herself to the cold concrete floor and break down in floods of tears, heaving sobs, she couldn't help but join her hands together in prayer and beseech the heavens above, to appeal to the Lord Himself.

"Why, why, why?" she cried in a mixture of languages she herself, up until that point in time, had no knowledge of whatsoever, as if the depth of her grief had inculcated her with universal polyglottal skills.

The reaction inside the cathedral was as unexpected as it was unprecedented. In a country of reserve and refinement – the home of Mozart and high watermark expressions of artistic achievement, of classical concerts and evening dress, of fine wine and exclusive restaurants serving the most exquisite foods – the well-dressed mourners (many of whom bore the deceased ill-will) were reduced to sobbing and moaning wrecks of people. As the first movement of his finest symphony rose to a crescendo, they were literally hanging from each other's shoulders, necks, and in some cases waists, unable to restrain the onrush of emotion. Great black mascara tracks ran down the cheeks of every woman of age. Grown men could barely console themselves. Children had collapsed to the floor, just as Milica herself had collapsed to the floor in floods of tears.

But perhaps most importantly of all – certainly from the Austrian government's point of view – the cameras were flashing and rolling, the heart-breaking scene of a nation mourning one of its most talented sons was being captured for posterity, to present to the rest of the world, to, in a very real and powerful way, rewrite history, to cut the more unsavoury parts of the composer's past life from his final epitaph, leaving him with an untarnished legacy. And whether that was right or fair, or in any way morally justifiable (in the sense of a great artist's work being far more important than his character and the acts he committed) is a question that no one can answer with any degree of certitude.

To show their appreciation – the success of the day had far exceeded even their most wild of expectations – the head of the Ministry of Culture, Josef Arnautovic, a suave, middle-aged politician with an aristocratic manner, had the professional mourning party driven to the banks of the Wien and taken on an extensive river tour, catered with the finest food and drink. In contrast to Robert Savović and Milica's father, neither of the brothers touched a drop of alcohol, nor ate in any way excessively. Clearly, Milica's example at breakfast had made a great impression on them both, to the extent that she felt, just as she had that morning, that she wielded far more influence over Radovan and Vlado than they did over her. And this ironical twist, that the captive now held sway over her captors, made the situation she found herself in all-the-more perplexing, certainly for her loved ones, who only learnt of the ambiguous dynamic of her relationship with the brothers many years down the line.

*

Later that evening, they flew to Milan for the funeral of legendary fashion designer, Valentina Totti. A veteran dressmaker of worldwide repute, Totti had not only built one of the most successful labels in the history of European couture, she had dressed everyone from pop stars to actors, to sportsmen and women, and revered politicians. She had even won an Oscar for the wardrobe featured in an American blockbuster movie. Her name was synonymous with daring design and bold colours that pushed the sartorial envelope. Even now, stars clamoured to be dressed in her latest creations. Totti was seen as the epitome of chic, glitz, glamour, and cutting-edge fashion. But that's not to say there wasn't a darker side to both her character and her past. Approaching her ninetieth birthday when she died of natural causes (heart failure), the designer had, over the course of her long and illustrious career, been associated with some very unsavoury elements. Most notably, her then-fledgling fashion house had designed and produced uniforms for Hitler's Wehrmacht. To compound the situation, photographic evidence existed of Totti in the Fuhrer's company. She was a guest at the Eagle's Nest in the Bavarian Alps on dozens of occasions. Whether rumours of an affair with the Nazi leader were in any way valid have never been confirmed – and, it must be stated, were rigorously denied by Totti herself. However, "He was, without doubt, the most interesting man I have ever met" was a quote directly attributed to the designer.

In some circles, she had received the harshest of criticisms for the role she played during the war. Jewish leaders felt that her contribution of clothing the troops responsible for some of the most reprehensible crimes in human history should be punishable in a court of law. And even though she was of Jewish heritage herself, she could never escape being tainted with the crimes of the Nazi regime. Living as a virtual recluse for much of her post-war life, vilified and lauded in equal measure, she still oversaw the day-to-day running of her vast fashion empire, she still designed clothes from a workshop just outside of Milan. Unapologetic and confrontational to the end, she received more widespread condemnation for views she espoused in a newspaper interview a few months prior to her death. Not only did she express her admiration for Adolf Hitler again, calling him "the last true visionary of our time," she was scathing in her denunciation of what she called "toothless politics." In her opinion, people had become enslaved, turned into "faceless automatons" by modern advances.

"Young people today don't have a worthy thought in their heads. There is no originality or spark. Everybody has been taught to conform or be damned. I fear for the next generation, I really do. That is why I never had children myself. I couldn't bear to put my own flesh and blood through such a torturous process, where every last vestige of individuality and creativity would be squeezed out of them by a society that died many years ago."

Regarding her affiliation with the Nazis, she was just as dismissive, if not insultingly blasé. "I could never understand what all the fuss was about. If I hadn't designed the uniforms, somebody else would've done it. Then, as now, I feel the religious groups were more vexed by the fact that the uniforms were so stylish and iconic, so beautifully made, that my interpretation of the Nazi party's vision, a world of strength and endeavour, purity of race, high culture, vigour, and advancement in every field, was perfectly realised. Put simply, I think they were jealous of Hitler because what he was trying to achieve was mankind's natural progression. His failure is probably the greatest tragedy in history. It set us back hundreds of years."

Naturally, her quotes reignited a debate which had lain dormant for many years. At the time of her eventual death, she was one of the most controversial figures in Italian public life. The older generation either saw her as a senile crackpot, or a dangerous old fascist of the most reprehensible ilk, while the younger generation didn't know what to make of her irreverent

189

views, prickly manner, how she wasn't afraid to speak her mind, to stand up for what she believed in, and say unpopular things that made everyone, no matter from what generation, feel incredibly uncomfortable.

The matter of the funeral, therefore, presented those in government with any number of problems. Opinion was divided. The more moderate or liberal elements felt that a low-key ceremony would be the best option; whereas the right of the Party (and, sad to say, nationalism was on the rise again in a country beset with many complex social problems) felt that Totti's life should be celebrated with a full state funeral. "Undoubtedly," they argued, "she was a divisive figure, but few designers in the fashion industry had such a spectacular and enduring influence. Moreover, she encapsulated the Italian spirit of creativity and individuality, and it would be wrong not to celebrate that in suitable style."

Romantic rather than practical arguments won out in the end. But when the date was set and all the plans put in place, the Party faced an unprecedented backlash in the press, culminating in full-blown protests on the streets that necessitated police intervention and the use of water cannons. Unable to back down and lose face by changing their plans now, the Party had no other alternative but to proceed with a deeply unpopular public event, which would no doubt be picketed and cause untold embarrassment on the international stage.

Enter Milica Stanković.

With their network of global connections, the Jakšić brothers had made it known to influential figures within the Italian government that they might just have the ideal solution to their problem – a professional mourning service. While initially dubious – the Italians, after all, are passionate, emotional people by nature, the mere idea of hiring a foreigner to express the intense feelings that are almost a national trait was anathema to them – senior figures, who had become increasingly desperate, decided to hire the girl's services. The way they saw it, such a provision would, if nothing else, prove diversionary, and might just deflect attention away from what they now recognised was a huge misjudgement on their behalf.

*

On the morning of the ceremony, the streets were lined with protestors rather than mourners. Many held aloft placards, shouted and chanted, booed and jeered, demanding that the funeral service be cancelled. Religious groups – Milan was home to a large Jewish community – had massed in Santo Steffano Square to express their indignation at the government celebrating the life of someone they considered to be a war criminal. Accordingly, the police presence, not to mention the deployment of several units of state guard, was extensive and intimidating.

Still, it wasn't enough to deter the stars of stage and screen, popular musicians from all over the world, Olympic champions, past and present, former statesmen and stateswomen, not to mention some of the biggest names from the fashion industry from attending. Half an hour before the official commencement of the ceremony, one fine automobile after another deposited the great and the good – some of whom were wearing Totti's exclusive designs as a tribute – outside the city's main cathedral. Clearly unnerved by the protestors, and in the hope of avoiding the projectiles (mainly rotten fruit and vegetables) that were being hurled from the mass of bodies hemmed in by well-marshalled crowd barriers, they dashed inside, shielded from the onslaught by hulking bodyguards.

Having been sneaked into the famous duomo long before the crowds had started to gather in such large numbers, Milica and the Jakšić brothers watched the mourners enter the grand church through a crack in the door of a small anteroom behind the main pulpit, where the deceased's open casket was now on display. With great interest – if not a profound sense of sadness – Milica observed the manner in which stony-faced men and women, the majority of whom were clad in black, walked over to the casket and appeared to mutter curses (well, certainly far from warm or respectful words) at the old woman's corpse.

To show such contempt and disrespect in God's house had the most powerful effect on Milica.

When she made her dramatic entrance, each sob, moan, cry, and gasp that she uttered as she prostrated herself before the casket reverberated not just through the stone and marble of the cathedral's structure, but through the skin and bones, heart and soul of every man, woman, and child present. It shook both rafter and conscience, the physical and the spiritual, the animate and inanimate, until the mourners themselves were in floods of tears, until they were hugging and embracing each other, until the level of their upset was so palpable, many started to choke and struggle for breath. And all the time Milica swayed and lamented before the casket, before God, lost, entranced, subject to shudders and shocks and spasms, as if she had been struck by a fork of lightning.

Up until that moment – the moment of Milica's dazzlingly poignant and wholly unexpected appearance – the service had been a stilted affair. From outside, the protestors' chants could still be heard. Sirens whirred. Shouts, screams, distorted staccato words through a loudspeaker, shattering glass (it was only later that it became apparent that some stores had been looted, their windows smashed) combined to create an oppressive, uncomfortable atmosphere inside the cathedral. On more than one occasion, the priest had to break off from his liturgy as what sounded like gunshots could be heard off in the distance.

"But the passing of a soul is a time for reflection…" he recommenced, only for a louder, bigger bang to interrupt him once more.

As for the mourners themselves, beyond the tension and discomfort of the situation, of not quite knowing what level of pandemonium was taking place outside, there was a distinct lack of remorse or sadness, or any of the finer feelings that should rightly be on display at a funeral. Whether merely unnerved, or truly disdaining of the deceased, they had started to whisper and talk amongst themselves. Some even laughed and told cruel, unkind jokes about Totti. To the point where the whole service was on the verge of descending into farce, like a classroom full of unruly pupils with no respect for the teacher's authority.

But all of that changed the moment Milica rushed from her hiding place.

And at the very height of that transformation, when even the most hardened of heart, those who bore serious (and, in most cases, wholly legitimate) antipathy towards the late fashion designer, were struggling to control their emotions, the cathedral's main door swung open. Somehow, half a dozen protestors had evaded both the barriers and the attention of the authorities with the sole intention of disrupting the service itself. Only when they were hit, sledgehammer-like, by that wall of grief, they were stunned to silence. Not quite comprehending what they were witnessing, they dropped their placards and cans of spray paint to the floor, their pieces of wood, their makeshift weapons, to both defend and attack, turned, and slowly walked out of the cathedral.

And it was this powerful image that adorned many newspapers across the globe in the coming days, an iconic photograph that would have significant ideological meaning for generations to come. In many ways, it symbolised a clash of the old and the new, of tradition and modernity. Young people coming face-to-face with a form of spirituality they had been taught to despise, because it was outdated, superstitious, oppressive, farcical, a figurative drug which stunted the growth and progress of society. Only there was something in the faces of those young people, the way they had dropped their weapons of protest to the ground, as if in surrender, that told a story all of its own. Whether there really is a supreme, omnipotent God didn't matter in this, or any other context, for that matter – the debate had been fruitless, and ultimately irrelevant since the dawn of time. If people could draw comfort, consolation, hope, if they could let that feeling of the unknown cleanse them of pain and uncertainty, then it could only ever be a good, positive, and powerful thing, something that should be embraced and nurtured.

*

Later that evening, as they journeyed to the airport in the back of a chauffeured Mercedes, Milica sat, deep in thought, replaying not just the day's events through her head, but the more philosophical considerations of what felt like a distinctly new phase of her performing life. As she would later confide to those closest to her, she had been struck by the depressing similarities between the Western and Eastern mourners she had encountered, and would go on to encounter, during her career. Despite the obvious contrasts, the higher standard of living in Vienna and Milan, the finer clothes, the cleanliness of the streets, the colourful shop windows stocked with all kinds of alluring goods, the efficient public services, and shiny automobiles on the well-maintained roads, the men, women, and children seemed singularly lacking in genuine sincerity, warmth, and kindness. The death of a loved one or associate stirred no tender human emotions in them (quite the opposite in some cases). All of which made her question exactly what she and the brothers were hoping to achieve. If all she could do was open people's eyes to the true sadness of death for a handful of hours, were they making any real, lasting, and worthwhile changes to their lives, their outlooks, the way they treated one another over the longer term?

"Something very special happened in the cathedral this morning," said Vlado. "I know you have reservations. But you must look past all negativity and doubt. You must endeavour to share your gift with these people, no matter how unworthy or ungrateful."

Milica shot him a quick, questioning glance, for he had very much articulated what she had then been pondering to distraction.

"The strongest and greatest amongst us," he went on, "stay true to their convictions. For good or for bad, they stick to what they believe in. You must do the same."

"I think I know what you mean. And regardless of the situation, I sense, deep down, that what I am doing now, being with you and your brother is the right thing to do. I can't explain why, it just feels that way."

"Good, I'm glad to hear it," said Radovan. "We travel to London this evening. Your services are required there. Hopefully, you don't feel too tired or drained of emotion. I know our schedule has been hectic. I know your thoughts must be with your family. After tomorrow, we will have an opportunity to rest and recharge our batteries."

*

Over the course of what constituted a long drive, Milica eventually drifted off into a deep sleep. The last thing she recalled with any clarity was being carried up some steps and into an aeroplane in Vlado's strong arms. After that, she remembered nothing of the take-off or any announcements from the pilot or safety instructions from the cabin crew. Exhausted by the rigours of not just the day, but everything that had happened since she was taken from the villa in the early hours of the morning, it was only a matter of time before she succumbed to a profound tiredness, both mental and physical.

But rather than just sink into a blank, empty form of unconsciousness, she was subject to the most disturbing of dreams. On a gloomy, overcast afternoon, she saw herself in a remote cemetery in the countryside, not unlike the cemetery she had visited in Sopot. Collapsed on the ground, she was sobbing and moaning and lamenting before what she soon realised was her own grave. Etched into the headstone were the words: *Milica Stanković, Beloved Daughter of Dragan and Nevena.*

Directly behind her stood her parents, Robert Savović, Miss Tadić, Father Miroslav, Sanja Babić, the Jakšić brothers, and a whole host of mourners from the different funerals she had performed at. But not one of these people displayed even the slightest flicker of emotion. They just stood there, completely unmoved, as if the matter of her passing meant little or nothing to them. And the more the Milica of the dream – the living, breathing version of herself – sobbed, moaned, and lamented before what constituted her own grave, the more disinterested and indifferent did those gathered appear. When this finally registered with her dream self, she swung 'round and started to yell at them, "Why aren't you crying? Why aren't you sad? Why aren't you showing any remorse? I did so much for you and your families. Why can't you shed a tear for me in return?"

And it was at that moment she woke up. And it was those final words that lingered long in her head. Even though she had secretly despaired at the thought of Robert Savović using her performances for financial gain, she thought the positive aspects far outweighed the negative, and was happy to continue up until the point Father Miroslav died, and she realised that she could no longer compromise herself like that, morally; and that whatever she decided to do in the future must be completely pure and worthy. But never had she pondered the deeper, more philosophical side of remuneration (away from the petty, grubby side to which she had been exposed), never had she turned the mirror around to herself and assessed her own personal motivations. Had she, all along, albeit unconsciously, displayed such heart-wrenching despair because she wanted something from people of far more value than money – pity, remorse, their finer feelings, their tears in return? In the same way all those dirty banknotes had filled Robert Savović's pockets, had she wanted to suck, vampire-like, the last vestiges of humanness from these unwitting half-people to satisfy a sinister form of vanity in herself she had never thought to question before? Had Professor Damjanović been right, after all – was Milica's gift or condition or whatever you cared to call it, no more than a form of mental illness, hysteria, that would go on to prove even more problematic in later years?

Alas, it is the curse of a sensitive, tender, and intelligent soul to question and probe, to wonder why certain things came into being, things which are universally detrimental to our collective health and happiness. It can be a torturous (and often unhelpful) process, especially when a person first starts out in life and doesn't really know their true purpose or path, why they seem to be drawn in one direction and not the other. But, as Vlado Jakšić had so rightly observed, the greater amongst us always stick to their convictions, they follow their heart and conscience, no matter where it might lead them. And even though Milica Stanković would suffer many more crises of confidence, dark moments when she didn't know if she was doing the right thing or not, she did summon the inner strength to stay true to herself and everything she most ardently believed in.

*

In the early hours of the morning, when Milica had finally dismissed those troubling thoughts from her mind, she stirred in her seat to find both Radovan and Vlado reading from bibles. Under the soft glow of the overhead lights, the brothers wore such contented, almost serene expressions on their faces, it showed just how much they were moved by each passage.

Sensing her eyes upon him, Vlado closed his leatherbound bible, turned, and smiled at her.

"You're awake. I hope you feel refreshed now. Would you care for something to eat or drink?"

Milica shook her head.

"Is something troubling you?"

"I was just thinking about my parents. I hate the idea of them being worried about me. They've always been very protective. For me to disappear without a trace will have caused them so much distress."

"I understand." He slipped a hand into his inside pocket. "Here." He handed Milica a blank postcard and a pen. "Write a few words to them. Don't identify yourself or sign your name. Just write something that they and they alone will understand, something that will let them know that it's you who has reached out to them, and that you are in good health. Understood?"

"Yes, of course. But why all the secrecy?"

"We were not the only ones interested in securing your services. Certain criminal elements – if it doesn't sound hypocritical for someone of my background to call them that – not to mention a number of government agencies were keeping you under strict surveillance. If we hadn't acted when we did, I have no idea what fate awaited you. For that reason, you cannot let anyone know where you are."

When they arrived in London, another chauffeured car transported them from the airport to another luxury hotel. Not that Milica took much interest in the sight of another great, big, dreary, grey city. She was still trying to compose a suitable message to her mother and father. Having requested a sheet of paper, she had written out a dozen or more drafts, only to scribble them out for fear of either being too explicit or too obscure for her parents to decipher.

In the end, she decided on the simplest and most straightforward lines she could muster:

Dear Uncle Dragan and Aunt Nevena,

I'm glad to tell you that the new-born calf survived the difficult birth. She is perfectly healthy and in good spirits now. You don't have to worry about anything.

I hope to see you both soon.

When she showed the note to the brothers, both nodded out their approval.

"Nicely executed," said Vlado. "That is sure to put their minds at rest."

*

After freshening up at the hotel and eating a plate of modest sandwiches, courtesy of room service, Radovan sought to explain the finer details of today's performance.

"I think it only right and proper that we give you a little background information about the deceased. Does Preemington Enterprises mean anything to you?"

Milica shook her head.

"Well, they are a global multi-national company with diverse business interests in many different countries. They have oil refineries, tobacco plantations, telecommunications networks. If you care to name any profitable line of commerce in the modern world, then Preemington Enterprises will no doubt have some kind of stake in its operation.

"The founder and CEO, Max Essien, has just passed away, leaving behind a multi-billion pound estate. But like many ruthless businessmen, those who have gone on to achieve great success, Essien wasn't the best-loved of individuals."

"Put quite simply," Vlado took up the backstory, "his methods, the ways in which he got the best out of the people around him – bullying, intimidation, scare tactics – were cruel and hugely demanding. And this was something he applied to his personal life as well. Two of his six children, from four different women, committed suicide as teenagers. His first wife died in circumstances so mysterious, many think that Essien himself was involved. Another spouse – the third wife, I believe – has been interned in a mental institute for the last fifteen years."

"He had many enemies," said Radovan, "both from within and outside of his business and personal spheres. Acting on the deceased's express wishes, the executives at Preemington want to lay on a lavish funeral, culminating with his body being buried at Highgate Cemetery."

"This is where we come in. If you could create a suitably mournful atmosphere at the graveside, it would make it appear that Essien wasn't a deeply hateful individual disdained by all those who knew him."

"But there is a twist," said Vlado. "You must be fully prepared for failure."

"Failure?" asked Milica.

"That is correct. These are not the kind of people who'll be affected by your performance. Most of the mourners will be paid actors, stand-ins the company have hired from a production company. The others will be family members and colleagues who were routinely terrorised by the dead man. It is our understanding, therefore, that there may well be a lot of hostility on display, perhaps even attempts to sabotage the event."

*

Although well-briefed, Milica didn't really know what to expect from the occasion. Ever since becoming a professional mourner, she had dealt with a whole host of bizarre situations. As Robert Savović remarked on more than one occasion, she had seen the very worst of humanity, money-grubbing relatives prepared to demean themselves in any way imaginable to secure financial remuneration. She had seen as many false tears as she had witnessed genuine and heartfelt emotion. Regardless, she always put her reservations to one side and performed to the best of her abilities. It was only later, when she not only reflected upon the events of the day but read about Essien's life in the newspapers, that she realised where all that hostility and bad feeling had come from, and just why her attendance had, for the first time in her career, been all but superfluous.

But we are, of course, getting a little ahead of ourselves.

Despite all the provisions that had been put into place, not to mention the deceased's vast wealth, there were only around one hundred or so mourners in attendance, many of whom, like Milica, had no association with the dead billionaire whatsoever. Moreover, the atmosphere had a dark, poisonous edge to it. Essien's surviving children and ex-wives, his closest associates, stood by the open grave, positively glowering at the casket as it was lowered into the ground.

"Ashes to ashes, dust to dust…" said a berobed priest, with all the solemnity befitting of the occasion.

On cue, Milica rushed over to the graveside, dropped to her knees, and sobbed with all the heartfelt entreaty and powerful earnestness of her previous performances. Seconds later, a woman who she later learned was the deceased's eldest child, a daughter in her late thirties, broke away from the other mourners, sunk to her knees beside Milica and began to hug her tightly and burst into floods of tears herself. Only her outpouring of emotion, while powerful, was in no way in earnest. In fact, she was mimicking and mocking Milica in equal measure, in what was a quite grotesque and tasteless parody of grief. Such was her hatred for her dead father, she shot to her feet, pushed Milica aside, and started to make the most hideous monkey-like noises, to posture and preen, to wiggle her behind in the direction of the grave, to make lewd gestures, to swear, spit, and curse. And all in the glare of the world's media, the flashing cameras, the assembled journalists hungry for a controversial story of this very kind.

"Straight to hell, that's where you belong. I hope you burn and rot and are made to suffer for all the pain you caused."

Even when two hefty security guards attempted to subdue her, she would not be easily restrained. She kicked out at them and clawed their faces with long nails painted a striking shade of red.

"Get your hands off me! Or I swear that I will send you to meet your maker, just like that evil bastard in the coffin over there."

For her part, Milica couldn't quite comprehend such a dramatic shift in the woman's emotions. A few moments ago, she was trembling in her arms, overcome by what Milica assumed was a wave of grief and upset so strong that she might be in imminent need of medical attention. But that had been no more than an act. Now, she was like a wild animal. Wheeling around, she jabbed a finger in Milica's direction.

"Go on, girl, you cry for that monster, because I certainly won't shed any more tears for him. I might have all his money now, but believe me, he took my soul. It's just been buried in that ground along with his stinking corpse."

It took quite some time, and a further barrage of insults and accusations, before a doctor was summoned to administer a powerful sedative to Essien's daughter. By then, the other mourners were in a visible state of shock. Some had been so shaken by the unpleasant scene, they sought comfort in each other's arms. While others, the more cynical or indifferent perhaps, struggled to keep their amusement to themselves.

"I knew this would be anything but uneventful."

"You know what they say – you can choose your friends, but you can't choose your family."

"Can't say I'm surprised. They're lunatics. Every last one of them. That's what too much money does to you."

These were just a few of the far-from-whispered or discreet comments which reached the ears of Milica and the Jakšić brothers as they readied to leave the cemetery.

"Don't let today's unsavoury events upset you," Vlado said to Milica. "You did everything in your power to create the appropriate atmosphere. Forget about that poor troubled woman's outburst."

But the events of the day stayed long in Milica's memory, both in the immediate aftermath, and in the years to come. Not for the first time, she had seen blind rage and outright hatred, feelings so strong and vindictive, they were not worthy of the name human – certainly not in the way Milica viewed her fellow woman and man. And it made her think back to the fight she had witnessed in the schoolyard when she was no more than a little girl, how those two boys had punched and kicked each other. Only they were mere children with undeveloped minds, subject to impulses neither of them understood, let alone were able to control. To think that those dark feelings could manifest in an educated, refined adult mind to such a violent degree truly saddened Milica, making her realise that some people were as far from their God as they were from themselves.

"Come." Radovan draped an arm around her shoulder. "We will go back to the hotel now. We can rest up and have something to eat."

"Our ultimate plan – ," Vlado pushed a leather-bound ledger across the dining table, " – is to redirect our finances to good and worthy charitable organisations without, of course, overtly championing any religious causes, let alone the reinstatement of the church as an institution in our country. That is our ultimate goal."

"Fortunately," said Radovan, "everyone in authority, from local officials to most high-ranking politicians, are still fond of taking bribes. The bigger, the better. Thus, we have been able to set up some promising initiatives without drawing much attention to ourselves."

Over the next hour, the brothers explained things in more detail. And even though the neat, ordered columns of figures on each page of the ledger meant little or nothing to Milica, the passion with which they spoke about the educational facilities they were currently constructing in the smaller towns and villages ('to give those less privileged a chance to better themselves'), the medical centres, the drainage projects to provide clean drinking water was truly inspiring, even if she wasn't quite sure how much she was actually contributing herself.

"But these are major construction projects. The fees for my performances must be a drop in the ocean in comparison. Surely, there is something more I could do to help."

"I think you seriously underestimate your reputation and earning power," Vlado replied, "and the unique Western psyche. The spiritual crisis they are currently experiencing."

"How do you mean?"

"That most of these people have been spoiled and pampered and lived such a decadent, immoral existence for so long, they crave a higher purpose in life, enlightenment, as much as some form of religious justification. The older they get, the more they fear the unknown judgement from up above."

"Although it may sound cynical," said Radovan, "we are fully prepared to exploit the situation. There are so many so-called 'successful' people over here who, to put it in simple terms, want to buy their own redemption, that we have been inundated with queries regarding your services. Make no mistake. You are one of the most in-demand performers in the world at the moment."

*

Over the course of a whirlwind eighteenth-month period, Milica performed in some of the biggest cities in Europe – and beyond. In towering cathedrals or beside graves in far more modest cemeteries, she displayed her trademark outpouring of grief and despair; she reduced hundreds, if not thousands of mourners to floods of tears. Like a star of stage or screen, the brothers insisted on dressing her in the finest of clothes, the best designer labels, always in black, and hewn from the most expensive of silken fabrics. During that period, she became quite well-known on the international stage. Newspapers in different countries ran stories on her unique services. They conducted countless interviews with the help of interpreters. The headline-obsessed Western press, as much as their insatiable audience, hungry for stories about anything out of the ordinary, were fascinated by the level of fame (or notoriety) she had acquired as much as they were by the social, and perhaps philosophical, aspect involved.

"Why do you think people hire you?" one reporter in Grenoble put what, in recent weeks, had become the most frequently asked question to Milica and the Jakšić brothers.

Even though she understood the general gist of these enquiries (during their extensive travels, they had, to pass the time, studied many different languages via textbooks and phrasebooks), either Radovan or Vlado would invariably answer on her behalf.

"It is not for us to question. We merely want to offer emotional support and help people during the grieving process. If we can console the recently bereaved when they are struggling to come to terms with the death of a loved one, we feel as if we are providing a good and worthy service."

There were always other questions, some not quite so easy to answer. Questions about exploitation, taking advantage of vulnerable people, of morality, of accepting large amounts of money for expressing emotions which should come naturally to people when a family member, friend, or colleague passes away.

Protective of their star attraction, the brothers were quick to rush to her defence. With no small degree of eloquence, they refuted the more dubious accusations. They spoke of Milica's past, as a child who couldn't stop crying, how she had always felt a powerful stirring of emotion whenever she encountered any pain or suffering in life, and how she wanted to do everything in her power to lessen the burdens other people carried around with them.

"In so many ways, this is her natural calling. We have simply harnessed her gift to try and do good in this world."

In truth, they had come to idolise the girl, to look up to her as if she really was possessed of divine qualities herself. For two men who had been involved in criminal circles since boyhood, who had seen (and done, it must be stated for the record) some truly horrific things, being around such a kind, gentle, and indisputably pure soul had a regenerative effect on them both. And whether this was merely delusionary, in the same way their moneyed yet morally decayed Western clients fooled themselves into believing they could change their ways to appease a higher spiritual power, to cleanse their souls of misdeeds, it made the brothers feel like better people, with clearly defined goals in life.

*

Back in their own country, Milica's exploits hadn't escaped the notice of a certain high-ranking government official. In fact, Dušan Srna received regular updates from several trusted sources. Unfortunately, the military operatives charged with her safe return always seemed to be one step behind her abductors, no matter how well-briefed regarding their current whereabouts.

"But, Colonel, my office has provided unlimited funding for your unit. You are supposed to be the finest, most resourceful specialists in the country. Why have you failed to deliver the girl to us? Intelligence from the West suggests that she is in the hands of a two-bit criminal organisation and that an operation to seize her could be undertaken with ease."

"I can only apologise, sir. We've been ready to act on numerous occasions, only for her captors to secret her away at the last minute. It's almost as if they're aware of our covert activities, down to the last detail. I have never witnessed anything quite like it before. If I didn't know any better, I would suspect that they had been tipped off by an inside informant."

This theory, even though Srna and his office were unaware of the fact, was indeed correct. The extensive network of politicians susceptible to bribery went all the way up to Srna and beyond. One simple overseas phone call or telegram was all it took to keep the brothers abreast of any secret military operations that directly affected them.

"Don't be so ridiculous, Colonel. These – ," Srna glanced down at a report on his desk, " – Jakšić brothers are hoodlums, black market traders, opportunists. How on earth could they infiltrate high offices in government? No. Your unit's operational performance has been flawed. You must've telegraphed your activities. I cannot even begin to express my dissatisfaction. As you well know, the leader has been in the grips of a debilitating illness for many years now. Somehow – and this has baffled the best doctors in the country – he has managed to hold on. But make no mistake, the end is near. Therefore, I must stand you down from the operation."

"But, sir, my men are –"

"Your men are incompetent, as are you yourself. The operation I entrusted you with was simplistic enough. To fail yet again is unacceptable. As time is very much our enemy, I have reached out to Moscow for assistance."

"Moscow?"

"That's correct. Our comrades are already en route to France. We anticipate a swift and satisfactory conclusion to the mission."

*

During their enforced separation from their daughter, life had not been kind to Dragan and Nevena Stanković. Despite persistent phone calls, and a string of increasingly desperate letters to the authorities, the police investigation appeared to have been all but closed. Due to a complete lack of physical evidence (the bedroom in which Milica had slept had yielded not a single fingerprint, and the only tyre tracks identified in and around the villa belonged to the ailing old van that had served Robert Savović so well over the last few years), and the absence of any eyewitnesses (there had been no reported sightings of a girl matching Milica's description in the area in the days and weeks following her disappearance), the general consensus was that the girl, whose troubled childhood and mental health problems were well-documented, had taken her own life. In all likelihood, by drowning, by sneaking out of the villa in the dead of night, filling her pockets with rocks, and walking into the ocean. And while no body had washed up on the shore, this sequence of events – a tragic case of suicide – was seen as the most probable explanation.

"But that don't make no sense," Dragan had argued during one of many heated telephone conversations with the police. "Milica wanted to dedicate her life to helping other people. Never once did she seem down or depressed. Never once did she say she wanted to do herself in."

But it was perhaps the way life in Velika Plana carried on as normal that proved more galling to the Stankovićs than anything else. Either through indifference, or a fear of upsetting the couple, none of their friends or neighbours asked after Milica anymore. They never mentioned her at all. If they had the uncomfortable misfortune of bumping into either

Dragan or Nevena in the street, they offered no more than a standard hello or a brief wave or nod of the head.

"It's as if they don't remember that we had a daughter," Nevena sobbed. "As if Millie never existed."

Devastated by her unexplained disappearance, Dragan began drinking particularly heavily. Not in the tavern with Robert Savović anymore, but alone in the apartment while Nevena worked long shifts at the chemist shop. As much financial (he had all but spent the money he had saved from the professional mourning business) as an inexplicable aversion to a man whose company he once craved (the same Robert Savović), Dragan would spend long hours slumped in an armchair, guzzling back strong spirits and drifting in and out of fitful sleep, reimagining his long walks with Milica through the forest and down by the river. So vividly would he replay their conversations (well, Milica's fascinating reflections on the great works of literature), it would bring tears to his eyes. Increasingly, he found himself responding to the lengthy, florid descriptions his daughter had relayed, in a way he had never felt capable of doing in the past, despite being mesmerised by her words and having any number of questions he wanted to ask, points he wanted to clarify. A sad irony, no doubt. How we, as people, often travel back to certain moments in time when we didn't do or say the things we dearly wanted to. A capacity for reflection is undoubtedly one of the crueller and more frustrating aspects of being human, all too human. To live a moment in time again, to reshape and reform a memory, acting with all the many and varied benefits of hindsight, until you have moulded a perfect event out of a happening, and, in particular, your role in it, which had always left you with a profound sense of disappointment or missed opportunity.

"But like you said, that poor woman shouldn't have thrown herself under that train. No matter how desperate a situation may appear, Millie, there's no problem that can't be solved if you have good people around you who love you."

And it was one of these dream visions, almost as intoxicating as the alcohol itself, which saw him finally arrest his alarmingly self-destructive behaviour. In this particular vision, Dragan saw his daughter – no longer a mere girl anymore, but a beautiful young woman, dressed in the finest silken gown, with her long shiny hair falling halfway down her back – walking through the capital city, waving to a huge crowd of people that had gathered on the streets. It was a dazzling sight, a public event or national celebration. The adoration that the common man and woman displayed towards Milica, the sheer noise they generated, the military guard surrounding her, the soldiers on horseback, the brass band striking up in the background startled Dragan into something approaching full sentience, a state he had not occupied for many weeks.

"I knew it," he mumbled to himself. "Millie is alive and well and destined for great things."

Half-stumbling over to the door, and sending a few empty bottles tinkling and tumbling across the floor, he felt he simply had to go and speak to his wife, to share his vision with her.

When he rushed into the shop, he found it empty. Nevena was sitting on a stool behind the counter, staring vacantly into space, so lost in her own thoughts, she hadn't even noticed his far-from-discreet or noiseless entrance.

"Nevena, I just had the most wonderful of visions. I saw our Millie. She were all grown-up, like a proper well-do-to lady, walking through a big city surrounded by crowds of people who were applauding and calling her name. She looked so pretty. I just know it were real, like a glimpse into the future."

Nevena, on shaking herself from her reverie, became incredibly excited when her husband's words finally registered (and he had to repeat himself on three or more occasions before he had gone some way to instilling his vision in her mind).

"It must be a sign from above. God is telling us not to give up hope."

"That's exactly what I thought, my darling. And listen, I know I've not been the best of husbands of late, that I've been moping around feeling sorry for myself. But all that stops today. I'm going to knock the drinking on the head, once and for all. I'm going to tidy myself up, have a proper wash and a shave, and, first thing in the morning, I'm going to try and get my old job back at the steelworks. Now more than ever, we need to have faith in Millie and whatever the good Lord has got planned for her."

*

The next morning, Dragan visited the steelworks for the first time since his controversial display in front of the disciplinary committee. More through luck than judgement, he arrived at a time of the morning when Pančev was not only in his office, but when he had no pressing administrative duties to attend to.

"Dragan Stanković! My word, is that really you?"

And while his words were friendly and effusive, they didn't quite conceal his shock and sadness at Dragan's physical decline. Now skinny and wasted, with a hollowed-out face of concave cheeks and a sickly pale pallor, he was almost unrecognisable from the robust, stocky, force of nature worker who was once held in such high esteem by everyone associated with the steelworks.

"What brings you here?"

"Well, to be perfectly frank, I wanted to ask for my old job back. I know I acted terribly all that time ago. I know I went down the wrong path. But things have changed. As you probably know, my daughter, our only child, went missing. It were a terrible blow for us to take."

Naturally, Pančev had heard about the Stanković's misfortune. They story of the mysterious disappearance had, in fact, been the talk of the town for many weeks now.

"Yes, I was sorry to hear about that. It must've have been a dreadful shock. And you've heard nothing since? The police haven't been able to track her down?"

Dragan shook his head. "No. They have no idea what happened to her. But if nothing else, it's made me see the error of my ways. I want to get back on the straight and narrow and do the kind of work I was born to do."

Pančev slowly nodded his head and ran a hand over his freshly shaved chin. This unexpected request presented him with a problem not easy to solve. As it happened, the steelworks were currently operating at full capacity. Moreover, they had a desperate need for new workers to keep up with the demand. Only Dragan was clearly in no condition to return to his old duties.

"I won't lie to you, Dragan, we could do with a man of your experience. But I couldn't put you straight back to work on the main production line. If agreeable, we could start you out on some lighter duties, and see how things go."

"Of course, I'd be happy to help out in any way I can."

"Good. I'm glad to hear it." Pančev stood up. "I'll expect you here first thing in the morning. It will be just like old times."

*

When Dragan returned home, he found a postcard on the mat in the hall. Ducking down, he picked it up and studied the postmark – *Sopot*. Ever cautious, the Jakšić brothers had arranged for the card to be sent from inside the country, to avoid arousing any suspicion. Unbeknown to them, however, the destination – the scene of one of Milica's most moving acts of kindness – stirred up such powerful emotions in Dragan, he didn't even need to read the message, or confirm that the handwriting did indeed belong to his beloved daughter.

"It's from Millie. She wants us to know that she's all right, and that we'll be seeing her again soon."

For the second time in as many days, he raced from his home, zigzagging his way through the town's busy main street, and hurtled into the chemist shop. Only today, a long line of customers stood in front of the counter. Impatient, hopping from one foot to the other, waving the postcard high above his head in an attempt to get his wife's attention, Dragan, nevertheless, had to wait a full five minutes before he made his way to the front of the queue and caught Nevena's eye.

"Whatever is it?" she asked, with more than a hint of concern. Due to his exertions, beads of sweat were pouring down his beetroot-red face, and his old work shirt (darned and repaired by her own skilled hand on countless occasions) was clinging to his back.

"Look at this." He placed the postcard on the counter.

It took no more than a handful of seconds for Nevena to understand exactly what the receipt of such a curious message truly meant, and the identity of the sender.

"How wonderful! Like your vision, Dragan, this is a clear sign that all our worst fears were unfounded. Who knows? We may be reunited with Milica any day now!"

This unexpected turn of events brought tears of joy to Nevena's eyes. Unlike her husband, who refused to even acknowledge the possibility that Milica might have wanted to disappear of her own volition, Nevena had feared something of the kind happening, ever since the professional mourning service had become such a big success. There was something in the way Milica looked at her father and, in particular, Robert Savović, when they returned from one of the funerals and started divvying out the money they had earned. Disappointment, distaste, and disapproval were all readily apparent as she trudged through to her bedroom 'to rest.'

On more than one occasion, Nevena felt compelled to broach the subject with Dragan, but something always held her back. Clearly, their daughter wasn't happy with their avaricious chortling ("This will certainly buy a good few rounds down the tavern, eh, Dragan?"). If she was honest with herself, the good woman would've acknowledged the stirring effect the sight of all that money had had on her in those early days. People who have never had much in life, those who routinely struggle to make ends meet, to put food on their tables, lose sight of their moral compass, if we can call it as such, when chance (and heavy) remuneration presents itself to them. They will overlook the cruellest and most exploitative of acts if it means that their own pockets will be lined with banknotes.

As such, her despair at the disappearance of her daughter had an even darker and more damning effect on her than it did her husband. By nature, the most selfless and loving parents are cultivators of their offspring's finer feelings. They want their children to grow into good, upstanding individuals. If the son or daughter, for whatever reason, falls below the standard of behaviour prescribed, parents of Nevena's irreproachable ilk cannot help but feel responsible. By the same token, if the child displays pure and worthy attributes, it makes them feel as if they had succeeded in the greatest of all tasks, bringing into this contrary, often violent and inexplicable world, a person capable of changing things for the better. For that reason, and many others that operated below the surface level of her consciousness, Nevena felt a disproportionate level of misplaced guilt regarding Milica's disappearance. If only she had acted sooner, if only she had confronted Dragan and Savović, if only she had voiced her concerns regarding her daughter's state of mind in the weeks before she vanished without a trace, then none of this would've happened.

Each night, she prayed before the ikons, pleading with God to return their daughter to them, safe from harm, begging, beseeching, condemning even, expressing her acute sense of injustice that one of His finest servants could be taken from her family so indiscriminately. When, after weeks of earnest prayer had garnered no positive response, tortured by insomnia and those guilty thoughts, Nevena could think of only one course of action.

To go and see Sanja Babić.

However, this wasn't the most straightforward of assignations to arrange. The long hours Nevena worked at the chemist shop didn't present her with an opportunity to leave her post for more than half an hour each lunchtime. Moreover, now that he was in advancing years, Mr. Vidić had become increasingly cantankerous and demanding. Whether his health was failing him, or whether he simply felt as if Nevena was duty-bound to display such dedication to her post, in consideration of his past kindnesses, amounted to one and the same thing.

To get around this wheezing, irascible octogenarian-shaped obstacle with failing eyesight and sporadic incontinence (for which, in fairness, he was taking one of his own concoctions to remedy), Nevena had to resort to methods she considered beneath her – she lied.

"I'm terribly sorry for the inconvenience, Mr. Vidić, but I have a doctor's appointment scheduled for late tomorrow morning. It's not something I can put off. Hopefully, it won't keep me away for more than a couple of hours."

"Doctor's appointment?" Mr. Vidić squinted out a brief, yet probing appraisal of her physical condition over the top of his thick glasses. "But you look perfectly fine, in the prime of your life. If something ails you, feel free to consult with me for a remedy. I have all the experience in the world." He flushed proudly and adjusted the very same spectacles. "Yes. Make no mistake. There's no condition I haven't seen in my time."

"Thank you, Mr. Vidić. Unfortunately, my, erm…ailment is of a rather delicate nature. A woman's problem, and I would feel much more comfortable discussing it with my doctor."

This was, of course, another lie – but an effective one.

Crotchety, old man Vidić may've been, but a semblance of good manners and discretion (qualities he possessed in abundance when Nevena first came into his employ) thankfully remained.

"Why of course. But please do bear in mind that Tuesdays can be dreadfully busy. If you could make your visit to your physician as brief as possible, it would be much appreciated."

*

The following Tuesday, late morning, Nevena tapped on the door of Sanja Babić's shack near the forest.

"Ah," said the old woman upon answering, "it be the Stanković woman. Mother of the blessed angel girl Milica. Come in. I've been expecting you."

Cryptic words Nevena didn't really dwell on or consider in any way ominous. Experience told her this was just the way the old healer expressed herself. But she would've done well to be wary. For no sooner had she taken a seat in the ramshackle abode than Babić qualified those words in the most frightening way imaginable.

"Your daughter is in grave danger. But not from those who took her. No. Them be protectors sent to lead her down the right path."

"Protectors? I don't understand."

"Nor shall you ever, mere mortal that you are. But listen carefully. The walls are-a-closing-in. That girl of yours will be subjected to a terrible ordeal. She will be at the centre of events that could change the world forever more."

*

At this point in our story, it would be remiss not to give mention to the activities of Robert Savović:

On their eventual return from the coast, he made all kinds of reassurances to Dragan and Nevena.

"I have friends in high places. I'll call in a few favours. Don't you worry. I'll leave no stone unturned. I'll make sure we find out exactly what happened to your daughter."

Empty, hollow words, for he had been directly responsible for Milica's disappearance. But words which filled the couple with false, if short-lived hope, that was both cruel and unnecessary in the circumstances; a pledge posited solely to make Savović feel better about himself.

Still, it would be wrong to say that he wasn't deeply affected by the kidnap plot, and the pivotal role he played in its execution. In the normal scheme of things, and certainly over the course of his eventful life, Savović was never a man to feel any guilt or remorse, no matter how heinous a wrongdoing he had committed. Like the world's most fearsome predators, he was programmed to exist in a certain way. While the shark and crocodile hunt and eat, Savović schemed and exploited. He had no fine or noble feelings. He felt no attachment to anyone or anything. If he had to connive, backstab, and ultimately betray those who had developed a particular liking for him, he would not have blinked an eyelid. But his feelings towards Dragan and Milica had been more complex and deep-rooted than even he could acknowledge at the time, and were perhaps linked to what was undoubtedly the biggest disappointment of his life, a wholly unedifying and humiliating experience that he had never shared with anyone else.

In his formative years, when he was part street urchin, part callow youth, Savović sneaked into the local theatre during the performance of a play, the story of a soldier doomed to die at the frontline, and his brief yet passionate love affair with a beautiful actress. And although Savović was never able to find out the name of the production, he was so moved by the spectacle, particularly the male lead's stirring and heroic performance, that he resolved, from that day forward, to become the finest actor in the world.

Back then, he had already been sucked into a life of petty crime (through necessity, it must be stated, the need to put food on his family's table, rather than any delinquent tendency per se). But unbeknown to the gang of youths he had become associated with, he attended weekly acting lessons with a well-known thespian who had a predilection for rough young boys from the wrong side of the figurative tracks. And it was the fallacious dynamic of this teacher-pupil relationship which had the most profound effect on the development of Savović's character, that made him the cold, cynical, conniving confidence trickster and general fraud that he went on to become. For all his bravado which, even then, saw him relay unlikely tales to his criminal brethren that would reduce them to gasps of astonishment or uproarious laughter, Savović was singularly lacking in any artistic talent. He couldn't transfer the charisma which defined him in the back streets and alleys, or the dingy taverns of his later years, onto the stage. Regardless, his acting coach, acting on desires which need no further elaboration in these pages, convinced his student otherwise.

"Beautiful, Robert. You read the part so wonderfully well. Such passion, such emotion, such verve! You're a star in the making, you really are."

Those unused to praise or kind words are particularly susceptible to compliments and encouragement of any kind. Within a matter of weeks, Savović was convinced that he was well on the way to fulfilling his most treasured ambition, that he was no longer destined to spend his life on the streets, but on the stage, receiving plaudits from adoring crowds in the country's finest theatre houses.

This delusion came crashing down all around him when he took a small part in a play at a provincial theatre. A last-minute replacement for a far more experienced actor who had been taken ill overnight, Savović wasn't so much struck with paralysing stage fright when he attempted to recite a few simple lines, but cataclysmically aware of his own lack of timing, projection, posture, assurance, delivery – the core essentials in the arsenal of all proficient actors. Every one of those words (a mere nineteen in all: 'If you kill me now, I will avenge myself in the next life. Of that you can be sure.') dribbled inarticulately out of his mouth, like drool down an infant child's chin. It was a crushing sense of realisation, knowing that he had wasted his time, that he had fooled himself into believing his acting coach's words of praise (and with this realisation came a true understanding of the man's interest in him), that he vowed to never set foot on the stage again.

Nevertheless, this disappointment, like any person's greatest failure, stayed with Savović for the rest of his days. He developed an aversion to flattery, pretty words, or flowery compliments. Life, as he had learned through bitter experiences, wasn't like that. It was a cold, ugly, hostile place where you had to be on your guard at all times. Every once in a while, though, no matter where he resided, he would drink himself into a state of melancholic nostalgia and visit the nearest theatre house. Concealing himself in the back row (an unnecessary precaution for someone who was essentially a stranger in a new town), he would look on awestruck as the actors, some far more accomplished than others, performed with all the timing, projection, posture, assurance, and delivery that he simply hadn't possessed as a much younger man.

Hence, his fascination with Milica Stanković, the deep-rooted complexity hinted at above. When he first saw the girl prostrate herself before an open grave, when he saw the sheer power of her performances, the grace, the movement, he felt a stirring of emotions he couldn't initially identify. Was it admiration? Respect? Or was it something much darker, bordering upon contempt? Did the frustrated actor in him feel jealous in the presence of someone blessed with the gifts he had so badly yearned for in his youth?

A failure in everything but life itself (and this, strangely, was no consolation to a man who had come from nothing), he devoted himself to the professional mourning enterprise because he was fascinated (if not obsessed) by Milica's natural talent, how everything came so easily to her. Just like her father, whenever she performed, Savović would analyse her each mournful sob and cry, the way she would clasp her hands together in prayer, and throw back her head and beseech the Lord above.

Why he did this was a mystery to himself. In the face of a superior talent, those of lesser abilities often look for any flaws or weaknesses – indecision, a lack of sincerity perhaps – chinks in armour of far superior construction and quality to their own. But in this respect, Savović never once saw Milica falter. And this was hard to reconcile for a wily, cynical man who had been brought up on the streets, who had only survived due to the quickness of wits and the ruthlessness of his code. For men of his background, there was no such thing as a pure heart, an untainted character, a person performing an act without an ulterior motive, without some form of personal gain involved.

From their first booking onward, whenever he watched Milica perform, he felt a surge of resentment so poisonous that only a veritable ocean of strong booze could temper it. On more than one occasion, when they were preparing for her entrance, he had a strong compulsion to strike out at the girl, to punch and kick and pull her hair. His bitterness towards her festered to such a degree, it was a miracle that he managed to restrain himself.

"And you say she never makes a claim to any of our earnings?" he asked Dragan after another hugely successful performance. "She doesn't want nothing to do with the financial side of things?"

Dragan shook his head.

"Still, she's aware of the benefits? She knows we're charging these folks a great deal for her services?"

"Of course, she's far from stupid. But I'll tell you something, without fear of contradiction, she would turn up at these here funerals and perform free of charge. Helping people, it's in her bones. Robert. It's what she were born to do."

Despite making a few agreeable comments, Savović remained unconvinced. Only the more he saw, the more he studied, observed, and scrutinised, the more he realised that Dragan had been right. There was no edge or angle or anything suspect or insincere about the girl. She simply did what she did because she wanted to help other people. But even confirmation of that failed to satisfy Savović, or dismiss the hostile feelings he felt towards Milica. Those who are rotten to the core cannot reconcile the idea of the irreproachable, incorruptible soul, for it reminds them of just how lowly and miserable they themselves really are.

In the early hours of the morning, long after Dragan had stumbled home from the tavern, Savović would lay in the silence of the backroom, on a makeshift bed, and think of ways he could hurt or humiliate, or, better still, unmask Milica as a fraud. He just couldn't accept that there wasn't a darker side to her nature. Next morning, when he partook of his first drink of the day, the most effective way to clear his mind and stop his hands from shaking, he no longer felt any malice towards Milica, just a desperate need to get her out of his life once and for all. If it hadn't been for the huge amounts of money she was generating for the business, he would've had no problem about leaving the town and trying his luck elsewhere. A maverick, nomadic soul, it wouldn't have been the first time he simply left a place without so much as a goodbye to those he had struck up a friendship with.

"There's no doubt about it," he often mused over that first drink of the morning, "that girl is having a negative impact on your well-being. She's putting thoughts into your head that you would never have dreamed of thinking in a million years."

It was with little or no remorse, therefore, that he was fully prepared to trade the girl for a handful of silver, in the same way a merchant would offload a shipment of highly sought-after goods.

Only now, when he reassessed the situation, he bitterly regretted having acted, not so much hastily, but so emphatically that there was literally no way back. He knew the reputation of the Jakšić brothers (although he was completely unaware of the spiritual epiphany that had seen them change their ways completely). He knew that men with their connections would be able to make far more money from her unique talents than he ever could. Put as simply as possible, he began to miss Milica because she had, for a brief period of time, made him a very rich man. Like Dragan, Savović had been far from sensible with the great wads of money that had come his way during that golden period. If being down to his last few thousand wasn't bad enough, he was, for the first time he could ever remember, totally bereft of ideas for new business enterprises.

But what perhaps made him regret that decision all the more was the morning three hulking men with strong Russian accents called into the tavern. Before they had even approached the counter and asked for him by name (which they most certainly proceeded to do), Savović felt a horrible sinking feeling in the pit of his stomach. One look at these fearsome characters told him that they placed little or no value on human life.

"We're looking for Robert Savović."

*

After leaving France, the Jakšić brothers took Milica on a trip down to the southern part of Italy. In the first-class compartments of an overnight train, they travelled to the one and only destination they would, in fact, reach: Naples. For Milica, this was an amazing excursion. From an early age, she had felt a powerful attraction towards churches, of which this devoutly Catholic country abounded. On almost every street corner or sprawling plaza, there stood places of worship, some dating back to the eleventh century. When they ventured inside the Sansevero Chapel Museum and stared in wonder at the dramatic, colourful frescoes on the ceilings, it was all too much for Milica. Rushing towards the front of the church, she dropped to her knees in front of the altar and began to prostrate herself before the image of Christ in such an impassioned manner, all the other visitors – local people and tourists alike – couldn't help but be deeply affected. In particular, two wrinkle-faced old women with kerchiefs covering their heads knelt beside Milica and began to pray and cross themselves with similar fervour. The general commotion this sight created saw two priests, clearly affiliated with the church in some way, appear from the nave or sanctuary situated directly behind the altar.

After a moment or two of silent contemplation, the older of the two priests shuffled over to Milica, reached out and placed a hand on her head.

"You are a special one, my child. The Lord has earmarked you for great things."

*

"For me," said Milica, "all churches, even the plainest and most modest, are places of true importance. But to see what artistic heights love and devotion to God inspired in the creator of the magnificent works of art here is truly humbling. How could anyone, no matter what their religious or political beliefs, not be moved by such a sight? How could they not realise that beauty on this scale could only have come from the Lord Himself?"

"I wholeheartedly agree," said Vlado. "Whether Catholic, Orthodox, Muslim, Jew, or whatever code you follow, when you tread the right path, when you apply the pure teachings of Jesus Christ to your life, there is nothing you are not capable of."

The wonderous frescoes and ancient churches were not the only things that caught Milica's eye during their tour of the city. She was also struck by the disparate ethnicities that mixed in the cafes and bars. Not until her travels with the brothers had she seen anything other than people with white skin. Moreover, for someone who, up until relatively recently, had never been beyond the borders of her own country, the vibrant streets of this impoverished city offered up some troubling sights. The pitiful state of the beggars, painfully thin and in threadbare rags, were hugely distressing for an idealistic young girl who so desperately wanted to eradicate any pain, suffering, and inequality from the world.

"I don't quite know what to make of this place," she said. "In the other cities we have visited, you could see a clear divide between the rich and the poor. The well-to-do and the workers. But here, there is a universal vastness to the underclass. Regardless, these people seem closer to God for that very fact."

"A thoughtful observation," said Radovan. "And it is most certainly true – to learn what is most important to us in life, we must truly suffer."

"Yes, I have felt that most strongly, ever since I was a child."

"That is one of the greatest challenges that we face," said Vlado. "No doubt, the world will become a more global and open place in the years to come. But people shouldn't fear or mistrust things simply because they're different."

"Vlado is right. It is our aim to foster more love and understanding. We want to bring people together. Even in the most turbulent of times, whenever we have faced any adversity, whenever we have needed comfort in our darkest moments, we have always looked to God.

"Now, more than –" but before he had the chance to finish his sentence, an unmarked van screeched to a halt directly in front of them.

A second later, the side door swung open, and half a dozen or more hulking men holding submachine guns leapt out into the middle of the road.

"Get in," shouted one, "or we shoot you in the street like dogs."

*

Back in Velika Plana, Dragan Stanković had just arrived at the steelworks for the first shift of his second tenure as an official state employee. Having not had a drink for a few days, and having not slept at all well the night previous, he felt a mixture of anxiety and excitement, a breathlessness in his lungs, and a queasiness in the pit of his stomach. Despite the nature of the work, the long hours and physical challenges involved, he had, in very different days, looked forward to each shift. He liked to test himself, to feel the sweat pour from his brow and his muscles ache, for it told him that he had just done a good, honest day's work, that the fresh bread on the table and beef soup simmering gently on the stove had been earned in the most honourable way.

But beyond his natural apprehension, potentially debilitating as it then felt, Dragan was struck by the sheer size and physicality of his fellow workers, some of whom had been at the steelworks for decades, former colleagues who he had once toiled beside. It made him painfully aware of his own physical decline, the way the alcohol and dissolute living had diminished his strength, making him an old man long before his time. In comparison to the steelworkers striding purposefully through the main gates, strapping fellows with rounded shoulders and bulging biceps, he felt sickly and inferior. He realised just how far he had fallen, and just how hard it would be to return anywhere near to his former standing.

To compound that sense of not really belonging here anymore, these workers, almost to the last man, failed to recognise him. In fact, they eyed him with suspicion, as if they couldn't quite understand what this old man with the shambling gait and uncertain manner was doing at the steelworks in the first place. It wasn't until Pančev rounded them all up and began to allocate the day's work duties that they received an explanation.

"Oh, and before you all get started," he said, tucking a clipboard under his arm, "we welcome back a stalwart worker from the past today. Come over here, Dragan." He ushered him over. "Many of you will remember Dragan Stanković, recipient of so many commendations for exceeding his work quota, we all lost count." He chuckled and patted Dragan on the back. "He'll start out on light duties for now, just until he's back into the swing of things."

As much as Dragan appreciated the introduction, not because of the generous words about his past accolades, more the way it identified him to old friends and co-workers to whom he had become a stranger, he was still stung by their general reaction. The shock and sadness he clearly discerned when they realised that the old man they had been casting such pitying glances at was in fact Dragan Stanković, the one worker they had (again, almost to the last man) looked up to and admired more than anyone who had ever stepped foot inside the steelworks. And while some came over to shake his hand and apologised for not recognising him, their gestures and words were underpinned with all the shock, sadness, and pity he noticed when Pančev told them who he was.

If that hadn't been humiliating enough, the nature of the duties he had been assigned – no more than sweeping up, and fetching and carrying inconsequential items from one side of the steelworks to the other – proved to be beyond his physical capabilities. Every few minutes, he would have to stop and catch his breath or, if nobody was looking, sit down on a wooden pallet for a quick rest. Whereas before, when he was in the prime of his life, he embraced the challenges of the working day, where he pushed himself and all those around him to their limits and beyond, now the challenge assumed the shape of merely staying on his feet long enough to sweep up a small pile of metal shavings in the storeroom.

But somehow, he made it to the end of his shift without collapsing and making a complete fool of himself.

"How was your first day back?" Pančev asked him, as they both prepared to clock out. "No doubt it'll take a little while for you to get back into the old routine."

"Yes, yes, of course." He smiled weakly. "It's been a long time since I did any physical work."

"Just you persevere. If you stick at it, I'm sure you'll build up your strength again, and be ready for more demanding tasks."

*

The next morning, Dragan awoke up with every muscle in his body aching. When he tried to move, to simply roll over onto his back, he couldn't muster the necessary force.

"Are you all right, Dragan?" asked Nevena. "You're breathing so heavily. It's not your heart, is it? You haven't had those chest pains again?"

"No, no, my love. Don't you worry. I'll be right as rain just as soon as I get up and about, just as soon as I get the blood flowing through my veins again."

But it took a truly Herculean effort, a painful stop/start process, just to swing his legs off the bed and sit up.

"I don't think you should go to work today," said Nevena. "Clearly your duties at the steelworks are too much for you now. Why don't you lie back down again and rest? We'll manage on my wage for the time being. You can look for something less physically demanding."

Her words stirred Dragan into action as much as they wounded his already-battered pride. Forcing himself up off the bed, he pictured all those pitying faces from yesterday and was determined to prove them wrong. Only he knew that he wouldn't be able to do it without a little help, a boost from a familiar and reliable source. But when he shuffled on his sore, aching legs into the bathroom, dug his hands behind the cistern, and looked for his secret hiding place, he remembered that he had long-since resolved to no longer keep any alcohol in the house, let alone conceal it. Disproportionately disappointed (although, perhaps, there is no disappointment comparable to that of a drinker who discovers that there is no alcohol readily available for their consumption), he slumped down on the toilet seat, put his head in his hands, and softly began to sob.

*

At this juncture, we need to learn the fate of Robert Savović. Not least because he was about to come crashing back into the Stankovićs' lives.

Even though he attempted to skulk out of the tavern that morning, unseen by the dangerous-looking, Russian-sounding strangers, his efforts proved to be in vain. Before he had made it halfway across the barroom in the direction of the rear exit, he felt a firm hand grab his shoulder.

"Not so fast, comrade."

The owner of the hand swung him around one-hundred and eighty degrees, so they were now facing each other in, most certainly from Savović's perspective, uncomfortably close proximity ("His breath was vile, Dragan," he later confided to his former drinking partner, "like death, like the grave, like he'd been feasting on human flesh").

"You look very familiar." The Russian took a black and white photograph of Savović out of his tunic pocket. When or where it had been taken, he had no idea, even though it was most certainly a recent picture. "We need to talk to you about the girl."

"Girl? What girl? There must be some misunderstanding. If this is about the incident the other evening, then I assure you everything was above board and consensual."

In his panic and fluster, Savović found himself précising a rather unpleasant sexual misdemeanour that had been troubling his mind for the last week. Local people, in his experience, can resort to drastic retributive measures when one of their own, especially no more than a teenage girl, is deflowered in such an unceremonious manner by a man old enough to be her grandfather.

"Silence." The Russian slapped Savović on the face with such force, he momentarily lost consciousness.

The next thing he remembered with any clarity, he had been dragged into the backroom of the tavern, the very same room that had served as his sleeping quarters and unofficial-office-cum-business-premises for the last three or four years. Having evidently been thrown down onto the concrete floor, the first thing he recognised, beyond the ominous instinctual fear hardwired into the minds of those who are no strangers to the most dangerous of situations, was that the three hulking men were now towering over him.

"Where is the mourning girl?" growled the Russian who had originally accosted him. "The last time she was seen in these parts, she was in your company."

"The mourning girl? Milica Stanković, you mean? Well, no one can rightly say. The authorities think the poor mixed-up child, who had a history of mental instability, took her own life."

"There would be no truth to the rumour that you sold her to the brothers Jakšić, then?

On mention of the Jakšić brothers, Savović, if he didn't know before, realised he was dealing with government operatives, or trained assassins in the employ of the brothers' rivals.

"Now you come to mention it, I did have a telephone conversation with two businessmen of that name. They wanted to obtain the young girl's services, and take her over to the West. But I never for one minute thought they were capable of kidnapping her, or doing anything underhanded."

"You lie," were the last two words Savović heard before he was subjected to the most horrific beating he had ever endured (and remember, this man was no stranger to being cornered in dark alleyways by gangs of vengeful drunks). With their heavy army boots, they proceeded to kick and stamp all over the far from robustly-built man cowering in their wake. And no matter how cannily he tried to defend himself, covering first his ribs, then his face, then his genitalia, he was never quick enough to prevent at least one full-bloodied blow from connecting with its intended target.

Within seconds, he was no more than a bloody, crumpled pulp of human matter smeared across that same concrete floor. But that wasn't nearly the end of his ordeal. Grabbing him by a handful of matted hair, the original assailant pulled him up to his feet and stared hard into his battered and bruised face, the nose of which had taken a decidedly circuitous journey (especially in the established anatomical order of things) towards his right ear.

"Where are they now? How can we contact them? We need phone numbers, addresses, everything you have."

But these, of course, were questions Savović couldn't answer. As soon as Milica had been removed from the villa, that was the last contact he ever anticipated having with her.

"I – I don't know…honest…I just took the money…"

"Unfortunately, we do not believe you. But perhaps, there is something that will make you talk." He unsheathed a huge hunting knife. "Let's try and make you *see* things from our point of view."

Without so much as pausing, or stopping to ask Savović another barrage of questions, he dug the knife into the poor man's face, gouging the left eye clean from its socket.

Quite why they searched out Savović in the first place, let alone beat him so savagely, has, or is unlikely ever, to be satisfactorily explained. Milica had already been captured in southern Italy, rendering the operation a complete success. Moreover, any information Savović could've provided them with was, in all likelihood, already in their possession.

Nevertheless, they left him half-dead in a pool of ruby-red blood, minus his left eye.

*

In the moments after they were bundled into the back of the van, Milica and the Jakšić brothers were incapacitated with a potent dose of chloroform. Where they were ultimately transported to, or how long they were on the road, therefore, was a mystery to them all.

When they eventually awoke, they found themselves in what looked like an empty holding cell at a provincial police station. Only there were no identifying clues on the walls, no signs in a language that would give them some indication as to where they actually were, if they were still in Italy, or had been transported over the border.

"My watch has been removed," said Radovan, checking his bare wrist.

"Mine too," said his brother. "Clearly, they want to disorientate us as much as possible."

"This is most irregular. If the authorities had wanted to arrest us, finally, why would we all be interned in a cell together? Why has Milica remained at our side? She has nothing to do with our criminal activities of the past."

"Agreed," Vlado replied. "Why would our government suddenly show an interest in us? We've been off the radar, so to speak, for many years now. And we have some of the most influential politicians in our pockets."

"All of which suggests that we weren't the principal targets."

They turned and looked at Milica who was, only then, shaking off the effects of the anaesthetic.

"What happened?" She yawned, stretched, and rubbed a hand across her face. "Where are we?"

As best as they could – for they too were still a little groggy and uncertain about an exact chain of events – the brothers explained that they had been, most likely, arrested. By whom, however, they had no concrete idea.

"Not to worry you unduly," said Radovan, "but whoever has locked us up here might, in fact, be interested in you, not us. And if that is the case, then we can only conclude that your performances have come to the attention of some very powerful people."

"Me? But I don't understand."

"Nor do we," said Vlado. "But operations of this type can only be undertaken with the full knowledge of senior figures in the government. For that reason, we feel we must confess something important to you about how exactly we came into your life. We made a deal with your former business manager, Robert Savović. Put simply, he sold you out to us, even though we had no idea that your professional relationship had in fact already come to an end."

"I see," said Milica, with eyes downcast. "I had my suspicions. Robert is a far from scrupulous individual. When I told him that I no longer felt comfortable performing for him, I sensed that he wouldn't simply walk away from the arrangement empty-handed."

"No. He is most certainly a shrewd operator. But by that point, we were incredibly eager to start working with you. We had heard such wonderful stories about the effect you were having on people from all walks of life, from the rich to the poor, and everybody in between. Money was no object, even if, as I said before, that Savović character's demands were hugely excessive."

"But what are we going to do now?"

"There is nothing we can do," Vlado said soberly. "In all likelihood, you will be returned to our country to serve whatever purpose you have been earmarked for…while we will be disposed of in the most expedient manner possible."

Milica shot to her feet. "No! Surely not."

"Calm down." Radovan drew her close and gave her a reassuring hug. "You shouldn't work yourself up into such a state, nor are you to be upset about our demise. You still have many wonderful things to accomplish in this life. As for us, we do not fear death. We know we are going to a better place."

"Besides, Milica – ," Vlado knelt in front of her and took hold of her hands, " – the life we have led, we knew we would always meet a violent end. It was as inevitable as the sun setting each evening."

"No!" She squeezed her eyes shut to battle back the tears. "It can't possibly happen like that. God will not allow it."

In the short time she had known them, she had come to see the good, pure, and worthy side of their characters. It pained her to think of them being erased out of existence in the same way someone would blow out a candle, banishing a room to darkness.

"Listen, Milica," said Radovan. "Think of life as a ledger. In one column, you have all the good deeds you have done. In another column, you have all the bad deeds. If our book were to be opened today, I'm ashamed to say that the bad column would far outweigh the good. But don't be sad, for we have seen the light, and feel truly privileged to have been able to have done some good deeds these last few years. Never more so than having had the pleasure of making your acquaintance, and being close to someone who has clearly been touched by the hand of God."

But his words only increased Milica's upset. Even though she had spent so much of her recent life knelt beside coffins containing corpses, young and old, she couldn't help but feel as if this was (Father Miroslav's painful passing withstanding) the first time death had ever touched her directly, and she was chilled by the prospect.

"Let us tell you a story," said Vlado, still holding her hands. "It looks as if we have a little time at our disposal, and it might help you to understand that death is as necessary a part of our existence as life itself, that, in some extreme circumstances, it is the only solution.

"When we were young men, just starting up our criminal organisation, we promised a beloved aunt that we would give her only child, Borislav, a job. Family has always been important to us. We came from an impoverished background, and had to do everything we possibly could to provide for our ailing mother and baby sisters. But we had our reservations where Borislav was concerned. He was a sly, underhanded character, a gambling man, as slippery as an eel and venomous as a snake.

"Foolishly, we let sentiment dictate. We gave Borislav a job. At first, he was charged with simply picking up payments from commercial businesses in the area that we had intimidated into paying protection money. But this, with hindsight, was a huge error on our behalf. To entrust a man like Borislav with bulging envelopes full of money, day in, day out, was to dangle temptation right in front of his nose.

"Inevitably – although we had hoped our family connection and already fearsome reputation as men not to be crossed would be enough of a deterrent – Borislav began to skim a little money off the top of the payments he was entrusted to transfer from one part of the town to another. At first, small amounts that wouldn't be easily noticed. But, of course, he soon became greedier and greedier.

"To put that into perspective, gambling is a truly evil addiction. In many ways, it is more devastating than drinking, or the use of narcotics. With a drug, you understand that a person is experiencing a sense of good feeling and euphoria – a chemical reaction in their body. Whereas, with the gambler, his rush or high, is in many ways, triggered by an intense craving for self-destruction. No logical mind could ever conceive of beating the odds in life, time and again. But it is that very headlong rush into disaster which drives the most ardent of gamblers on.

"Anyway, I digress. In a matter of weeks, we realised what was afoot – that Borislav was stealing money from us. In the normal course of events, we would have dealt with him in the most severe manner possible. Only we loved and respected his mother too much to, for instance, break one of his legs or arms, or leave him in a permanent state of disability. Instead, we took him down to the banks of the river, put a gun to his head, and told him that if we ever saw him again, we would kill him.

"Terrified, he begged for mercy, he assured us that nothing like this would ever happen again. He told us that he needed the job, that without it, his children (Borislav had fathered half a dozen or more children from four different women, offspring our aunt, his mother, absolutely adored) would starve.

"Regardless, we stood firm. There are no second chances in an operation like ours, where you meet danger at every corner. You simply can't have unreliable people close to you.

"But again, with hindsight, cutting him off like that was the worst thing we could've done for our family. In the days after we parted ways with Borislav, he went on a huge petty thieving spree in town. He looted stores, burglarised houses, snatched purses from old ladies in the street. All to fund his gambling addiction. He was arrested, somehow escaped the jailhouse, and continued to loot, break and enter, rob and steal. Only not just from strangers now. He crept into his own mother's home in the middle of the night and took, not only her life savings, but one of the gold teeth from her mouth (and how he went about this without waking her was as feat in itself, a display of light-handedness that beggared belief). He kidnapped one of his children from the apartment of his former partner and sold the girl, only eleven years old at time, to a local brothel.

"It got to the stage where our aunt came to see us at the kafana where we conducted the day-to-day running of our various business interests. As soon as we saw her, we feared the worst. We had heard all about Borislav's activities and were certain that she would ask us to take him under our wing again, to try and calm him down and make him see sense. But that didn't prove to be the case. So outraged had she been by his actions, auctioning off one of his own children, selling her into what amounted to sexual slavery, she looked us both square in the eye and said, 'You must stop him from hurting anyone ever again. No matter what it takes'.

"Now, we both knew exactly what she meant, and how much it must've cost her to, in effect, put a death sentence on the life of her only child. But we also knew, Milica, that it was the best possible course of action. Borislav was a lost soul. He had no control over his addiction. Moreover, he showed no remorse for his actions. All he could think about was getting money for his next bet."

"So you killed him?"

Vlado shook his head. "We didn't have to, even though we sought him out with that express intention. Later that day, we had it on very good authority that he was staying at a cheap hotel in one of the most notorious parts of town. Naturally, we made our way straight over there. A slim wad of banknotes was all it took for the porter to point us in the direction of Borislav's room without, of course, notifying the occupant himself. Wanting to get the unpleasant business out of the way as quickly as possible, we simply kicked the door down and rushed into the room. Only –"

"Only what?"

"Only Borislav was already dead. In a last, desperate attempt to get his hands on some big money, he had offered

244

one of his kidneys to a rival gang who traded in illegal organ transplants. We found him sprawled out on the bed, lying atop blood-soaked sheets, with haphazard stitching up one side of his body. The procedure had been as botched and clumsy as it was fatal.

"An ignominious, and no doubt excruciatingly painful, end to his pitiful life. But it taught us a valuable lesson. It taught us – ." Before he could reveal the finer details of that lesson learnt, the main door swung open.

Two men entered the room, both of whom were dressed in high-ranking military uniforms.

"Russians," Vlado whispered.

"Ah, gentlemen, young lady," said the taller, leaner, and perhaps more senior of the officers, "you are finally awake. Apologies for any discomfort you may have suffered over the last twenty-four to thirty-six hours. In the circumstances, it was unavoidable."

He stepped forward into the light. A man of around fifty, with dark, narrow eyes, he stood very erect, studying them intently for a minute, maybe longer, before he spoke again.

"As you've no doubt surmised, we need the services of your little religious zealot there, the girl who has made such a reputation for herself by crying her eyes out at strangers' funerals. Just when you thought Christianity couldn't get any more backward." He chuckled, as if to himself. "But each to their own. Gentlemen, we take it you voice no objections?"

Knowing the question was facetious to the extreme, the two brothers showed not a flicker of emotion, let alone were forthcoming with a word or gesture that could serve as a response.

"Good. I'm glad you are in full agreement. The girl comes with us."

Two soldiers entered the room, marched over to the cell, unlocked the door, and gestured for Milica to stand up. Her first reaction was to resist, to cling onto the arms of the Jakšić brothers, but a stern look from each, in turn, told her any such resistance was as foolhardy as it was futile.

"Go, you must," said Radovan. "If you ever need us, we will always be watching over you. Now, don't look back and don't shed a tear. Like I said before, you still have great tasks to accomplish."

"No!" She swung around and shouted in the direction of the officers. "I will not go anywhere unless you guarantee the safety of my two friends. If any harm were to come to them whatsoever, I will refuse to perform ever again!"

"Understood, young lady." The officer smirked and plucked a piece of phantom dust from the sleeve of his tunic. "You have my word. We are not mercenary barbarians, but honourable military men with orders to follow. If you would be so good as to come with me, we can transport you to your destination. In due course, your friends will be released."

While still reluctant, Milica nevertheless walked out of the cell and followed the officers into the corridor.

"May the Lord be with you," the brothers shouted after her.

No sooner was she well out of earshot, in the back of a Mercedes speeding off into the blackness of the night, then one loud bang, a gunshot, quickly followed by another, sounded from the depths of the holding cell in which she herself had been so recently incarcerated.

*

Before we re-join Milica on the final leg of her journey, we must first return to the backroom of the tavern. Very much left for dead, sprawled out in a pool of blood – this wasn't, however unlikely as it may seem, the last act of Robert Savović's life. Shortly after the band of Russian mercenaries had brazenly walked out of the tavern's main door, one of the serving-girls, Karika, a somewhat flighty young woman of five and twenty, and someone far from immune to Robert Savović's charms, rushed to his aid.

"My God! Robert, what have they done to you?"

With skill, tenderness, and consideration, she managed to both stem the worst of the bleeding, and manoeuvred the severely injured man into an upright position, thus unblocking his airwaves and allowing him to breathe with a modicum of comfort.

"You poor thing," she said, running a wet cloth over his face. "There'll be no saving that eye of yours…and there's blood flowing from your mouth. You must be all broken up inside, too. The only place for you is the hospital. You'll need proper medicines, maybe an operation or two to put you right."

Outright refusing the medical attention he so badly needed ("I don't want to bring no attention to myself. If the law get a

247

sniff of this, they'll ask too many awkward questions and I'll be back in clink, never to see the light of day ever again"), Savović persuaded Karika to dress his wounds (even the horrendous eye injury, the now empty socket she referred to a moment ago) and patch him up as best she could. With a bottle of rakija in hand, the stoic chancer managed to dull the intense pain with strong alcohol and, quite incredibly, get to his feet.

"You're a diamond, you are, Karika. I know people don't see much worth in you, girl, that they put you down and gossip about you behind your back, but I won't ever forget what you did for me today. Near as damn saved my life. But there's something I've got to do, somewhere I've got to be."

"What? No, Robert. You're in no fit state to be out of doors. Wherever are you to go? You can hardly walk."

"Sometimes a man has to cleanse his conscience. In so many ways, what happened today, I had coming to me. It were payback for all the dodgy deals and underhanded shenanigans I've been involved in. And it's certainly opened my eyes – or eye, I should probably say. Ha! – to a great wrong I perpetrated against a good, honest man who offered me his hand in friendship. The purest gesture any of us can make to another person. Fate, Karika, it catches up with us all in the end."

"You're talking in riddles. You're talking nonsense. Tell me. Where are you going? I'll be worried sick if you don't at least let me know where you're headed, and what time you'll be back."

"I'm going to see my old friend Dragan Stanković. I'm going to take him by the hand and tell him the truth. He, more than anyone else in this world, deserves that."

By the time Savović had limped across town to the Stankovićs' apartment building, it was close to midnight. Regardless, both Dragan (in that contrary state where he was so fatigued by another shift at the steelworks that he couldn't actually sleep or rest up in any significant way) and Nevena (knelt before the ikon, praying fervently for Milica's safe return) were awake and rushed to answer the two loud knocks upon their front door.

"My word!" cried Dragan. "Is that you, Robert? What on earth has happened to you? Come in. Take my arm. Let's get you in a chair."

"Thank you, old pal. Sorry to impose. But there's something I need to say."

Once Dragan had helped him across the room and eased him down into an armchair, Savović did indeed have the courage of his convictions.

"Dragan, Nevena, again, forgive me for intruding on you at this ungodly hour. But as you can see, I've finally had some wisdom beaten into this stupid old head of mine today." He tapped two fingers against his skull and smiled, revealing a mouth missing at least four or five teeth. "But don't you feel sorry for me. We all get our just deserts in the end. And the reason I appear before you now in such a pitiful state is because I were responsible for your Milica going missing."

"What?" Dragan and Nevena said at one and the same time.

"It was me. I arranged for her to be taken. Some big-time gangster-types had contacted me some time ago, wanting to know if they could take over management of her career. But I knew that the girl were a goldmine and I told 'em she wouldn't ever perform for no one else but us.

"Only when she were adamant that she didn't want to continue no more, I decided to cash her in. I contacted the Jakšić brothers – that's what they're called – and made a deal. I arranged the whole trip to the seaside just so they could whisk her off over the border.

"I know you must hate me for what I done. And in truth, I'm so hollowed out and empty inside, I don't feel any remorse or guilt for the great wrong I committed against you. But I know how worried you've been and felt that I simply had to put you out of your misery. Milica didn't walk into the ocean with her pockets full of rocks. She were taken over to the West to perform for the capitalist folks."

Very calmly, Dragan listened to everything his friend had to say. But when he had finished (and this took quite some time, so often did Savović break off to catch his breath and compose himself anew), he didn't feel any anger or an urge to shout and scream at the man, or even grab and strike him. Neither shocked nor relieved to know for certain that Milica was alive, he felt subject to a cold, numb sensation, an emotional no man's land where the capability to express himself, to think and feel, negatively or positively, were beyond him. Perhaps this was a natural reaction. Betrayal of that kind, the realisation that someone you considered a true friend could harm you and your loved ones in the most devastating way imaginable is hard for anyone to take, a set of emotions impossible to assimilate so quickly. But perhaps the overriding feeling Dragan Stanković was subject to at that moment in time, immediately following Savović's confession, was one of resignation. Knowledge that the only thing people have been put on this earth to do is exploit each other for their own gain. Perhaps he knew this long before he met Savović, perhaps it was instilled in him during many a long backbreaking shift at the steelworks. But for the one person he had thought to be above such scheming to be of baser and more venal stock than anyone else, knocked what little resilience was left out of Dragan for good.

It was Nevena who became upset, angry, who shouted and screamed, who berated Savović for what he had done.

"How could you, Robert? After all the money Millie made for you. And how could you let us suffer like we have done ever since she disappeared? How could you look us in the eye? How could you have said all those things about helping us find her, when you knew all along where she was? You're an evil, despicable man. I want you out of this apartment right now."

*

Back in the capital city, Dušan Srna's political aspirations hung in the balance. While his rise through the ranks had been conducted with an almost phantom-like stealth, he now needed to put a few more building blocks into place before he could fulfil what he saw as his historical destiny. In that respect, his approach could not have been better planned or executed. Nobody in high office saw him as a particular threat. Nobody took much notice of the handsome, immaculately dressed young man at all, despite his seeming ubiquity. For not a single high-level meeting, Party congress, or full-blown military parade passed without him being in attendance. Scrupulously polite, almost suspiciously up-to-date with current political affairs (he could've conducted in-depth discussions with ministers from departments as diverse as cultural enlightenment to public sanitation), he seemed to glide in and out of focus. Had anyone been paying particular attention to his activities, they would've found the way he oscillated between the company of General Kostić and Filip Todorović, chief of the secret service – the two main leadership rivals should the present incumbent pass away – highly unusual to say the least. The enmity between the two giants of the Party was well-known, bitter, and long-standing.

Having plotted and schemed for so long, Srna hated the idea of not pulling off his own spectacular coup d'état, by playing the ageing military leader off against his younger secret service counterpart. If you let two cockerels loose in a pen, they will, as everybody knows, proceed to peck each other to death. The person to pick up the pieces would profit the most. And Dušan Srna, about whom some still had the temerity to call a junior minister, had put himself, through the light personable channels of charm, compliments, and lavish wining and dining, to the darker (and, admittedly, far more effective) arts of bribery, blackmail, and threats, in the optimum position.

But he still had that one monumental problem to contend with – both the leader and current regime had never been so unpopular.

To succeed, he needed to create a spectacle. He needed the country to fall in love with their leader once again. But considering that the now-invalided, half-vegetable of a man had not appeared in public (not genuinely, anyway) for years, this would be a difficult situation to manage. Undoubtedly, the old man had been an incredible politician in his considerable pomp, someone rightly renowned and respected. Like a trapeze artist, he had trod a tightrope between Moscow and the West, brokering lucrative deals with each party that generated millions in revenue for the nation. Who cared if most of it went into his own personal coffers? He gave his people self-respect, an identity they could be proud of, simply because they were associated with such a wily, sharp, and intelligent political manoeuverer.

Only memories, in any walk of life, are indeed short. Then again, if you've earned x amount of money at a factory for ten years without a single raise, and the cost of living has rocketed up three hundred and seventy-eight percent over the last eighteen months, you have legitimate cause for complaint. Factor in the disgruntlement in the countryside – the peasant farmers who had seen one bountiful harvest after another requisitioned to feed the cities, to the extent that they couldn't feed themselves through the winter – and you had a veritable powder keg on your hands.

Unlike some of his more complacent contemporaries – and Kostić and Todorović were most certainly counted amongst that number – Srna was well aware of the problems the country now faced. In actual fact, he was one of the few high-ranking politicians who had ventured out into the towns and villages. With all the sly, ingratiating cunning their ailing leader displayed when he ascended to power himself, Srna had made unlikely allies, and formed solid connections with disgruntled local government officials (of which there were many). If any strike action or demonstration were planned, he was always the first to know. At meetings in rundown town halls, in back alley kafanas and gloomy taverns, he made pledges and promises to those who, although they weren't aware of the fact, could ultimately prove to be kingmakers, if and when the leader passed away and the battle for accession became as primitive and prolonged as Srna assumed. Like Stalin all those years before, he had, through painstaking political brinksmanship, assembled a powerful following, an inchoate yet primed government apparatus in the making. All he had to do was ensure that the political goodwill swung back in the leader's favour.

In that regard, he relied on hour-by-hour updates from the old man's most trusted personal physician – 'stable but critical' being the almost constant refrain for nearly two years now. And, as the social and political situation worsened, as the bickering and posturing became pettier, more puerile and pointless, an idea started to take shape in Srna's head. Call it chance or coincidence, but he happened to overhear a perfectly innocent conversation in the canteen one lunch-time.

"The provinces are becoming more backward by the day. Do you know what I heard last week? The common folk are employing professional mourners to bawl and make a general display of themselves at funerals now."

"Whatever for?"

"A throwback to their religious beliefs, no doubt. It's infuriating. To think they still worship a crowd-dwelling fairy, especially when one considers the giant steps socialism has made in recent decades."

Possessed of what might well be called a photographic memory in modern parlance (or at least 'admirable recall' back then), Srna remembered a report he had from the provinces many years ago. The ramifications of which have already been outlined in these pages – his somewhat obscure meeting with Professor Dejan Damjanović, and the tentative arrangements for the celebrated physician to take the young lady in question into his care again.

Only now, infuriatingly from Srna's point of view, not only had the girl disappeared, but the leader somehow, bafflingly and inexplicably, seemed singularly incapable of dying. Like a lot of great men in life, he clung onto what remained of his existence with a stubborn resilience that not one of the specialists who examined him could readily explain.

"The heart beat is faint, the breathing shallow, he has lost control of his bodily function six times in the last twenty-four hours, he is almost completely non-responsive. He is, without any shadow of a doubt, the closest patient I have ever seen to a living corpse in my thirty-three year medical career."

Yet what Dušan Srna perhaps didn't appreciate, so stretched thin had his patience, and resources, been in recent months (for no man, no matter how charming or influential, can plot a political coup of any magnitude in perpetuity) – is that things have a contrary habit of changing very quickly.

Two knocks sounded against his office door, heralding one such swift and emphatic change.

"Enter."

A moment later, his personal secretary, Adam Popović, walked into the room.

"Sir, we have just heard from our friends in Moscow. They have the girl."

∗

Within thirty-six hours of leaving the deserted prison cell in a still-classified Western European location, the final resting place (even though she would never be made fully aware of the fact) of the Jakšić brothers, Milica Stanković found herself sitting in Dušan Srna's office.

"Ms. Stanković," he began, "I must first apologise for the no doubt distressing nature of your transit back to your home country. Unfortunately, matters of national importance are at stake."

"National importance? But what could that possibly have to do with me?"

"More than you could imagine. Let me be frank and completely upfront with you. Despite the reports you may have read in the newspapers, our leader is gravely ill. Due to the uncertain political situation in the country, his death may trigger not only a long and potentially bloody fight for power, but a full-blown civil war.

"To avoid the worst-case scenario, we need, for want of a better expression, to make a martyr of him. We need the people who once held him in such high regard to look favourably on him once again. We need to bring the country together rather than drive it further apart. If not, the consequences could be devastating, not just for the current generation, but for many generations to come.

"Look, Milica, I won't lie to you. Personally, I'm a very ambitious man. But I'm not like all those other politicians, the stuffy bureaucrats you've no doubt seen on the television. I came from a very religious upbringing myself. I respect the traditions of the church and feel that both institutions – the church and the Party – can peacefully coexist."

"How do you mean?"

"That the Party's approach was far too radical. We didn't take into account centuries of tradition. It was cruel and barbaric to try and separate a people from their God like that. And it has done untold damage to our communities. This region has a unique geographical position in Europe and is composed of a diverse mix of ethnicities, blood lines, and religious communities – some of whom have a natural antipathy towards each other. For those reasons and more, we need to unify our people.

"That's where you come in. We want you to perform at the leader's funeral, when he finally passes away. We want you to express the kind of profound sadness and grief you have expressed at other funerals in the past. I fear it is the only way of healing our broken country, and bringing not only stability, but hope, back to the lives of ordinary men and women."

Of all Milica's gifts, perhaps the most valuable was her ability to look into someone's eyes and quickly gauge their sincerity. Most certainly – and it took only a fraction of a second for her to make this assessment – she knew that Dušan Srna, this singularly impressive, well-spoken man with his fine-smelling cologne, soft, blemish-free skin, and immaculately parted hair – was not only a phony and a fraud, but a highly dangerous man. In the aforementioned flash, she knew that he had never stepped foot inside a church in his entire life, let alone had any spiritual connection with the Lord. She could clearly envisage the kind of society he wanted to create; she could see long queues of dirty-faced, malnourished, and destitute people standing outside stores that had little to no goods to sell; she could see young men massacred on a bloody battlefield of the future; she could see pain and uncertainty, brothers fighting against brothers, the smoking ruins of cities and towns no longer familiar to anyone. She saw, felt, experienced, in an almost visceral manner, the complete and utter dejection and unhappiness of her countrymen and women – a hopelessness so all-encompassing that their belief in God was all but eradicated, sending them back into the dark ages that no amount of social progress or technological advancements could ever address.

Regardless, like her mother when she wanted to visit Sanja Babić, Milica did something which she had never done before – she lied.

"Of course, Mr. Srna. I would be only too happy to help our country. I will do whatever is necessary."

She didn't know why she told him such a blatant untruth (at that moment, she felt such a powerful aversion towards the man sitting opposite her, it shamed her to the very fabric of her being), the words simply flowed from her mouth like a river flows into the sea – naturally and uninhibitedly.

"Excellent," said Srna, beaming with all the rank complacency he had recognised in Kostić and Todorović, but, just like them, singularly failed to recognise in himself. "You'll be doing your country a fine service. In the interim period, you'll be allocated living quarters in the main parliament building. If you need anything, all you have to do is ask. I, personally, am at your service twenty-four hours a day.

"To help you prepare mentally, I thought it might be a good idea for you to talk to a learned physician who has already taken an active interest in your case. Professor Dejan Damjanović."

Milica gave a start. That name stirred memories from her childhood. Not that Srna seemed to notice.

"For now, I'll have my personal secretary take you to your quarters, so you can freshen up and rest for a while."

*

The following morning, after a fitful sleep troubled by dreams about the Jakšić brothers' welfare, Milica was escorted across the city to the lavishly decorated office of Professor Dejan Damjanović.

"Ah, Ms. Stanković, please take a seat." He gestured to the visitor's chair situated on the other side of his grand mahogany writing desk. "You may not remember me, but I actually visited your family home many years ago. Then as now, I was most fascinated by your case. But had you told me that we would meet again in such changed circumstances, I'm not sure I would've believed you.

"As for our current working relationship, our friends in government felt it prudent for you to undergo an informal psychological assessment. If my sources are correct, you've been through quite an ordeal over last year or so. Therefore, we wanted to make sure that you have come through those challenges unscathed."

Over the next fortnight, Milica met with Damjanović each morning at eleven o'clock sharp. During these 'interrogations', as she began to refer to them, the Professor tortured her with (among other tedious psychoanalytic banalities) a repetitive form of word association.

"Parents."

"Kindness."

"School."

"Learning."

"Religion."

"Truth."

And although Milica always tried to answer honestly, and not be in any way obstructive, or even hostile to the Professor's treatment (as she had every right to be in the circumstances), all that she really took away from the sessions, all she really felt was a profound sense of sympathy for whom she had come to see as the most deluded of individuals, someone who had spent his whole professional life constructing an elaborate self-serving facade, with its own language and terminology and symbols and definitions, like a form of psychological Esperanto, that was as nonsensical as it was contrived and ineffective. For the medical community, as far as Milica's experience of it went, had lost sight of the very people they were supposed to help. They had got so deep into theorising and dreaming up new concepts to make a professional name for themselves, they barely took the patients' welfare into consideration, or gave much practical thought to finding a cure for whatever ailed them.

"Diseases of the mind," he sought to explain during one of their sessions, "can only ever be managed. By that I mean, we can only ever help the patient function on a day-to-day level. Of course, there are often many factors to consider – the development of the condition itself, the socialisation process, the family background, any traumatic incident that may have acted as a trigger point, to name but a few causal links in any given chain."

"Yes, I've often thought the ability to think and feel to such a profound degree is both a gift and a curse. But coming from a working-class background, I can't help but think that most of our problems, the diseases of the mind, as you called them, are linked to inequality and injustice, to poverty, to not seeing any light at the end of the tunnel, in terms of improving your own life and that of your family."

And Milica's mind wandered back to the early days of her professional mourning career, when she had looked on from the backseat of that decrepit old van as her father and Robert Savović counted out the big wads of money they had just received. The change in her father's demeanour, outlook, and general overall mood was such, it even had a positive effect on him physiologically. No longer did he walk around, all hunched over and with his head lowered. Now, he puffed his chest out, and had what could almost be described as a spring in his step, if not a touch of swagger.

"How delightful." Damjanović clapped his hands together. "You sound more like a Marxist than a Christian. My treatment is clearly having a positive effect."

Milica smiled good-naturedly in return. Ever since she was a little girl, she had been aware of the inequality she mentioned a moment ago, but also – and again, she thought of her father – the dignity of labour, the spiritual connection between toiling for your bread, suffering, and understanding the deeper, more important things in life.

"But in all seriousness, Ms. Stanković, we must be realistic above all things. Take your own situation. When I deliver my final report to my superiors – and I have no qualms about being completely honest and upfront with you, completely transparent – the underlying conclusion will be that you are of sound mind, that you are an intelligent and perceptive young lady with, most importantly, an exceptionally strong moral conscience. If, for instance, you were asked to perform a great service for your country, I would have no doubt that you would act according to your aforementioned conscience and take the right course of action."

*

Every afternoon, Srna – who had been greatly heartened by the positive comments contained in Damjanović's interim reports – would visit Milica in her room. Ever charming and personable, he arranged for her to go on guided tours of the city's churches, museums, and art galleries, excursions he felt would both impress her and stave off any boredom when, to all intents and purposes, she was being held like a prisoner under house arrest. At the end of each of these visits, he would ask Milica if there was anything she required. As demure and undemanding as he was charming and personable, she simply shook her head, thanked him, and said that she was perfectly fine.

Towards the end of her second week in the capital, however, she completely wrong-footed Srna as he prepared to take leave of her living quarters. In response to his standard enquiry as to any potential requests or requirements on her behalf, she did indeed ask something of him.

"If possible, I would like to visit my parents. The town is only around one hundred kilometres away, thus a return trip wouldn't take more than a few hours, half a day at the most. I know they have missed me terribly, and it would mean a lot for me to put their minds at rest, to let them know that I am alive and well."

While answering with the pleasant evasion typical of the modern-day politician – not agreeing to the request but certainly not declining it either – Srna, with the thoroughness he applied to every facet of his life, personal or professional, made some discreet enquiries via some local officials in the town. To his dismay, he learned that the girl's mother, Nevena Stanković, had just been diagnosed with a virulent form of cancer, and given just weeks to live.

"The prognosis is particularly bleak, sir," said Popović. "By all accounts, the poor woman had been concealing a tumour the size of a grapefruit, just so as not to worry her husband."

This put Srna in a most unenviable position. If he told the girl the truth, it could have a terrible effect on her mental well-being. To the extent that she may be of little or no use to him should the leader pass away (and this, despite the many false alarms over what constituted the last two years, looked to be a very real and imminent prospect). But to have withheld the information felt profoundly wrong, even to a man whose moral compass had never been properly aligned in the first place.

To help come to a decision, he summoned Damjanović to his office.

"Most interesting," said the Professor. "During our last few sessions, the girl has made many pointed references towards her fears for her family's health and overall welfare. She told me she had been troubled by a series of dreams and waking visions of her mother being in terrible pain."

"Really?"

"Yes, a most curious of coincidences. Not for a single minute do I give credence to any second sight, clairvoyance, or spiritual mumbo jumbo. Clearly, the girl's enforced separation from her parents – and we must remember that she was not only taken against her will but had never spent a single day away from her family before – her longing to see them again, trigged these irrational fears for their well-being."

"I see. That makes some kind of sense, I suppose. But what, in your professional opinion, should we do regarding her request to visit them? Do you think it would be too traumatic, and have a potentially damaging effect on the girl's mental health?"

Damjanović shook his head. "Not at all. In fact, I would positively encourage you to inform her of her mother's illness. If you feel uncomfortable relaying such news, I would be happy to so myself. In the interim, I suggest you make arrangements for the sick woman to be transferred to the finest hospital in the region to ensure she gets the best possible care during the last few weeks of her life. Not only would it be a kind and worthy gesture, but it would, no doubt, be so incredibly well received and appreciated by the girl herself, she would feel as if she were indebted to you for the rest of her life, and be duty-bound to do anything you wanted her to do."

*

Later that day, Popović escorted Milica to Damjanović's office.

"I'm afraid I have some bad news," the Professor told her. "Your mother has been taken seriously ill. It doesn't look good,

264

I'm afraid. But rest assured, the government has moved her to the finest hospital in the region, where she will get the best possible care."

Milica felt a horrible sinking sense of the inevitable, like a car sliding across an icy road, destined to crash. As Damjanović had relayed to Srna, she had been subject to distressing thoughts about her family's welfare, gloomy premonitions of pain and suffering.

"When can I see her?"

"Right away. A car is waiting for you outside."

*

"Millie!" Dragan shot up to his feet, only to slump straight back down in his chair again. "Is it really you?"

The weary, sleep-deprived man, hunched over and prematurely aged, had to look and look again, rub his eyes, and repeat the process.

"Yes, Father, I came as quickly as I could. I would've been here sooner, but it was beyond my control."

Unlike her husband, Nevena had seen her daughter enter the room, not like a spectral vision but as the pretty young woman she had become. Already, the illness had taken a cruel and exacting toll on her. Although awake and lucid (despite the many painkilling drugs awash in her bloodstream), Nevena looked pale, gaunt, and terribly thin.

"I knew you would come, my darling." She took hold of Milica's hand. "I'm so glad you're all right. Me and your father have been awfully worried."

"I'm fine, really, I am. You don't ever have to worry about me."

But her belated reassurances had never been heeded, not in the distant or recent past, not ever. A born worrier, Nevena had always let the unimportant, trivial, insignificant aspects of life trouble her to distraction. That was perhaps why she fell ill in the first place.

"You're very sick, Mother." Milca put her free hand to Nevena's face. "But do not fear. Your faith has always been strong. It's been such an inspiration to me. Your warmth, kindness, and goodness have been like a beacon in the night, guiding me along my true path in life. For that, I cannot even begin to thank you."

As mother and daughter embraced, Dragan Stanković couldn't help but ponder everything that Milica had just said. Ever since she was a little girl, he had noticed a distance, a reserve or restraint, an indefinable something which had held the girl back from expressing her true feelings towards her mother. Not that he for one moment suspected that Milica didn't love Nevena, or that there wasn't a deep bond between them. There was just something in her manner, especially as she grew older, which often troubled Dragan, for he knew how much a spontaneous hug or kiss would've meant to his wife. On occasion he thought about broaching the subject, never more so than during the long walks they used to enjoy when Milica was younger. But far from the most articulate of men, or someone particularly adept at talking about his feelings, he had never been able to find the right words or moment, or perhaps, the right combination of those two essential elements, to go about it.

Now he felt as if the truth had been revealed. Whether it was linked to her unique gift or merely instinctual, Milica knew that her mother would be taken from them far too soon, that she was destined to live a tragically short life. And being in possession of that knowledge, she had erected an emotional barrier between them, to prevent both herself and her mother from getting too close to each other. Only now, they were nearing the end of the path, those powerful feelings had come pouring out of her, letting her mother know exactly how special the bond between them had been, and would be forever more, in both life and death.

Unable to restrain himself a moment longer, Dragan shuffled over to the bed, put his arms around them both, and hugged them tightly.

*

"They have grand plans for me," Milica told her mother, shortly after Dragan had gone off in search of some tea. "I feel incredibly conflicted. Like I will have to make a decision which may not seem right in the short-term, but will be of greater benefit in the future."

"You must listen to your conscience, my darling. Don't be swayed by any of their fancy talk. Do only what you feel is right and proper."

Even though these words mirrored, almost verbatim, those of Professor Damjanović, Milica interpreted them completely differently.

"Ever since you were born, I knew you were special. We both did, me and your father. But our lives aren't defined by one big moment, no matter how important it may seem at the

267

time. It's the little things we do, each and every day, that make us who we are. Even if it's just a kind word or act, multiplied over the years, it can make the world a better place."

*

Timing in life is everything. A cliché, granted. But often such sayings attain that status for no other reason than that they have proven to be true over the course of the millennia.

Three hours after Milica had returned from Velika Plana, and was (presumably) sleeping in her room, Dušan Srna received a phone call from the leader's most trusted physician.

"The old man has finally breathed his last. I officially pronounced him dead approximately two minutes ago."

To describe the fireworks that went off in Srna's head after he had put the phone down – the uplifting symphony music he heard, rising crescendo-like, the one-hundred-gun salute, the champagne corks popping, the wild cheering that wouldn't have been out of place at a major sporting event – would be crass to the extreme, especially when considering that an old man had just passed away. But such was his excitement at the prospect of years of methodical planning finally coming to fruition, he found himself strutting around the office in an arrhythmical pastiche of any number of popular dance steps, from the tango to the waltz, through to jerky Polish-style mazurkas. He jabbered to himself. He mouthed lyrics from the popular folk songs of his youth.

"This is it," he muttered as he slowly came back to his senses. "I cannot falter. I cannot show any indecision or weakness."

Rifling through his desk drawer, he withdrew the death notice he had drawn up nearly three years ago. Despite the relatively gargantuan time lapse, he was still more than satisfied with the feverous tone he had painstakingly cultivated. Phrases like 'Now is the time to take our great nation kicking and screaming into the modern age…What we need more than anything during this incredibly sad time is new ideas, new blood…We must build on the great victories of the past to forge a brighter future for every man, woman, and child.' But the vital ingredient, what, in private moments Srna called the 'coup de grace of my coup d'état', was the leader's last will and political testament, naming – among many other almost inconceivable requests – Dušan Srna as his successor, the man he wanted to replace him as the new head of government.

I have thought long and hard about appointing a successor, went one passage which Srna had, in fact, composed himself, *but on assessing the strengths and weaknesses of the most likely men, I didn't see one truly outstanding candidate. Kostić is far too set in his ways, he has a fiery temper and sexual proclivities that would shame Caligula. Whereas Todorović, like many men who have advanced through the secret service ranks, displays psychopathic tendencies. He is a sadist who would drag our country back to the dark ages of the previous century.*

After much deliberation, however, I was drawn to the one truly shining light of our Party, a young man who embodies everything our great nation represents. Dušan Srna.

The man in question broke off from reading to dust some tears from his eyes. It was perfect. All he had to do now was push one metaphorical button to secure power all for himself.

Crucially, in the immediate aftermath of the leader's death, he delayed informing Kostić and Todorović of the news for the best part of twenty-four hours. During that period, while both men were recovering from brutal hangovers (Srna had arranged for the general and head of the security service to be visited by a number of alluring Party devotees, young women of irresistible feminine wiles, equipped with a fierce arsenal of contraband rakija), Srna had secured support from all branches of the armed forces, the all-important media, and an interim government that had been in almost perpetual recess ever since the leader originally fell ill. Within that same twenty-four-hour timeframe, he was all but confirmed as the de facto leader of the country.

Even when Kostić and Todorović learned the finer details of his plot and sought an audience with whom they saw as an arch-usurper and crook, Srna simply had them arrested, tossed into the nearest prison cell, and then summarily shot through the back of the head the following morning.

It was just the beginning.

In hundreds of dawn raids, anyone (and this included some of the greatest political and scientific minds of their generation) that Srna felt was a conceivable threat to his power was rounded up in cattle trucks and transported to the hard labour camps of the east.

All that was left was for Srna to organise a state funeral on an epic scale.

But in truth, this was probably the most straightforward part of the whole operation. Every other week, or so it seemed, when the leader's health looked to be in a perilous state, Srna had contacted all the relevant government agencies. They had been put on high alert so many times, the practical arrangements were now embedded in their minds. No sooner had Srna, alongside the attending physician – the trusted doctor who had been at the leader's bedside with no significant break for nearly three whole years – addressed the nation, everything down to the last detail had been put into place.

"Comrades, it is with great sadness that I have to inform you of the death of our mighty leader…"

And even though Srna went on to speak for a long time (three hours and twenty-six minutes are recorded in the official records, although both the master tape and only copy of the actual address were mysteriously destroyed during the first painful few months of his tenure as leader), and even though he cut such an impressive and eloquent figure, literally nobody in the country had any idea of who he was, or who he would go on to be. Regardless, his glowing words, his teary-eyed reminiscences, the picture he painted of their 'finest son', an 'incredible statesman and political genius', a man 'who had locked horns and outwitted one capitalist behemoth after another', had the desired effect.

Within moments of his stirring address concluding, most of the population had decked their doors and windows with a national flag bound with a black mourning band. For people who had nothing to live for, for so long, who had scrimped and half-starved, who had worked themselves to the bone for a handful of coins, even the death of a man whom many of them considered a cold-hearted tyrant and despot had the contrary effect of bringing them closer together than they had been for years. Neighbours on not particularly good terms, those whose collective apartments had demarcation points like a no man's land in a theatre of conflict, forgot about all their lingering resentments.

In terms of the media response – the journalistic and broadcasting puppets Srna now had on a string – non-stop tributes, bulletins, and reports dedicated to the former leader's life were aired: archival footage of him as a young man working in a steelworks, stirring addresses to lively groups of lumpenproletariat baying for the blood of the bourgeoisie; inspiring still shots of him helping rebuild the country's great cities following World War Two; many a triumphant parade; a slow panoramic then and now collage of everything he did to well and truly put the nation on the worldwide map; culminating with a never-before-seen video (clearly shot on a home camera) of him giving Josef Stalin (much to the Russian leader's visible chagrin) a comprehensive drubbing at table tennis while vacationing at a luxurious Black Sea resort.

But it would be premature, not to mention misleading, to suggest that this created a universal tidal wave-like surge of national pride, that people simply forgot about the troubles which blighted their present and immediate future, and looked back to the past. There were still voices of dissension that had to be quelled – and Srna was well-aware of the fact. In constant contact with a vast network of militia and underground spies, he kept himself well-informed about any potential unrest, any planned protests which might knock the rose-tinted spectacles from the very noses of the people Srna was determined to get on side.

The last piece of the jigsaw came in the form of a certain young woman, namely Milica Stanković. If everything went to plan, her show of anguish and grief at the passing of the leader

272

would unite the nation, even if only for a short time – but that was all Srna needed to cement his position.

*

A few hours after he had not only seized power, but liquidated, imprisoned, or exiled any potential leadership rivals, he went to see the girl in her room. Whether complacent, conceited, or euphoric, or a contrary cocktail of all three unhelpful mental states, he was perhaps guilty, for the first time in the last twelve hours, of misreading the situation, of not picking up on – 'reticence' would be the wrong word to describe Milica's reaction, because she readily acceded to his request – but her distraction and restlessness. When someone doesn't appear to be paying full attention, they invariably have no interest in what you are saying.

"Milica, I'm so glad you're up and dressed." He smiled with a warmth so forced and unnatural she could've sworn she heard either his skin or teeth crack – or perhaps both. "First things first, how was your mother? Comfortable, I hope. It's such a devastating and indiscriminate disease, but you have my assurances that she will continue to get the very best treatment and care."

"Thank you. You've been very kind."

"Don't mention it. It's the least we could do in the circumstances." He let out a loud, mournful sigh, as manufactured and counterfeit as his smile of a moment ago. "As you've probably heard, our great leader has indeed passed away. This is a time of huge sadness for our country. But unfortunately, we don't have the privilege of being able to sit and reflect and mourn as we would like. No. We have to take action to prevent a national disaster."

He walked over to the window and looked out at the neat, well-tended gardens to the rear of the parliament building. With his back to Milica, he began a short speech which he had rehearsed many times before – not just that morning, but from the moment the plan took proper shape and form in his head.

"As we discussed previously, we need to put on a spectacular show to mark the leader's death. If you could perform like you have never performed before, in that towering mausoleum of white marble, in front of the world's press, we could bring the people together, and nip any potential insurrection in the bud.

"You need only look at the Russian or Chinese models. Leadership battles following the death of a long-standing and powerful figure can have devastating consequences. More than anything, I want to steady the ship, to help the country navigate through these choppy transitional waters. What we are asking you to do, therefore, Milica is of huge international importance."

"I understand."

Srna gave a start, as if he had forgotten that anybody else was in the room. He turned around.

"You do?"

Milica nodded. "Ever since I was a young child, I had an unusual premonition, like a recurring dream. I saw myself in a palace of white marble pillars, knelt before the coffin of an important personage. You have nothing to worry about. I feel as if this was the moment I was born for."

*

Two days later, the leader's funeral took place in the capital city. To truly make it a spectacle that everyone would remember for years to come, Srna went to extreme lengths to create the gaudiest and most ostentatious ceremonial scene imaginable, an event that had more in bearing with an American theme park than a sombre day of national mourning. At dawn, four hundred volunteers, in the main, hunched-over old women whose memories predated the last great war and the country's 'phoenix from the ashes' rise to international prominence, scattered the petals from over one million white roses along the main roads. Every street corner within a three-mile radius of the funeral procession was decked out with huge murals depicting the leader in the prime of his life, dressed in a brilliant-white uniform, with impressive epaulettes and a chest emblazoned with full military honours. Thousands of children were bused in from the provinces and positioned all along the streets leading to the mausoleum where the leader's body would be laid to rest. Dozens of camera crews had set up at twenty or thirty metre intervals, to ensure that not a single frame of footage was wasted, as the event would be televised all over the socialist world. There were brass bands, mounted soldiers, a sequence of full military salutes, a flyover by state-of-the-art fighter jets, the late leader's pride and joy. Renowned figures, statesmen, acclaimed actors and actresses, sports stars, writers, and academics crammed inside the mausoleum to pay their respects.

Everything was in place.

One after another, veteran politicians and national figureheads, those of the same vintage as the leader, stood on a lectern beside the open coffin and delivered speeches and eulogies celebrating the life of such a unique and visionary leader, a man ahead of his time in so many respects.

"Sadly," said one of his closest aides, wiping a tear from the side of his wrinkled cheek, "we shall never see the likes of him again."

As these lengthy and moving speeches finally came to an end, the main door to the mausoleum swung open. Everyone turned as Milica Stanković made her entrance. Dressed in brilliant-white, not the traditional black gown she had been instructed to wear, she cut an incredibly radiant figure, an almost angelic vision surrounded by a nimbus-like glow. It was a moment of wild drama and pathos. One celebrated journalist described her slow walk towards the coffin with florid and poignant references to the palpable outpouring of grief that reverberated through the white marble pillars, how it felt as if each teardrop that fell from the collective eyes of a nation could be heard hitting the ground, like 'figurative pins dropping in a silent room'.

But it wasn't until those gathered took a closer look at the girl that they realised something was seriously amiss. Although most of the mourners were some distance away, it became increasingly apparent that she had done something quite grotesque and appalling to her face. Namely, she had drawn great big black circles around her eyes with eye pencil, and applied so much crimson-red lipstick to her mouth, smearing it haphazardly, that it looked as if she was bleeding profusely, like something zombie-like or vampiric. Regardless, it wasn't a fact that registered in its vaudevillian totality. The vast majority of those gathered were anticipating a performance of some kind, maybe not that of a full-blown professional mourner, but perhaps a hymn or recitation of a eulogy.

But rather than burst into tears and prostrate herself before the coffin, Milica did something truly unexpected. She turned around to face the hundreds of well-dressed mourners crammed inside the mausoleum, and – the full effect of her ghoulish appearance now in evidence – she put a finger to her lips, as if to shush the already-silent people who stood before her. Then, very deliberately, very slowly, she walked out of the mausoleum with – and again, we quote from the same journalist – 'each one of her soft footsteps echoing on the marble floor like a death knoll for the former regime and all it stood for'.

It was a simple gesture which not only baffled the entire nation and the millions of people watching on television around the world, but completely altered the dynamic of the day. Granted, no one except Dušan Srna and a few members of his inner circle had any idea what this strange-looking girl's appearance at the funeral represented. But after she left the building, they most certainly knew that something quite profound had just passed, as if this mere girl really had heralded the end of an era.

"What – what are you doing?" Dušan Srna shouted after her. "Come back. You can't just walk out like this."

But, of course, his words were as belated as they were ineffective. The irreparable damage had almost certainly been done.

*

Although a direct correlation between one young woman's refusal to cry at an admittedly huge state funeral cannot be blamed for the collapse of a nation and an entire political system, mere straws have been known to crack the sturdiest of a camel's vertebrae. What cannot be denied is that the power of her gesture had a huge effect, especially, on those watching events on television at home. Rather than join their friends and neighbours for the planned street parties to celebrate the leader's life (and here Srna had, once again, been incredibly astute, giving each citizen a generous 'free' alcohol allocation), they conducted heated discussions, and debated the significance of what they had just seen. Who was that girl? Why had she been granted access to the mausoleum? What was the meaning of her putting her finger to her lips like that? Did it symbolise the end of what many had come to see as a repressive regime that was wildly out of touch with the people?

Those debates raged on. To the extent that there was mass unrest, strikes, marches on the capital. To the extent that Dušan Srna's interim government only clung onto power for a handful of weeks.

To this day, those in the former leader's close circle speculate about another course of events, an alternative reality. They wonder what would've happened had Milica Stanković performed with all the gut-wrenching anguish which had defined her early performances in the provinces. Would it have been enough to uplift a nation's flagging spirits? Would she have sparked such an outpouring of collective grief that it would've made people forget about their worries, their poverty, the fundamental rottenness of a social structure that had kept them enslaved for years?

That is something we will never know.

The system did indeed collapse.

*

278

Now that we have reached the end of our story, all that is left to do is to reveal the fate of the main players in our unlikely cast.

Like many people who have been fortunate enough to find their soulmate in life, Dragan Stanković was so devastated by the loss of his wife, he only lasted six months after she passed away. During that period, he could be seen walking aimlessly through the forest, or sitting on the banks of the river, overwhelmed by such a heavy burden of sadness, the townsfolk could almost see it weighing on his shoulders, dragging him down towards his own grave.

"Mark my words, that one ain't long for this world either."

And they were, of course, correct.

At a funeral attended by barely a dozen mourners, Dragan Stanković was buried alongside his beloved wife. For hours after his coffin had been lowered into the ground, his daughter knelt by the graveside, deep in silent prayer. Only when she had finally stirred did a slightly-built old man approach her to offer his condolences. It was Robert Savović, dragging one foot after him (a permanent reminder of the vicious attack which had almost cost him his life) and with a patch over his empty left eye socket.

"I didn't want to disturb you while you were paying your respects." He bowed nervously, took off his cloth cap, and tucked it under his arm. "I just wanted to apologise for the past. I'm far from a good man and I have many faults that I can do nothing to remedy now. But I just wanted you to know that your father was a lovely man, great company. We enjoyed many a fine evening together at the tavern. And I know you probably don't want to hear about our drunken shenanigans, but no matter what happened between us, we really were great pals. I miss those times, as I miss Dragan now, and will always miss his friendship."

"Thank you, Robert. I know my father loved you. For that reason, I love you too, for bringing laughter and happiness into his life. You have as many gifts as shortcomings. I only hope you will enjoy some peace in the autumn of your years."

As regards to Savović's own eventual demise (not two weeks after Dragan Stanković's funeral), he died in the most peculiar of circumstances, an unlikely chain of events that would have graced one of his more preposterous stories. Having married the serving-girl, Karika, and settled into a fairly ordered domestic routine – Savović dealt in highly profitable black-market goods now readily available due to the political turmoil following the leader's death, and Karika brought in a reasonable wage and healthy tips from her job at the tavern –

the couple, even though the much older husband had no end of physical complaints, enjoyed the kind of rampant marital relations that would've put the vast majority of twenty-year-olds to shame. During one of their more intense trysts, Savović attempted a sexual manoeuvre he was both poorly positioned and physically unable to perform, which resulted in him falling out of bed and breaking his neck on the hard wooden floor.

"Say what you want 'bout that old rogue," said the townsfolk, "he certainly went out with a bang."

But that wasn't the only shocking and unexpected occurrence in Velika Plana during that challenging and uncertain period. Due to increased production demands, a lack of experienced workers, and a universal flouting of health and safety protocols, the steelworks burnt to the ground one evening, killing over thirty men, including Dragan Stanković's old friend and supervisor, Mihailo Pančev. Where the original fire started, or why one of the giant smelting pots exploded, was never satisfactorily explained. All that really emerged from the public enquiry was that the men had been worked far too hard, far too often. In fact, some of their weekly quotas were almost impossible to fulfil. But, because of financial restraints, the result of mismanagement and corruption, there was no money available to rebuild the factory. Hence, the biggest employer in the town had literally gone up in smoke. All of which decimated the area, resulting in mass unemployment, the closure of stores, and a general disenfranchisement that would be sadly replicated all across the nation.

And what of Dušan Srna?

Hounded into exile (there was no way he could remain in the country after his coup failed so spectacularly), he ended up in the United States. Philadelphia, to be precise, via England and a three-week steamboat passage. Fascinated by the capitalist economy, this land of plenty, where the shelves in every store were stacked with goods, he quickly forgot about his former political beliefs, the ideological purity into which he had been indoctrinated from an early age. A capable man, as has been well-showcased within these pages, with a gift for language acquisition, he soon secured gainful employ as a translator, editor, and proof-reader with a popular academic press. A conscientious worker, he married a wholesome American girl and started a family. Two boys were born within a year of each other.

One evening, however, as he walked his usual route home, he was approached by a transient, an evangelist-type whom he had often seen on street corners in the neighbourhood, drunkenly proclaiming Christ as the saviour. Confused, not understanding what this dirty-faced buffoon was ranting and raving about, Srna lost his temper and, in no uncertain terms, told the man to be on his way. On hearing Srna's heavy Slavic accent, this street corner evangelist started to rant and rave with even more convicted incoherence than before.

"You commie bastard! What are you doing in God's country? Hey, hey…" he tried to gain the attention of other passers-by. "Looky here, we got ourselves a shit-stinking red, a Russian commie spy on the streets of Philly. He be looking to spread socialist poison in our communities. We gotta stop him, kill him, grab him. We gotta do the Lord's work!"

Words which quickly, and fatally, from Dušan Srna's point of view, drew a huge crowd of burly drinking men out of a nearby bar. On learning that a communist was walking their streets, they wasted no time in setting about Dušan Srna, kicking and beating him so ferociously that they killed him outright.

Come half-past five, when their husband and father would usually return from work, a wholesome American housewife and her two angelic-looking sons, very much possessed of their father's good looks, were left staring at a front door that he would never pass through again.

As for Milica Stanković, after her father's sad death, she remained in the family apartment and made her living by taking in washing from neighbours and darning and repairing clothes. For decades she lived the kind of sparse, austere existence she had always dreamed of living. Never marrying, nor having any kind or romantic involvement, the townsfolk referred to her as the 'nun'. But unlike before, when she was a young girl, they always treated her with respect. Even those who were too young to remember the role she played in events of national importance – that simple yet powerful gesture which brought the curtain down on an entire belief system – sensed that there was something special about the sprightly woman who bounded around the town, her arms laden with freshly laundered sheets.

Every once in a while, there would be a knock at the apartment door, and a recently bereaved member of the community would ask Milica to attend the funeral of a loved one. As always, her heartfelt and sincere outpouring of grief brought all the mourners together and helped them rid themselves of all the painful emotions they had been bottling up ever since their father or mother, husband or wife, uncle or aunt, son or daughter passed away. But whenever they attempted to show their appreciation, by way of a thick wad of banknotes, Milica would politely decline them.

"No, please, it was my pleasure and privilege to share this sad day with you. If you ever need to talk about your loss, my door is always open."

Death, the great mystery of life, will continue to baffle and confound us until the end of time. But if a person can believe in something that helps them get through the pain, be it a belief in God, a religion, or simply that there is something better awaiting them on the other side, then surely that provides more consolation than any sober intellectual denial of anything spiritual and inexplicable in an existence which is defined by those very concepts.

About The Author

Neil Randall is a novelist and short story writer. His debut novel, *A Quiet Place to Die* (Wild Wolf Publishing), was voted e-thriller Book of the Month for February 2014. His first collection of short stories, *Tales of Ordinary Sadness* (Knox Robinson Publishing, 2016) received much critical acclaim. One story was short-listed for the prestigious Wasafiri New Writing Prize 2009, another long-listed for the RTÉ Guide/Penguin Ireland Short Story Competition 2015. His shorter fiction and poetry have been published in the U.K., U.S., India, Australia, and Canada.